Bleeding Navy Blue

By
Christopher R. Smith

PublishAmerica
Baltimore

© 2006 by Christopher R. Smith.
All rights reserved. No part of this book may be reproduced, stored in a retrieval system or transmitted in any form or by any means without the prior written permission of the publishers, except by a reviewer who may quote brief passages in a review to be printed in a newspaper, magazine or journal.

First printing

ISBN: 1-4137-9091-7
PUBLISHED BY PUBLISHAMERICA, LLLP
www.publishamerica.com
Baltimore

Printed in the United States of America

To my family for all your help and love.

Special thanks to:
David D. Coe III

Prologue

Allah was smiling on him and his men today, showing the way to freedom. Every one of Raceme Mohammed's men was primed to fight and die for his cause. The men were carrying old but very reliable AM 94 assault rifles, the follow-up to the Russian AK 74, and some men had smoke grenades. The truck stopped one block from the targets, an American ambassador and a team of inspectors who were pillaging the country. Raceme was especially proud of his little fifteen-year-old brother Kallime, who was on his first mission for Allah.

Twenty-five armed men used the buildings for cover as they moved towards the last inspection sight, the location of which Raceme came by from a woman friend of his, working in the inspectors office at the U.S. embassy. The inspection team would arrive in ten more minutes and he had to have all his men in place. The plan was to let the team come into the building with their marine guards and surprise them with a quick assault. They had to kill the marines, but they wanted the others as hostages to bargain with the U.S.

Just as planned, the building was empty when he arrived and he moved his men up the back fire escape onto the second floor, and to the ambush site. Kallime went up to the roof with a radio in order to signal Raceme when the target arrived.

"Are you set, little brother? We're going to make history today." Raceme smiled into the radio, knowing his little brother could feel his excitement of being a soldier of God.

"Yes, Raceme, Allah will be proud of me today." Kallime settled in on the roof and watched diligently for the target. He was scared, but determined to make his brother proud today. This was his rite of passage, and he planned to become a man.

In the building, Raceme's men were ready to trap the inspectors in a large room that originally had been a dining hall or cafeteria, hiding behind the serving lines and in the kitchen. Previously, this building had served as a mission, but recently closed because of rampant disease that had devastated the country since the war. The team of American delegates was trying to test for harmful bacteria and poisons left over from the fighting. Fortunately, Allah shined his light on Raceme's cause, catching the ambassador when her guard was down. For her it was a public relations tour with the inspectors, trying to win support for the new government and the U.S. in the process.

Kallime radioed for the men to be ready to strike when he saw the American delegation arrive. Standard operating procedure would have been for the marine detachment to secure the building before the team entered, but this was the last stop and there had been no sign of trouble all day. Furthermore, the ambassador had ordered her team to enter quickly and finish the day, which had been hot and long. The word spread quickly that the team had entered the building, and Raceme's men were poised and ready to fight and die for their cause, awaiting their fates.

The entourage entered the building and tested the first floor for any sign of disease, unaware that a firestorm awaited them on the next floor. Finished on the first floor, the team walked up the stairwell right into the trap. Raceme carefully waited as the armed guards formed a perimeter around the ambassador's team. He held his fire as the troops began to talk amongst themselves, having no idea that they were about to die a horrible death. Some of the lower-ranking men went so far as to place the stocks of their rifles on the floor, sealing their fates.

Raceme stood, took aim at the ranking NCO, and shot him in the back of the head, killing him instantly. Every one of his men stood from their hiding spots and opened fire on the marines, who didn't know what hit them. The marines, all well trained, could not escape the trap set for them and the ambassador. In a matter of seconds, by the hands of Allah through his loyal servants fighting Jihad, the marines became another casualty of the war, and the ambassador and the inspection team became prisoners. The kidnappers rounded up the remainder of the team, placed hoods on their heads, and bound their hands behind their backs. They moved the prisoners to the trucks and off to their compound. Allah was proud of his army as they struggled to be free from the control of the Americans.

One of the numerous spy satellites that the U.S. had orbiting the earth, tasked almost exclusively to this part of the world, spying on a region of constant turmoil, captured the abduction and sent the feed from the satellite to a top-secret listening post in nearby Turkey. Form there the post passed the feed on to the different government intelligence agencies in the United States, the largest being the National Security Agency, Defense Intelligence Division, and the Central Intelligence Agency. The satellite coverage of the area was no accident, being necessary during the war, and after, given the constant threat of terrorist attacks, and the government could not abandon the region even after years of civil war.

The encrypted digital video of the attack, sent via secure satellite to a briefing room in the White House, made its way to the president and his aides, who conferred with the joint chiefs of staff on the proper response to the attack. The chiefs all agreed that the U.S. had to respond with a covert operation to rescue the ambassador and her inspection team, at the same time punishing the terrorist for attacking a peaceful mission. They left the details to the commanding officer of the Navy Special Warfare Unit or CNSW, Vice Admiral Christopher Townsend, a decorated SEAL himself with over thirty years in the navy. Tasked with the retrieval of the inspection team and instructed to minimize American casualties, he had a formidable task.

Townsend assembled his men in the operation room, a large conference room with individual computer monitors around an oval oak table. Every one of the people in the room Townsend trusted and tested, with a single exception. Alfred Cormier, a NASA physicist, sat in the corner of the room with an envelope in his hands. The envelope contained orders for Admiral Townsend from the president himself. Cormier was in charge of the experimental transporting system that the joint chiefs wanted to test on this mission. Even before Cormier delivered the orders, the technicians had begun installing his system in the operations room, but Townsend luckily didn't know that fact just yet.

The team sat and prepared to begin the session. Charged with the task of formulating a plan for the mission, the usual procedure for these high-level sessions involved the discussion of logistical and intelligence information, rather than operational details. In this case, however, Dr. Cormier's transport device dictated the logistics of the mission

"Excuse me, this is a closed meeting." Townsend had just noticed Cormier hidden in the back of the room.

"Yes, I know. I have orders from the chiefs concerning the method of transportation. Perhaps we can speak in private."

"That's not necessary, just do what you came to do and leave."

He handed the papers to Townsend, who read them and promptly excused the rest of his staff, excepting his aide, who would keep an accurate record of the conversation.

"Dr Cormier, isn't it?" He didn't give the doctor time to respond to his question. "I'm not going to allow my men to be guinea pigs for NASA and its pet projects."

"Admiral, the orders are clear and they come from the highest authority. My transport method is safe and was tested in the lab. It will save lives among your men."

Townsend read over the procedures and test documentation, finding a stellar record, but what else would he find? The orders also called for the use of the new electromagnetic pulse rifle. Townsend had wanted to see the new rifle in action for some time, so he reluctantly gave in and ordered the use of the transporting system and the new guns; in reality he had little choice in the matter, but he had to make it seem as if he had the final word.

"Dr. Cormier, I want this system monitored at all times."

"It will be. You won't be disappointed." Cormier left the room with a spring in his step and a smile on his face, a smile that would disappear very soon.

With Cormier gone, Admiral Townsend had to form a plan, one that would call for the use of his most experienced and best SEAL team, led by Commander Chase O'Sullivan. Chase and his team rotated from combat duties, and Townsend assigned them to training at the base, but the terrorists changed their designation, propelling them into combat once again.

After Cormier had solved the logistics problem and Admiral Townsend had picked his personnel, Townsend's job was complete. He had learned long ago that it was best to let the team, which was going to be involved with the operation, formulate the tactical details, under supervision, of course. He had a window of forty hours to assemble the team, perform a rehearsal for the operation, transport the team, and retrieve the hostages. Cormier's transport system allowed him to use the best available SEAL team in the country, but at what cost?

Chapter 1

A brilliant flash of light lit up the dusk desert sky, clearly displaying every color in the spectrum. A team of U.S. Navy SEALs transported onto the roof of a two-story building inside the compound of the army of Allah. Intelligence indicated that the hostages were inside the building, and the higher vantage point of the roof gave the team a tactical advantage. They used thermal imaging from an overhead satellite to pinpoint the location of the package just to make sure the team was free from any possible ambush. The team began to take sporadic fire soon after they appeared on the roof. Luckily, the men on the ground were disorientated and confused by the fact that a team of SEALs, the U.S. Navy's elite Sea, Air and Land operatives, had appeared on the roof of a building as if by magic. This gave the team the opportunity to organize and attack.

"Alpha team leader, initiate retrieval," Commander Chase O'Sullivan, the leader of the mission and the team, shouted into the satellite transmitter. The retrieval plan was simple. Alpha team had to rappel down the side of the building and into the window of the room where the hostages were located, surprising the guards in the process. Unfortunately, there was not enough time to rig the rappelling harnesses to the roof as the volume of fire increased. Bullets were hitting the edge of the roof with greater frequency, forcing some of the men to take cover. The SEALs returned fire, covering the rescue attempt, but more were taking cover than not.

"Commander, Alpha team is pinned down; we can't initiate retrieval. We need suppressing fire."

Chase surveyed the scene and realized that most of the fire was coming from the corner building. Steady streams of Arab gunmen poured onto the street in groups, the gunmen having no regard for their own lives. One by one, the SEAL team shot and killed the gunmen and two by two, fresh fighters emerged to defend their homes and country. It had been less than two minutes since the team had transported in, but Chase, with his experience in the war, knew that they were in trouble. At first glance, the roof appeared to provide good cover because of the two-and-a-half-foot lip that extended up from its base. Most all of his men had taken cover behind the lip and were trying to obtain fire superiority over the army of Allah, but little by little, pieces of rock and mortar were being chipped away and with them the safety of the group and their fire superiority.

"Chief." Chase called on his most experienced and reliable operator.

Master Chief Robert James ran towards Chase as bullets whizzed past his head, hitting the dirt and mortar roof at his feet, and dove in to Chase's position, mimicking a headfirst baseball slide. Master Chief James was a formidable operator. Everyone called him Jesse, however, because he was the man whom you wanted next to you in a gunfight. The chief and Chase could not have looked more different. Chase was five feet eleven inches tall and built like a body builder. He was formidable at worst and downright scary at best. Jesse, on the other hand, was six feet one inch tall, but looked about six-four because of his lanky build, being one of those people who had absolutely no body fat and could eat whatever he wanted in any quantity without gaining weight. Because he was so lean, most people, when they first met him, would remark on how he didn't look like a SEAL, but he would kick ass in training and combat with no problem. Taking off his shirt removed all doubts about his physical abilities as he was one solid muscle from head to toe. One had only to look into his dark brown eyes to see that he was a hardened warrior in every sense of the word. His hair was bleached blond and always cut high and tight. Some of his men thought that he had it cut every day.

"Chief, get Bravo team to concentrate their fire on that building in the corner with the EPs. Light them the fuck up, Jess." Chase pointed to where the Arab warriors were pouring out.

In a matter of seconds, a wall of fusion-ignited phosphorus rounds devastated the building from which the gunmen were emerging. It looked like the finale of a fireworks display on the Fourth of July. Chase watched in awe, realizing how wrong he had been about the new rifle. It was like having portable artillery. He wondered why he ever had questioned the new electromagnetic pulse rifle and its potential utility. The gun fired molten phosphorus through a very high-powered electromagnet, ejecting the plasma at three times the speed of sound. The weapon thought to have a few advantages over other more conventional weapons was highly regarded as the rifle of the future. First, it had the capacity to hold over 50,000 rounds of ammunition because the weapon used anhydrous phosphorous and not a solid projectile, allowing the individual soldiers who used the weapon to carry other essential equipment other than ammunition. This was necessary in order to compensate for the diverse environments in which a soldier could find himself, quickly besieged with chemical and biological weapons, as well as unforeseen changes in the weather. Secondly, the rifle had a higher rate of accurate fire, aiding in gaining fire superiority. Lastly, the plasma fired from the weapon caused a high amount of physical damage to the victim, lowering the enemy's morale and will to fight. Phosphorous ignited when it encountered oxygen and one could only extinguish it by removing that oxygen supply; this was usually done by submersion in water. Therefore, if the victim survived the initial trauma of the shot, it took a concerted effort to extinguish the plasma and a large amount of money tending to them in a hospital.

Approved only last month, this was the rifle's first operational use. Chase and other SEALs, including the chief, thought that the EP was a bit too heavy and lengthy to be effective in close quarters. The brass viewed this mission as an ideal opportunity to test and evaluate the gun's performance, having no field tests or its corresponding data. Most of Chase's team resented the fact that their superiors would send them into battle with a weapon that was untested. Chase and Chief James even went so far as to pack the more conventional, battlefield-tested, U.S. built, M 29/ME assault rifle. This mix between a machine gun and battle rifle had served the teams well for almost forty years. The rifle fired case-less ammunition electrically instead of mechanically, giving it a much higher cyclic rate and allowing for a larger magazine. In addition, the absence of a bolt eliminated jamming and misfires from dirt and water getting inside the chamber. Case-less ammunition had the propellant and projectile in one package, producing a high-powered weapon that left no shell casings for its operator to contend. The weapon had been designed in the early twenty-first century as the complete battlefield combat system. The original version of the M 29 fired standard high velocity, NATO .223 caliber, 5.56 by 45-millimeter rounds and the larger 20-millimeter, depleted Uranium armor piercing round. In addition, it featured an integrated optics system that could be used in a conventional sense or coupled with a helmet and camera system that was able to look around corners. Soldiers fighting in an urban environment could literally target and kill enemy combatants from the safety of cover. The weapon had proven its reliability in the past, enjoying the trust of the teams for years. The ME, or Miniature Electric, version was basically the same rifle scaled down to better accommodate CQB, or close quarter battle. Moreover, it featured the electric firing system and case-less capability. Lastly, the targeting system was replaced with an updated conventional tri-mode optics package. The rifle's optics featured a 20x magnification conventional sniper scope, thermal imagery, and night vision capability.

The contractors that produced of the EP450, in addition to the Pentagon, insisted that using the rifle didn't produce a harmful radioactive discharge, and the mini reactor only produced enough power to melt the anhydrous phosphorous and electrify the magnet, which was used as an ejection mechanism, making the EP450 completely safe to use. Chase's SEAL team would soon find out if the manufacturer's claims were true because the weapon was firing 950 rounds per minute, on full automatic, into the Arabian Desert fortress.

Alpha team, commanded by Lieutenant Lance Palmer, an up-and-coming operator who very well might represent the next generation SEAL group commander, rappelled through the open window on the far left side of second floor, finding only two guards. Palmer, the first in, surprised the guards, taking out the first one, who was perched on a chair by the door, with a single shot to the head from his navy issue 10mm Sig Sauer handgun. He didn't see the other guard until it was too late. The guard had been standing out of Palmer's line of sight against the wall where Palmer had rappelled through the window. The first round fired by the guard went through Palmer's thigh, shattering his femur, and the second bullet hit his chest, nipping his body armor, which saved his life. The rest of his group arrived before the guard could get off a third shot, chopping the man down in a hail of fire. Palmer writhed and screamed in pain as his blood, his life, spilled out onto the dirt-filled wooden floor.

"Man down, man down," Chase heard through the COM set. "Team leader's been hit."

"Calm down, Ensign. The package?"

"Affirmative, sir. The package is in hand."

"Alpha Team, move to the west side of the building for extraction, copy." There was no answer to Chase's order. "Ensign, collect your downed man and the package and move your team to the alley west of the building for retrieval." The ensign, obviously shaken, acknowledged Chase's order. It was his first operational command situation, and he had much to learn about being a SEAL and a leader.

"Chief, on me, Alpha team needs covering fire in the alley on the west side of the building. Get the rappelling harnesses rigged on the double, Chief."

Chase had to get the roof team home if he was going to surprise the Arab Army and safely retrieve the package. "Command, this is roadrunner, over. Command, this is roadrunner, do you copy?" Chase yelled into the COM set over the gunfire, trying to get command to transport Bravo team back to base.

"Roger, roadrunner, this is command. Go."

"Command, package is in hand, prepare for transport, over."

"Sir, the harnesses are ready, short time, let's go!" Chief James shouted from across the rooftop, ready to save his men inside the building.

The enemy army converged on the rooftop, lobbing grenades at SEAL team Bravo, but the Arabs were unaware that the rescue team was waiting on the west wing of the building. "Command, this is roadrunner, activate retrieval for Bravo team, over." Just as quickly as they had appeared on the roof, Bravo team transported home. The shooting rapidly died out as the Arabs tried to figure out what had just happened. With one half of the team back at base, the chief and Chase rappelled from the top of the roof to the alley without taking any fire. The diversion had worked, but wouldn't fool the Arabs for very long.

"Alpha Leader, there are friendly forces on the ground in the alley, over."

"Roger, sir, we are inside the door and ready to go on your command, over."

Suddenly, from behind their position, where Chief James was covering, shots rang out from his EP450, and like a sudden gust of damaging wind, the compound again was alive with stifling automatic weapons fire. Bullets hit the side of the building and above Chase's head. He looked around the corner, watching five or six targets pour out into the street at once, racing to his position, and he wasn't in a position to take them down. If they got a grenade into the alley, everyone would die and the mission would fail. There was no way that Chase could ever let himself or his teams fail a mission. Chase jumped out from behind his cover, taking a knee, and keying on his first target: a boy, no older than fifteen. Aiming for his center mass kill zone, he depressed the trigger. Without hesitation, he pulled the trigger, using his new EP450. The phosphorous round went through the dark-haired boy like a knife melting through butter. The second target was completely different—an old man, probably in his seventies. The second shot from Chase's rifle took the man's head clean off his body. Oddly, it seemed none of the targets knew the correct way to fire a rifle, because in a matter of seconds, Chase, who had not taken any accurate fire, killed four targets and scared the others off the street without a scratch.

Chase wondered why he had ever taken the time to finish his PhD in history and military science, being Navy through and through. He loved the danger, the combat, not so much the fighting, but outthinking and then outperforming an adversary. This was much the same attitude he'd had as a competitive wrestler in college. Whoever was faster, smarter, and quicker, had trained the hardest, and had the most weapons in his arsenal would vanquish his adversary. That was one characteristic that Chase had always possessed: a swagger that only the best had. He had the look that informed the rest of the world that they didn't stand a chance against him. No matter what the arena, he was going to win, at any cost. This engagement was no different for Chase; he would complete his mission, having never failed to achieve the objective of an operation.

"Commander."

"Go, Ensign."

"Sir, I'm taking massive fire from our left flank, through the walls of the building. I have four men down, one serious and one hostage hit. Sir, there's another problem. The ambassador and an aide are confined in the building across the street."

"Roger, bring your team into the alley and initiate retrieval. The chief, Rodriguez and I will get the ambassador." Chase knew that his chances of making it home safely had just become more remote, but he had to do his duty for his country.

"Aye, sir, Rodriguez is coming out followed by the team and the package, over."

"Chief, covering fire." Almost at the first utterance, both men had their EPs on full automatic and were lighting up the now darkening sky with fireworks. Rodriguez joined them as Alpha team vanished.

The road was about as wide as a three-lane highway but made of dirt and gravel, giving the base the feel of a town in the Old West. Across the street, the building, which at a height of four stories was unlike any other building in the compound, had only one viable entrance point: on the right corner of the front side of the structure. The three-man team would have to cross the street and go room to room with everyone else in the compound after them.

Chase reflected on how he consistently found himself in such precarious situations in the name of his country as he waited for their best opportunity to cross the street. How could one man come so far and not know how he had gotten there? Chase's childhood idea of how he was going to live his life differed greatly from the bullet-ridden reality that he lived. After high school, he had gone to the University of Pennsylvania on a full academic scholarship. He'd had numerous athletic scholarship offers, but Penn had the best team and the best reputation, but only awarded academic scholarships, so he'd decided to attend and became a three-time All-American and national champion wrestler, a sport that had been in his family for generations. He was very intelligent, but the only reason he had gone to college was for wrestling. One day, after he had won his national championship, the school awarded him a Bachelor of Arts degree in government and history. It had been just an afterthought to Chase, but it was unavoidable; he had to have a degree to get the job that he had wanted. He had wanted to teach at a university and coach wrestling. Now, on the eve of his thirty-third birthday, terrorists, who had kidnapped an ambassador and her inspection team, were shooting at and killing his men.

Chase was a young-looking thirty-three, with light brown hair that was just a bit longer than navy regulation. He was quite handsome with his athletic demeanor. When you met him, he was very intelligent and affable. In fact, most women would tell you that he was a big, sweet teddy bear, but other members of the covert operations community feared and respected him.

He wondered what had gotten him into this shit—the SEALs, the navy. Then he remembered: war. War had gotten him into the navy and competence kept him there. Before the war, Chase had been in graduate school at the University of North Carolina, working on his PhD in history and coaching, when his country had called. At the time, he had been such an ardent patriot, the kind only a young man could be, the kind of patriotism that war hammered out of a young man. Chase had wanted to be the best, and be around the best, so he had volunteered to become a SEAL, a covert operator, one of the people upon whom the country called when the shit hit the fan and didn't want to get their hands dirty. Chase had fought with distinction against the Arab

Coalition in the four-year war. America decided it had had enough of the constant warring in the Middle East, between the Arab Coalition's member nations and Israel. The wars had begun when the Word had switched from fossil fuel dependence to the limitless energy of cold fusion, negating the only source of wealth that the region had. The U.S. had decided, with the secret backing of the United Nations, to stabilize the region. There was no official international support for the action, even the British officially were against it, but no one did anything more than file a grievance and wait for the conclusion. America had achieved most of what it wanted from the war: overrunning Iraq, Iran, Saudi Arabia, and Palestine, while the smaller nations, including Kuwait and Jordan, peacefully agreed to be annexed.

Chase never really understood why he had fought in the war. Being a student of history, he realized powerful nation-states never heeded the lessons that history taught. The United States, the most powerful nation ever, was no different. There had been political upheaval in the Middle East for hundreds of years, and the only things that the people understood in that region of the world were the sword and the bullet. Diplomacy was not going to change that fact, so the U.S. gave them the sword and the bullet, only strengthening their resolve to purify the world in the name of Allah. Chase understood all too well his place as an instrument of United States foreign policy, and he had the scars to prove it. Now things were different; warriors like Chase were an anachronism. Smart weapons had taken over war for America. The whole point was to eliminate casualties, but that never happened. For some reason, they always came back to Chase. No matter how sophisticated the weapons, he was their go-to guy.

"Listen up. Lay down covering fire while I cross the street. Then the chief and I will lay down the fire for Rodriguez. The chief is last. Is everyone clear?"

"Sir."

"Yes, Chief."

"Night vision, sir. We can see targets, but they can't see us."

As Chase put on his goggles, he wondered why he had not thought to utilize the night vision. It was his job to keep everyone safe and come up with the strategy. Chase felt stupid and it showed on his face. Just then, he felt a hand on his shoulder.

"That's what chiefs are for, sir. Are you ready to go?" The sound of gunfire filled the air and deafened the remaining team members.

Chase darted out into the street, not worrying about firing his rifle, but about speed. His legs had never felt so heavy; carrying an extra rifle and its ammunition while attempting to outrun the gunfire was a difficult burden to manage. The extra rifle and its ammunition took their toll on Chase's legs, thumping clumsily one after the other until he was behind the stone porch that jutted from the four-story building. He rolled to a prone position and checked himself for bullet holes, finding his uniform and flak jacket were ripped on the right side about five inches from his arm pit, but with no sign of blood. Once checked, he opened fire, covering the other two. The EP was easy to use and had no kick, but the light discharge blinded Chase because he was wearing the night vision equipment. He began to fire without direction or line of sight, but the sheer volume of fire held the Arab army at bay. He felt the first and second body roll over him.

"Chief, the light bursts are fucking up the night vision. Break out the MPs." Chase had known that they would come in handy, and he smiled with satisfaction that he was right and the brass was wrong.

"Already done, sir...Rodriguez, two smoke grenades in the window." He pointed in the open-air window in the first floor. " Sir, on three."

The three-man fire team ran the length of the structure to the door without missing a step. With the bravado of Jesse James, Chief James barreled through the door, rolling and coming to a prone position. Two guards came down the stairwell, and with two controlled bursts, the chief was able to dispense his targets before they were able to see him through the smoke and the night.

"Clear. All clear." The other two swept in, clearing the rest of the room to the stairwell, where erratic fire began to come down the stairs and either hit the wall or fall short of Chase, who was squatting below the sight line of those firing from upstairs. He lobbed a stun grenade up the stairs in the direction from which the fire was coming and immediately ran up the stairwell. Once upstairs, he saw two men hunched over, coughing uncontrollably. They were boys in their early teens. *No wonder the fire was inconsistent*, he thought as he flung them to the ground, kicking their weapons across the room. That same moment, first the chief and then Rodriguez ran past him. Chase took out two pair of plastic restraints and bound both the hands and the feet of the children. He had killed children, one just a few minutes before, but killing when it wasn't necessary was where Chase drew the line.

"Clear," Rodriguez yelled as it echoed in his COM set.

"No sign of the ambassador, sir," Chief James yelled as he inched up the next set of stairs, with Chase and Rodriguez in tow. At the top of the stairs, the chief fired three rounds from his M 29/ME and motioned Chase with a hand signal to come up. Two scared hostages sat bound and gagged in the corner farthest from the door, with a dead guard lying on the floor next to them. Chase ran over to the ambassador and unbound her, pulled her to her feet, and rushed her towards the window. His team formed up at the window, nearly dragging the second hostage behind them.

"Command, this is roadrunner, over."

"Roadrunner, this is command, go."

"Package 2 is in hand preparing for retrieval." Chase placed the transporter guidance platform on the head of the ambassador while Chief James did the same for her aide. Then, Jesse donned his guidance platform and ran out onto the fire escape, securing the site. The others squeezed out onto the small platform to await retrieval. This was necessary in order for the satellite to secure the uplink needed to initiate the system, requiring line of sight in order to gain a strong enough signal.

"Command, this is roadrunner. We are ready for retrieval. Over." Chase was about to complete another mission; a thought that he'd had earlier, this one would be premature as well.

In mid-sentence, Chase watched as a lucky shot from a terrorist hit Rodriguez. The bullet ricocheted off the steel of the fire escape and hit Rodriguez squarely in the neck.

"Roadrunner, this is command, over."

"Roadrunner, go."

"We cannot fix on your position. What is your location? Over."

"Stand by, command."

"Chief, put pressure on that wound.

"Command, we are outside the third floor of the structure, on top of an escape ladder. Over."

"Roadrunner, you need to move to open ground. We cannot pick up your transporter signature. Over."

Chase's first instinct was to go to the roof, but the fire escape only went as high as the fourth floor. The only way out was down—into the teeth of the enemy. This action would require the EP450 electromagnetic pulse rifle.

"Chief, get one of the hostages on the EP and have the other support Rodriguez. We have to go down to an open space."

The chief forced the ambassador's arms around Rodriguez, using her body to support his weight. He quickly placed a field dressing over the wound in Rodriguez's neck and then showed her aide how to use the EP450. Jesse removed his night vision and led the way down the fire escape to the corner of the building. Chase was in the rear as they huddled together, searching for cover. Chase looked down at the ambassador's aide, the newest member of his team, from the last step of the fire escape. Chase had no idea what his name was, but from the looks of him, he was in his middle to late forties and about fifteen pounds overweight. His eyes, which showed complete terror, were bright blue and filled with tears. His left hand was shaking as he rubbed it over his slightly balding head, letting the gun almost fall from his other hand.

"Snap to, we need that gun for cover fire. Do you understand?" His body came to attention as he took the rifle firmly in his hands after he wiped off his face. "The chief and I are going to lay down covering fire. When we have it established, I want you to lead the ambassador and my man to our position, covering yourselves with fire as you come. The transport system will activate as soon as you hit open ground. Do you understand?" The man, still obviously frightened, nodded his head in agreement, and Chase went off with his gun-slinging cowboy friend at his side.

Again, the night sky lit up in a storm of electromagnetic pulses of plasma that ripped gaping holes in the sides of buildings. The unlucky people hit by the rounds were either cut in half or in some cases lit on fire. Chase and Jesse were in the middle of the street, firing in all directions like the cowboys of the Old West that Chase had enjoyed studying in school and in his spare time. These were the types of movies where the good guys had a showdown in the middle of a town with the bad guys. Little did his enemies know that this modern Jesse James was a SEAL. The chief took a kneeling position, managing not only to place covering fire, but also to pick up and dispense targets with extreme malice. He was one hell of a soldier.

"Roadrunner, we have you locked. Stand by." Chase looked over his shoulder and saw the aide, scared, but firing into the night. Chase gave him the thumbs-up sign and answered command.

"Roger, command, any fucking day!"

"Two, one, energize."

The five remaining members of the ground team disappeared into the night as the last of the rounds fired from the EP450 lit up the night sky for another second.

Chapter 2

Transporting was a new form of travel. The public wouldn't even know about this technology for quite a while, but the government would use it for special operations to beam across space and time to a corresponding destination. Thank God for Mr. Einstein and his special theory of relativity. Scientists over one hundred and fifty years later were just beginning to understand some parts of his theories, let alone finding ways to put them to practical use.

The discovery of transporting had been pure serendipity. NASA physicists had been experimenting with the boundaries of Einstein's special relativity theory, trying to propel particles at velocities greater than the speed of light, when they had stumbled onto transporting. They had found that it was not possible with the technology they'd had available to them to accelerate particles to these velocities without discovering a shortcut around the energy-mass problem that existed. Einstein's theory dictated that as an object approached the speed of light, its mass would approach infinity.

The problem was, as an object's mass approached infinity, the amount of energy needed to increase its velocity also approached infinity. Obviously, the idea of creating an infinite amount of energy seemed impossible.

The scientists at NASA, though, had found that, at extremely high energy levels, their experimental results had begun to deviate greatly from what Einstein's equations predicted. Several years of intensive research by NASA into these high-energy anomalies, as the physicists took to calling them, had showed some astounding results that would lead to transporting and a great leap in the knowledge of quantum physics. Initially, the scientists had found that small amounts of mass would seemingly disappear, without the corresponding release of energy that would have indicated that the masses converted directly into energy. As their experiments continued, the scientists began to theorize that they were seeing the behavior that some believed one of Einstein's equations predicted.

This behavior, which Einstein himself had recognized his equations might allow, and which he described as "spooky action at a distance," allowed for some subatomic particles to travel faster than the speed of light. The difference in the scientists' work was that they seemed to be able to generate this spooky action at a distance with whole atomic structures (i.e. molecules). After more years of work, the scientists had begun to be able to use this method to transport small living things across large distances. This breakthrough, though, was not the end all for which the scientists had hoped. As they had begun to transport animals with higher cognitive function, like mice, they had found that the transportation produced only a molecular copy of the organism. In other words, any memories or knowledge that the organism had developed seemed to disappear in the transport process. This discovery had represented a complete roadblock to the continuation of the work at NASA that had lasted for several years.

At that time, an incredibly gifted young neuroscientist named Frank Cornell had come to NASA. He had begun to look over the results produced by the transport scientists, and to speak with them about their experiments. Dr. Cornell had attempted to further the research, applying his vast knowledge of the higher-order brain functions. Within two years, he and his team had developed a completely new model for the relationships between the cells in the brain and nervous system (it was this work for which Dr. Cornell would be awarded the Nobel Prize—at 35). This new model allowed the cells in the brain and nervous system to successfully transport along with the rest of the cells in a living organism.

Dr. Cornell had demonstrated his confidence in the new transport system in a most unusual way. He had allowed his beloved family dog, Abby, to be transported using the new system. His family had been going on vacation, and he had asked his team to transport the dog to their vacation spot in the Grand Tetons. Dr. Cornell had done this in secret, surprising his young children with the rather sudden appearance of Abby. It had been clear to him, once the children had begun to play with Abby, that the dog had suffered no ill effects from the transportation, and the boldness he demonstrated had convinced all remaining skeptics at NASA of the promise of the new technology. Dr. Cornell's experiment with his dog also became a legendary tale that, due to the secrecy demanded by the Department of Defense and the Central Intelligence Agency, only in a group of about fifty people at NASA and in the uppermost levels of the government was it shared.

Though Cornell and his team had solved the basic problems with the technology, there were years of testing still to be done before science would deem it safe. The military, and the Central Intelligence Agency, seeing the obvious advantages such a system would offer them over their adversaries, had eagerly volunteered to test the technology. The transportation of Chase's team into the Middle East was the first operational test, and it was the largest number of people yet transported using the new system.

"Sir, guidance was a no go. The team energized, but the satellite never picked up the signal. Commander, they're not in the system. We have no positive pod signature."

As the young lieutenant commander picked up the phone, shivers went up his back. He had heard the battle on the satellite radio and watched on the satellite video feed. "How could the men just dematerialize like that?" The navy was supposed to take care of its own and he had just given the order that seemed to have killed five people.

"Admiral, there's been a problem with the retrieval. I think you should come down to the pod room, sir." The line went dead and the watch officer sank into his chair, pulling at his full head of red hair and shaking his head from side to side.

"Attention on deck." Every member of the room stood at attention, facing the door where Admiral Christopher Townsend entered.

"As you were. Son, what happened?" Before the sullen lieutenant commander could respond, the transport chief answered the question for him.

"Sir, chief of the watch, Gloria Summers. The guidance system dropped the signal in mid transfer. The signal from the ground team disappeared after the pod energized. They just vanished, sir."

"Commander, call Dr. Cormier, on the double. Have him meet me in my office and keep me informed on the search."

"Aye, sir."

The admiral should have been an actor, turning and walking out of the pod room towards his office with a lack of emotion typical of a sociopath. He entered his office, closed the door, and lost control of his emotions. He flipped over the table in the corner, shattering the vase that his wife insisted he have in his office. This wasn't enough to tame his rage, and he kicked at a leg of the overturned table, breaking it but not detaching it. His emotions taking control of his body, he grabbed the broken leg on the table, violently tearing it from the base and flinging it through the window, which shattered the glass pane. Tired and angry from the episode, he slowly slid to the floor with a tear running down his cheek. He remembered the day that he had met Chase. Chase was such a promising officer, and through the years, he had come to think of Chase as his protégé, like a son who would take over the family business. He was on the fast track to make admiral. "What a waste."

"Admiral?" Cormier poked his head through the door. Dr. Alfred Cormier, the NASA physicist who had stumbled onto transporting, was an older man, and he wore a gray wool suit threadbare on the lapels. He was slender with spotted graying hair that at one time had been jet black. He had a look about him, one that might cause grade school children to make fun of him but older people envy his brilliance.

The admiral stood immediately and brushed off his uniform. "Come in, Doctor."

"They briefed me on the ride over. I'm sorry."

"Sorry! What the fuck happened? I have the two best SEALs in the country, another member of their team, an ambassador, and the most respected medical chemist in the world gone. They vanished into thin fucking air! I have to tell the president that his ambassador is dead, and then I have to tell the families of the SEALs the same Goddamn thing. I don't want sorry! I want answers, and I want them now. Mark my words, Doctor; your head will roll with mine. Do you understand me?"

Cormier stood in front of Admiral Townsend in silence. No one had spoken to him in that manner since he was a child, and he wasn't quite sure how to react. Five people were gone, and his technology was the vehicle that had caused it. He felt that humility was the proper response.

"We'll find out, Admiral. Did we get the battle on the Sat.?"

"Yes, follow me."

Dr. Cormier turned and walked towards the door. Out of the corner of his eye, he saw a picture of the admiral, Chase, and the admiral's family having a barbecue in a park. Cormier understood why he had just been chastised, forgiving Townsend for what he had said.

Cormier watched the satellite film of the battle and was awestruck at the bravery and talent of the chief and Chase. He felt immense sorrow at the fact that his technology had killed the brave SEALs. His emotions overcame him when he saw them transport into nowhere. Tears ran down his face, demanding an answer from himself. The technology had worked hundreds times before with no problems. "Why was this time different?" Early experiments had used monkeys, and from time to time, the signal was lost, but they always turned up somewhere, once at the exact location of the North Pole. "Where was the SEAL team?"

By this time, the survivors of SEAL team Alpha and Bravo were huddled in the back of the op-room in silence, wondering what had gone wrong. After many hours of waiting, being used to having no sleep for extended periods, the men were still intently paying attention to what was being done in the command center. Conversely, the admiral, who looked worse for the wear, was quietly sitting in the corner of the room with his head down. His usually perfect uniform, now wrinkled and stained, bore the reminiscence of one of a dozen cups of coffee. His eyes looked shut, swollen as they were from complete exhaustion. Moreover, his usual military posture had transformed into something like the slump of defeat.

"I got it." Cormier yelled at the top of his lungs as the whole room came alive. It was like awakening a sleeping beast. Everyone in the room circled the doctor as he started his explanation.

"The guns, the goddamn guns did it. The electromagnetic rifle, I think it did something to the transport. I don't think they're dead."

"Doctor, if they're not dead, where are they?"

"That, Admiral, is the million-dollar question. Do you know anything about quantum physics?" There was no answer, just the look that a person gives someone, out of annoyance, when trying to communicate using different languages.

"Doctor, please explain it so that we all can understand."

Cormier gathered himself. "At NASA, we've been refining the transporting method for some time now and have developed a way to zero in on exact longitudinal and latitudinal coordinates using GPS equipment and a modified guidance platform. Instead of the other transport feed picking up the signal, a special satellite directs the pod to the exact location programmed. Albert Einstein believed that time and space exist together on a plane or line, and that a person, given the right vehicle, could travel to any part of that line. The theory, considered extremely advanced quantum physics, is difficult to understand at best, but your boys might have stumbled onto the greatest discovery since we split the atom. I need to get my colleagues from NASA to examine the data, but we may be able to harness this thing and get your boys back."

"That still doesn't answer the question of where they are."

"Sir, I honestly don't know where or when they are, but I do know that there is a good chance that they are still alive. I need NASA on the phone now, and I would ask that you clear this room so that I can think. Also, please get me one of those new pulse rifles."

Chapter 3

The realization that he was alive was a slow one. Dr. David Persons was the first to awake. He felt wet and sticky, but he couldn't yet focus on his reality. As he pulled himself to his knees and tried to rub the fuzz from his eyes, a sharp, burning sensation overtook him, feeling like he had just walked through an old, but still pungent, cloud of mace. He crawled over to where the ambassador's body was lying, face down, and nudged her repeatedly, with no success in getting her to stir. He then rolled over the SEAL team member, who was lying on his side next to the ambassador. Persons wanted to see the man's face so that he could identify which of the SEAL team members the man was. The pale face of a bloodless corpse greeted him. Dave suddenly knew what was all over him: blood. Rodriguez had bled out, which meant that they must have been unconscious for some time. Persons looked down, confirming that another man's blood covered him.

Doctor Persons, who had completed the MD/PhD program at Case Western Reserve University, had chosen to devote his life to research. He hadn't seen a patient since his internship and residency at Johns Hopkins, but he was still used to the smell of death. It didn't bother him, but the fact that this brave man had given his life to save him made Persons' stomach turn. Persons next stumbled over to where the chief and Chase were lying, motionless. He grabbed the shoulder of the first man, and just as he did, he found himself on the ground with his face in the dirt, dropped in one motion by the chief. Both SEALs were awake and lying motionless in the tall grasses, staring out at the harbor. The harbor was bustling with dockworkers and ship builders, building what looked like the beginning of an iron hull for a battleship or some other large metal ship. The United States hadn't built a battleship since before the end of World War II. The *Iowa Class* battleship was the most powerful dreadnaught ever to sail the seas, but the last of that class, the *Missouri*, had been retired after the Gulf War in 1991. Another irregularity, which Chase couldn't quite place yet, was the buildings. They were made of non-symmetrical stone and wood, almost a colonial décor. Dr. Persons settled next to Chief James and looked on in awe as visions of old movies and historical documentaries flooded his head. No one dared say a word and avoided stating what each was thinking.

The last person to awake was Ambassador Margaret Knox-Harriman, a slender woman with brown hair and bright green eyes. The eyes were the sort that reminded most people of a woman who in her prime had been beautiful and had aged gracefully in her fifty-four years. Her height, at five feet eleven inches, intimidated many men, and her demeanor propelled her to the top of her field. The president had named her the ambassador to the Arab Coalition just to infuriate them before the start of the war. Many people had thought that the appointment was political, but she proved them wrong. Margaret, the front-runner for the vacant post of Ambassador to France, had thought she would hear of her appointment on the day of her kidnapping, but it was not to be. Becoming the French ambassador was a very prestigious position, which in her present situation never would happen.

The first thing that Margaret saw when she regained her senses was the lifeless body of the SEAL whom she'd had to carry down the stairs in the compound. It was a task that she had not had time to protest in the heat of the moment, but about which she had planned to speak to Chase's commanding officer when they all returned to base. She swivelled her head towards the other three men who were lying in the grass, not knowing what to expect. Fortunately, she was still the highest-ranking official in the party, and she was going to get some answers from the SEAL commander. She stood and aimlessly walked towards the harbor and the other three men of the team. Just before she would have blown the team's cover, Chief James grabbed the petrified ambassador and threw her to the ground, dragging her to where the others were hiding, holding his hand over her mouth to keep her from screaming.

"We're going to move to the woods on the other side of the field and wait, under cover, until dark." Chase whispered to the group, pointing to the west as the chief gathered Rodriguez's body and gear and disappeared into the woods. The rest of the group followed with Chase in the rear entering a large pine and maple forest that afforded the team better cover.

"Commander, what's the plan?" Dave was doing his best to stay calm and impassive.

"Doctor, we're going to bury my man and then under the cover of night, we're going to the closest city. Hopefully, there we can find something to help us figure out what the hell is going on." He turned to Jesse. "Chief, we need to do an equipment check, and then I need you to go on into town and do some recon. The doctor and I will bury Rodriguez and wait for your signal."

"Aye, sir." First, Chief James stripped down his dead friend, then himself, organizing the group's equipment, putting the equipment in a pile with Chase's, and sifting through it.

"Commander, I demand to know what's going on right now! Who are those people and why are we in the woods instead of back home?" Margaret's voice gradually got louder until she was yelling at Chase, demanding that he give her some answers.

"Madam Ambassador, you need to stay calm. When it is dark, we'll have the answers you want. Either sit down quietly, or help us dig this grave." Margaret settled down on the base of a tree, propped her back up against it and watched as the rest of the group worked diligently.

Chief James finished his equipment check quickly. "Sir, I've got some good news and some bad. The bad news is that the new pulse rifles are not working but show full power, which I find odd. I don't have enough experience with them to repair the equipment. The good news is that the rest of the equipment is operational."

"Give me the equipment list, Jesse."

"Three M 29/ME assault rifles with five hundred rounds total, three 10mm navy-issue handguns with forty-five rounds each, three night-vision goggles, seven phosphorous hand grenades, eight stun grenades, two mace grenades and assorted C40 high explosive charges. All three repelling harnesses are operational. We also have three survival kits, each with a compass, ten-inch knife, gas lighter, fishing line and hooks, rain poncho, and insect repellent. We have one water purifier that luckily Rodriguez had in his pouch. Three operational communication units, five retrieval units, three medic kits, three MBA's—multipurpose breathing apparatus—and three environmental suits."

"Excellent, Chief. Take a handgun with three clips and a night-vision set-up and recon the town. It appeared to be down the road about ten miles."

Jesse James left with a quiet "Aye, sir" and disappeared into the forest.

The past few months had been very lucrative for Thomas's father and by extension for Tom himself. Being the only child of a New York banker who had moved his family to South Carolina after the war for the promise of inexpensive land meant that Tom had never to worry about his financial situation. He had a confident posture about him, one attributed to his upbringing in a well-to-do family and he was proud of the fact. Tom had to wash and shave every day, which in that time was virtually unheard of. It was a necessity that Tom be immaculate at all times; wearing the latest New York fashions, he stuck out like a sore thumb. A handsome, cultured man with red hair and freckles, Tom wasn't much for riding and shooting because his father simply hired people to it for him.

"Mr. Tidwell, Mr. Tidwell!" a dirty outdoorsman riding at full gallop yelled from around the bend in the road. Then Tom saw him as he galloped into sight, bleeding from his shoulder and riding low in his saddle. "Turn back! There are bandits coming. Turn back!" His arm waved from side to side just before he fell from his horse face down onto the road. Tom rode his horse to where the man had fallen, trying to help, but before he made it, his eyes fixed on seven men wearing all black including black masks. There was no time to turn the wagon; they would be on the group in a matter of seconds. He ordered his father's men to empty the stagecoach and tip it over, giving them some much-needed cover. George, Tom's father, and Elizabeth, Tom's soon-to-be wife, crouched behind the wagon as his hired guns readied themselves for combat.

"Tom, go for help. We need help quickly."

"No, Father, you need my gun, and I am not leaving Elizabeth behind."

"Then take her and go to town for help. It's only a few miles."

"Dad, I want to stay with you."

"Obey me, Tom. Now go, ride hard!"

Tom pulled Elizabeth onto his horse and spurred the animal into a full sprint. Over the hill and out of sight, he rode to town, knowing that he wasn't getting help, but rather saving himself and his wife.

George had never actually been involved in a raid. He always sent his men to scare people off their land, but now he was going to reap what he had sown for the past year. The masked men dismounted and split up into two different groups, each taking a different flank and converging on the wagon. Tom had seen only seven, but there were twenty men still hidden from sight around the bend in the road. The first ten dismounted and joined the flanking groups, and the last ten came straight on at full gallop. The shooting started, and it was each man for himself. No amount of money was enough to die for, especially for a man like Tidwell.

"Come back, you scoundrels," George yelled as his hired mercenaries dispersed.

The bandits were organized and skilled, one by one killing the fleeing men. George started to return fire from behind the cover of the carriage, hitting three raiders before the gunmen overran the stunned carpetbagger. His last vision was that of a masked man wielding a saber from high on his horse. At that moment, he wondered if there was a heaven. The saber hit him in the neck, but due to the awkward angle at which the blade struck, it didn't cut off his head. Instead, the sword sliced a large gash in his chest. It was a slow death, and a painful one, but the men, who had followed the Tidwells from South Carolina, had extracted their revenge. They might have lost the war, but they were not going to lose their land without retribution.

A group of five men on horseback chased after Thomas and his fiancée. The masked men rode well and had fast steeds; they caught up to him and began to shoot in his direction. The weapons that the bandits used weren't very accurate at longer distances, but little by little, the munitions became more accurate. The extra burden of a second person on his horse slowed down the steed just enough for the raiders to be able to gain ground on them, improving their aim in the process. From the top of a hill, Tom could see the town in the distance, and he knew that he was almost home free. He spurred his horse, hoping that it would go just a little faster, but it was futile. Just as the horse crested the last hill before the two-mile flat sprint to the town, a round hit it in the hind leg, rearing back and throwing Elizabeth, forcing Thomas to make a life or death decision. He had to go back for her, risking his life rather than dying in disgrace and ruining his family his name by leaving a woman behind. Tom was sure he was going to die, but Tidwell men didn't leave women behind; besides he loved Elizabeth. Tom dismounted, grabbing Elizabeth, but it was to late; he closed his eyes, hoping it would all be painless.

The chief was only two hundred feet away from the woman, under cover and trying to ascertain what was going on when she hit the ground, and he ran to help, arriving just a few seconds after Thomas and was greeted by five men on horses, shooting in his direction. The men had just crested the last hill and bore down on the group, guns blazing. The veteran SEAL simply reacted, pulling his 10mm pistol from its shoulder holster and firing in the direction of the riders' muzzle flashes. Chief James' weapon and skills were far better than those of the raiders; he picked off each of the targets as they bore down on the distressed couple. One after the other, with the help of his laser-sighted handgun, the chief killed the five men without any second thoughts. Five horses, all without riders, came to rest ten feet from the chief. He glanced over at the object of the raiders' actions. The man was holding an unconscious woman in his arms, his eyes shut and bracing for an impact that would never come.

Tom realized that the raiders had not hit him, and he slowly opened his eyes. An older man who was dressed very peculiarly greeted him. "Thank you, sir. They attacked my father and I down the road a bit. I have to get help," Tom franticly mumbled.
"Son, let me take a look at the girl." James leaned down to the girl and took her pulse, reaching into his pouch and taking out a smelling salt. He waved it under her nose. Elizabeth popped her head up, but just as quickly laid it back down.
"Honey...Honey, are you alright?" Tom pulled her body further onto his lap, hoping for an answer.
"Yes, I think so," she answered feebly.
"Can you move? We must go back for Father." Thomas lifted her onto one of the horses, forcefully abandoned by the mysterious gunmen, and turned to the chief. "Will you come with us? I can pay you for your services."
"I am going that way anyway. I'll go ahead and scout the position." Jesse James cumbersomely climbed onto a horse, almost sliding off the other side. He kicked the steed and it took off. He held on for dear life as the animal ran down the street. It was all he could do not to fall off.

The group of former Confederate soldiers waited for their brothers to return, but hearing the gunfire, they feared the worst. They were leery that the law had found them; having killed the father but let the son escape, they would have to run and hide until the coast was clear and then finish the job another time. The leader decided to hide in a prearranged location not far from the ambush site where the rest of the battalion was bivouacked until things cooled down. The raiders would hunt for the missing Tom Tidwell once they were certain it was safe as he now was the only thing in the way of the return of their land.

"Men, once again we have performed a successful raid on the Yankees, but we have failed to complete our whole mission. Come with me and reclaim what is rightfully ours." Captain Buford Jennings Walton was eloquent and persuasive. Having led his men this far, he was determined to win the battle and regain their land.

The Rebel war cry filled the dusk air as the men rode off.

Tom's new horse, courtesy of the dead bandits, had tired some. It slowed to a trot, and bucked a bit under the weight of two people. He heard the war cry in the distance and pulled back on the rein, stopping his tired mount. Both riders dismounted and hugged, partly because they were still alive and partly out of sorrow. After a few moments, they walked to the top of the hill and found the chief standing over a pile of dead bodies, mostly of men whom Tom had traveled with and counted on to protect him. Tom approached slowly, wondering who would protect him now, hoping that this strange man would have a price, one he certainly could meet.

"No, please, not him. He's my father, don't touch him."

"Someone will have to do something; he is still alive."

"Can you help him? Please don't let him die." Tom had no idea what to do for his father and realized that he had spoken too soon; hopefully his new friend would not hold that fact against him.

"I don't know. What happened here anyway?" Chief James tended to George Tidwell the best he could but had not planned for this contingency, therefore was not equipped with the proper medical supplies.

"They attacked us; we were just trying to go home."

"Who is us?" the chief asked without looking up from George and his wounds.

"My name is Thomas Tidwell, and this is my fiancée, Elizabeth Thompson; most of these other men are my father's hired help-guards if you will. They…they were all murdered by those bandits." Tom was shaken and disoriented from his experience, but managed to kneel by his father's side and take his hand.

"There isn't much I can do for him. I'm sorry." The chief knew that he should have never involved himself and the rest of the group, but he had been brought up in a good Christian family, which was a paradox in his life as a SEAL, his life as a killer—a fact that he readily accepted. Besides, it was on his way and the kid couldn't be older then twenty years old. What else could he have done—let them die?

"Please, sir, certainly you can do more for him. Don't let him die." Tom was desperate to save his father. "I can pay, whatever you want, I can pay."

"Son, I don't want your money, but I might know someone close by who can help.

"Commander, what's that noise? It sounds like…"

"Shh. Holy fuck, its gunfire, lots of it…Jesse? Let's go, we're moving out! Doctor, grab the third pack and weapon, on the double." Dr. Persons was on the move, slinging the pack over one shoulder and then the other, picking up the M 29 and the 10mm handgun and securing them in the pack.

"Ready to go!" Adrenaline was pumping through his veins as he stood and ran over to Margaret. He had not felt the power of Chase's favorite drug—adrenaline—in some time and he liked the way it made him feel—fearless.

"Commander, I'm the ranking official here and I order you to stay and wait for your friend to come back." Margaret was not going anywhere, especially if she was ordered to go.

"Lady, I have a man unaccounted for and he might be in danger. You can stay if you want, but the doctor and I are going to find out what the gunfire was about.'

"I'm going to have your commission; you can't speak to me like that, I'm an ambassador." Margaret was not used to her orders not being followed to the letter and resented Chase's lack of regard for her position of power.

"Let's go. I have no time to argue with you now." Chase grabbed Margaret's shirt and pulled her along with him until she was running. The group ran down the road towards the source of the gunfire. "The shots are not too far in the distance—three or four miles. Try and keep up." Chase was already looking over his shoulder at the other two members of his group.

Chase was in the lead, well in front of the doctor, and the doctor was at least twenty meters in front of the ambassador, who was still pouting. Chase never let himself get too far in front of the others, about the length of a football field. He would rather have the two non-combatants in the rear, rather then up front where the action was. Regardless, they were still his mission and he would not risk them being injured. As a result, he made sure they were in the rear, but always in sight, killing two birds with one stone.

He came to a bend in the road and slowed to investigate the situation. Chase definitely did not want to run blindly into an ambush. He put on his night vision equipment, motioned the others to stop, and crawled on his belly around the corner, trying to lessen his shadow reflected in the moonlight. Chase watched three people stand over a fourth person, who was obviously hurt. He scanned the figures for the chief's Special Forces friendly combatant signature. It was placed on the uniform of SEALs and other elite units so they would not take friendly fire from people wearing night vision equipment. The nice thing about the signature was, it was only visible with American equipment and was not visible in normal light.

"Chief!" Chase yelled at his friend from around the corner. He could not help himself; he was so glad to see him alive. Chase put his night vision in his front pack and waved to Jesse, who motioned Chase to hurry.

"We need the doctor's help."

"Doctor, on the double; there's a man injured."

The doctor ran at full speed down the road, mumbling that he was a researcher and did not practice medicine. He arrived and looked down at George, who was pale and struggling to breathe. The doctor bent over him, assessing the gaping hole in his chest, and whispered a prayer in his ear.

"I'm sorry, there is nothing that I can do for him except put him out of his misery. He simply has lost too much blood."

"I'll do it. He's my father; it should be me." Tom drew his handgun, a Star, double-action army 44 caliber, and pointed it at his father. "Please, I need to do this in private." No one said anything, walking away from Tom and his dying father, tending to their own business.

"Jess, what happened? You didn't do this, did you?"

"No, but there are five men down the road who I shot dead. I couldn't turn him down. He was so scared, and he had a woman with him. He said they were attacked by bandits with masks and that his father sent him for help."

"What else did you find out in town?" The chief handed Chase a wanted poster and pointed to the headline. Just then, a shot rang out into the stillness of the night.

Chase looked at the date on the poster: November 12, 1865. Chase could not believe it. *This is insane,* he thought. *How did this happen, and why? More importantly, how old is the poster?* The group did not even know the date.

"Chief, we need to gather the equipment and some of the stray horses, and go into town to figure this all out."

"Aye, sir." The doctor, Chase and the chief flipped over the wagon and harnessed the remaining horses to the rig, gathered their belonging, including Tom and Elizabeth, and started to town. The trip was made in silence with everyone piled in the back of the wagon.

Chapter 4

Who were the men that helped the Tidwell boy? Five of his friends were dead, and he wanted revenge. However, his orders stated to observe and report any movement at the ambush site. Sergeant Joshua Harden looked on with keen eyes, sharpened in the lost civil war. *That thief, George Tidwell, had killed three men who had lived through the entire war. They were hungry, battle-scarred men, and a banker had killed them,* he thought while surveying the battle scene. Harden took mental notes as the dead bodies of his friends found their eternal resting place and Tidwell's now repaired wagon started towards town. The group seemed to be going into town, but the rest of Harden's group was too far away to intercept and destroy the Yankees. *The captain will have a plan; he always does. No matter how difficult the problem, Captain Buford Walton has the solution.* Waiting until they were out of sight, Joshua walked slowly to where his friends rested for eternity, knelt, and spoke a prayer.

"God, in your infinite wisdom grant these men the peace that I could never give then while they were alive." Finished, he mounted his horse and headed to the hideout, knowing Captain Walton would have a plan and that he would follow him until they completed their mission.

"Sir, I did as you requested. I got the men whom the boy killed and put them on the wagon outside the camp. Sir, why aren't we giving our soldiers a decent burial?"

"We will, but first they're going to help us get our land back and avenge their deaths all at the same time. Cover their bodies and inform the sergeant when he gets back that I wish to see him."

"Yes, sir."

Buford visited every one of his men before he settled down to rest. It was going to be an early start, but he was used to that. He drifted off to sleep—a soldier's sleep, with one eye open and one ear listening at all times, waiting for danger.

"Captain Walton, sir."

Buford jumped to his feet as if something was wrong. "What is it?" He seemed perturbed at the interruption of his sleep. His friend Josh Harden stood over him with a look of disgust directed towards the loss of life, rather than Buford's tone of voice.

"You wanted to see me when I got back, sir?"

"Joshua, I apologize. You startled me. Did you discover anything?"

"He seems to be headed into town with some of his men. I think that they are his men. I have no idea where they would have come from otherwise."

"Good, even better. We'll go into town before dawn, so get some sleep. I'll need you fresh for tomorrow. Post guards and pick a detail to go with us, fifteen men or so."

"Yes, sir." Harden smiled at his friend as he turned to go. He had a plan—a plan that would lead them to victory, which had eluded them in the war.

The town was beautiful to look at, resembling something right out of a textbook studied in school. It had quaint buildings made of brick and stone that gave one a feeling of warmth and hospitality. The residential homes had waist-high, black cast-iron fences around them with grass and what looked to be spring and summer gardens that now were mounds of recently thawed winter mud. Moving from the outskirts to the town center, the street, which had been dirt and gravel, became cobblestone, connecting the vast shops that cluttered the downtown area. Many of the buildings were new, most of the older structures having met their destruction or burned in the war, and construction continued as far as the eye could see. The biggest building in the town was the hotel, which was where Thomas headed. Not many people were out at this time of night, but inside the hotel lobby, a party raged. Drinking, girls, and gambling occupied the men who, for one reason or another, visited the town.

Thomas pulled on the reins, stopping the wagon directly in front of the hotel. He handed the reins off to Dr. Persons, who was surprised to be holding a team of horses and showed it on his face, but played the part as best as he could.

Tom jumped down from the wagon and started to the door of the hotel, turning just as he was about to enter. "How many rooms do we need altogether? I figure three—the two ladies in one and the four of us pair up and take the other two."

"Aaaah, that would be fine, kid, but we don't have the money for the rooms," the chief answered hesitantly.

"You saved my life. The least I can do is give you a bed to lie your head on for the night."

Chase and the chief exchanged looks of disbelief, saying at the same time, syllable for syllable, "There's no place like home. There's no place like home." Everyone in the wagon erupted in laughter, save Elizabeth, who gazed out at Tom with a confused look on her face.

Tom disappeared into the hotel with a stagger that said he was glad simply that he still was alive.

The hotel manager approached Tom with a confused look on his face. "Mr. Tidwell, how nice to see you again. We didn't expect you back so soon. Did you forget something?"

"No, no. I would like to rent three rooms for the night and have six baths." Tom handed the proprietor more than enough to cover the bill. "The rest is for our privacy." He held the bill in his hand until he received a nod and a smile.

"This way, Mr. Tidwell. I have the perfect set of rooms for you and I can have the baths drawn at eleven-thirty."

"That will be fine. Thank you." Tom opened the door to one of the rooms and inspected it. It seemed to be satisfactory. This was where he was going to sleep tonight.

"Oh, one more thing. Please ask my friends outside to come in, and we will need our luggage brought in as well. One last request: have someone take care of my horses and wagon," he said to the hotel manager, holding another ten-dollar bill in his hand.

"Right away, Mr. Tidwell. I would be happy to." The man took the bill and disappeared down the staircase.

The group of displaced time travelers looked around the town in amazement and pondered their fate, each lost in their own minds until a portly man exited the hotel and approached the wagon, snapping the group back into reality.

"Excuse me. Mr. Tidwell asked me to show you to your rooms and take care of the horses. If you would follow me." The manager pointed in the direction of the door and ordered his help to get the bags. Chase ensured the help did not take his bag, which contained the equipment from 2099, eliminating a possible problem, something Chase didn't need any more of that evening.

In silence, one after another, the group entered the hotel, wondering what was going to come next. This had to be a surreal dream; an after effect of transporting was on most of their minds, but everyone knew it really wasn't the case. Either way, they would know in the morning after a well-deserved rest.

Tom welcomed his friends with a smile on his face and arms wide open as if he had saved the day. "A bed, a bath, and gentlemen, some company if you desire."

"Thomas, we appreciate the bed and the bath, but I think that we can stand to be alone tonight." The chief and Chase opened the door to their room to find that there was just one bed. They flung the bag containing the equipment that they dared not leave in the wagon onto the floor and both looked at the bed like they were both dying of thirst and there was just one small glass of water.

"I'll flip you for it, sir," the chief suggested, taking his good luck 2099 quarter from its plastic cover attached to his dog tags.

"Chief, I might have to pull rank on you this time," Chase said, cracking a smile. "We've been in worse places than this and with worse people. I think I can manage curling up with a dirty old man for one night." Both tired men stripped off their uniforms and fell asleep before they had an opportunity to have the bath that they desperately needed.

That wasn't the case for Margaret Knox Harriman, who welcomed the chance to get the grime off her body. She slipped into the tub and started scrubbing her skin. Each part of her body got the same attention and each part of her body was becoming raw. It wasn't enough for her. She wished she could scrub to the bone, but the process became too painful to tolerate.

"This is all just a very bad dream. Tomorrow I will be back at the embassy," she insisted to herself.

"Did you say something?" Elizabeth didn't know this woman's name, a strange woman, one who wore slacks and a shirt and tried to give orders to those men. She seemed well mannered and well versed in matters of society, if a bit forward. "What is your name? Why were you wearing men's pants?" Elizabeth added under her breath. "I wasn't able to ask in all of the commotion."

"My name is Margaret. Now if you don't mind, I would like to take my bath in peace." She continued her scrubbing and began to cry, something that she hadn't done in years. Margaret was a strong woman who never showed her weaknesses. In her line of work, she couldn't afford that luxury, and her ordeal was starting to take a toll on her, cracking her usually strong armor.

Elizabeth listened from behind a paper and cloth divider that wasn't much of a sound barrier. She was certain that something strange was going on, and she was going to find out what that was. First, though, she was going to get her much-needed sleep.

The gravity of the night's events finally hit Tom, and he cried into his hands at the side of the bed. He was going to lose everything that he had ever wanted: money, power, and land. His father was gone, and someone wanted him dead, but he was not going to lose his life. The best thing to do would be to hire his new friends to take him and Elizabeth back home. *That's it.* He would report the ambush and the killings in the morning and start back home with these men. *They are quite strange*, Tom thought. *They dress oddly, and the one couldn't ride a horse at all.* In fact, he was even worse than Tom himself. *No matter—he was good with a gun, and that was the important part.* Tom wiped his face and crawled into the bed where Doctor Persons was already sound asleep.

Chase awoke before dawn to the sound of metal clinking together. He opened his eyes to see the chief cleaning their weapons. The man was a machine, never breaking down or faltering under pressure. He was the perfect product of the U.S. government. He paid a high price for that perfection as a SEAL. *The chief has no family, just a new woman in every port, so he says. He lives and breaths the navy, just as I do; that's probably why we are such good friends,* Chase thought as he sat up in bed.

"Good morning, sir. Our baths are ready in the next room. They're cold, but I'm sure that you're used to that."

"Chief, you don't have to call me sir when we're alone, especially if we really are when the hell the poster said we are."

"We are. I went downstairs and looked around a bit. Everything is surreal. I had to use an outhouse in the back."

"Chief, call me Chase. I don't want people to wonder. These people wouldn't understand. Hell, I don't understand what happened." Chase rubbed the sleep from his eyes and looked out the window at the quiet, predawn town. For the first time in quite a while, he had no idea what to do or how to get out of the mess in which he found himself.

"I'll call you Chase if you stop calling me Chief all the time."

"What do want me to call you? Master Chief?" Both men laughed. It felt good to be able to laugh in such a taxing situation. "Alright, I'll stop calling you Chief if you tell me where the outhouse is." They couldn't control their laughter; both men, warriors by trade, laughed like two schoolchildren at recess, trying to find something funny about the situation in which they found themselves.

Both men were up, dressed, and ready to begin the day before any of the others even thought about waking up. The whole point of being up early was to get a head start on everyone else in town, but that wasn't the case this morning. They watched as two men went into the sheriff's office just as the sun started to show over the horizon, lighting up the countryside.

By 9:00 a.m., everyone was up and ready to go. The question, though, was where they should go. Should the team stay put and wait, or should they move and attempt to find their own answers? No one speculated about what had happened yesterday. In fact, for some time no one uttered a word at all.

"You guys need some new clothing. You can't go out in public wearing that." Thomas pointed at the combat uniforms that they both donned and smirked. "Here, take this money and go to the shop for some suitable clothes for traveling. Then meet us at the stables. I'll prepare the horses."

Chase grabbed the money with his left hand, and, turning to go outside, he patted his friend on the back, pushing him out the door. "Let's go. *Robert!*"

The chief had just opened the door when three men stopped him in the doorway, two with guns drawn. On the first man's lapel, a shiny tin star reflected the early morning light. The last of the three men stood to the side, pointing at Thomas

"That's him. He's the one who killed my brother."

"Are you sure, Mr. Walton? He seems harmless enough."

"Yes, sir, I am. He killed my brother. I saw it with my own two eyes."

"Mr..." The sheriff trailed off when he realized that he did not know the man's name.

"Tidwell," Tom answered the sheriff in a shaky voice as though he were just starting puberty.

"Mr. Tidwell, I'm not sure what happened here, but murder is a serious charge, so I'll have to take you in so that a judge can sort this out." The man reached out with handcuffs and affixed them to the wrists of a very frightened Tom Tidwell.

Tom wanted to tell him about the ambush, but every time he opened his mouth, nothing came out but a low, tonal noise. The sheriff gripped the chain links of the handcuffs and escorted Tom in the direction of the jail, leading him like a disobedient dog. The chief watched as Buford Walton smiled and tipped his hat with a satisfaction similar to that of a man who had won a long contest with many difficulties.

"Chase, what was that?" Dave Persons asked crossly.

"I don't know, but we're going to find out. First, Jesse and I are going to buy those new duds, and then when we look like we belong, we'll go to the jail house and find out what is going on."

"Captain, what's the plan? If he's in jail, we can't get to him." Confused, Sergeant Harden looked out at his mentor, wondering what magnificent plan he had this time.

"Joshua, I want you to go back and get the men together and come into town at two o'clock. Make sure that they come in peacefully and leave four of the men to help me."

"Yes, sir." With that, Joshua departed to complete his orders. Joshua was loyal to a fault, and he wanted to impress that upon the captain through his actions. What he didn't know yet was that these orders would save his life. Just to be safe, he left his four best men in the town and set out for the hideout.

Buford had other plans for Tom; the law wasn't enough for this land-grabbing pig. He was going to have his revenge.

In his study of history, Chase had always been fascinated with the Old West and took this unique opportunity to play the part to the extreme. He looked like a Hollywood version of the ultimate dark and mysterious hero. His pants were jet black, and his shirt was also black, but it had shiny silver buttons on it. He sported a gunfighter's jacket made of tan cow leather that came down to his shins. In addition, he had to have the tan leather gauntlets that cavalrymen wore. The crowning piece of the outfit was his hat, which was black with a sliver band around the base. He slightly modified his gun belt to house twin futuristic 10mm semiautomatic handguns with laser sighting, one hanging from each side of his waist. The chief indulged himself as well and had almost the same exact costume, except that his included a tan hat, which matched his coat. In addition, he carried only a single holster around his waist. The pair truly were a remarkable sight, seemingly straight out of Hollywood in the 1950s. They also purchased a third set of clothes for Dr. Persons, who was preparing the horses and wagon for their departure.

"Chase, I'm going to go scout the location and report back here. You make sure that everything else is ready."

"Giving orders now, Robert?"

The chief turned his head so that he looked Chase right in the eyes. "With all do respect, sir, fuck you." Without missing a step, Chief James disappeared around the corner. Chase knew that he was just kidding and went about his business.

Buford Walton was determined to get Tom, and he hoped to capitalize on the fact that this was a Confederate state. He entered the jailhouse, where the sheriff was playing solitaire.

"Sheriff."

"Mr. Walton, what can I do for you? The judge won't be in town until Tuesday." The man stood and shook Buford's hand.

"I know, you told me this morning. I was just wondering if you served in the recent war because you look similar to a gentleman whom I served with in the Virginia 10th."

"You must be mistaken. I was in the Virginia 8th, but it's a pleasure to meet you regardless. I have a great respect for the 10th. I remember a time when—"

Buford interrupted the man as he didn't want to go any further into his lie. "Actually, sir, I'm in need of a favor from you."

"What kind of favor?"

"The kind for which I would pay handsomely. That man in the jail is a carpetbagger, and he stole my family's land after the war. I want revenge and my land. I want him dead."

"Sir, I'm not about to kill someone in my own jailhouse."

"No, sir, I wouldn't ask that of you. All that I ask is that you turn your back or go to lunch so that I can bring him well outside of town and kill him."

"You said that you're willing to pay for my services?"

"Yes, how much would it take for you to leave the door open when you and your deputies go to lunch?"

"Well, I would have to pay off my deputies. Hmm, I figure three hundred would do just fine."

Buford hadn't expected that it would be so much money, but he was almost done with the mission. He took his money from his billfold and counted out three hundred dollars, handing it over to the greedy sheriff. "Go to lunch at one-thirty; at one forty-five your jail will be empty."

"I'll put the keys in the top left drawer." The sheriff smiled as he recounted his money.

"Good day, sir." Buford tipped his hat as he turned for the door.

Chief James hurried around the corner and down the alley, away from the jail, where he had just overheard Buford's plan to kill Tom. *We will have to break him out*, he thought. Jesse already had saved him once; he had to lead the boy out of danger again, or the five men he had killed would have died for no reason. He immediately went to the stables to find Chase and tell him about what this Buford Walton was planning.

"We can go in before the others and steal him right from underneath their noses. Fifteen minutes is plenty of time to get in and get out. We'll send Persons and the women out of town and stash the horses around the corner in the alley I just surveyed." Jesse had rehearsed his sales pitch on the way to the stables.

"In and out, what do you think? Five, maybe six minutes at the most," Chase responded, pondering the logistics of the operation. "That sounds good, but I want the M 29s just in case there's trouble."

The plan and players were set. Dr. Persons readied the wagon and horses. He would hide the getaway mounts in the alley behind the jail and take the women out of town after they first had visited Thomas to inform him of the plan.

"Margaret, we need to get you some more appropriate clothes to wear into the jail. You look about my size—a bit taller, but I have a dress that has not been taken up yet that would look beautiful on you."

"Elizabeth, I'm perfectly fine the way that I am. I am in no way in need of your handouts."

"I thought you would be more comfortable in something clean, plus Chase told me to give you something."

"I do not follow orders from that man like everyone else does. He can go to hell."

Elizabeth couldn't believe the pompous woman she had to deal with. "I don't know who you are, but proper women do what they're told. That's my fiancée in there, and if your friends don't get him out, he is going to die." She started to cry, trying to convince Margaret to follow the plan. "Please don't let that happen. I'm pregnant, and we're not getting married for another three weeks. If he's dead, then I will be an outcast."

"All right, for you I'll put on this stupid dress, but I'm not going to wear one of these all of the time. I could care less about Chase and fitting in."

At fifty-four, the ambassador looked no older than forty. She kept herself in shape, and in Elizabeth's dress, she looked pretty. The blue-and-white pattern wasn't a winter design, but it was the only dress that Elizabeth owned that would fit Margaret. The wire in the dress made it hard for her to move around, but after Elizabeth was finished with the makeup and hair, she fit right in, as had been the plan. Both women went to the jail and did exactly what Chase had told them to do.

"Excuse me, Sheriff, my name is Elizabeth Thompson. I believe you have my fiancé, Thomas Tidwell, in here. My mother and I would like to see him."

"Of course, but visitors are limited to ten minutes, and I'll have to check you for weapons." This part the sheriff enjoyed. He frisked the two women thoroughly and instructed them that they couldn't touch the prisoner.

The two women passed through a doorway into the cell room. The room was surprisingly large, and there was more then enough lighting from the lanterns outside the cell. The cell itself was just that—there was only one bench on which the prisoners could sit or sleep and no windows, which made it far more difficult for people to escape. Tom was sitting in the corner on the floor. He was elated to see Elizabeth and ran to the bars, clutching one in each of his hands.

"Elizabeth, what is happening? They wouldn't listen to my story about my father. They said that I had to wait until Tuesday for the judge to return." He reached for her through the bars, but heeding the sheriff's instructions, she took a step back.

"The sheriff said that we couldn't touch, Tom. I have a message for—"

Margaret interrupted Elizabeth in mid-sentence. "We're leaving town and she came to say goodbye."

"Leaving town? Why?" Tom was scared and confused.

"Tom, we are all leaving town today before two o'clock." Margaret knew that the sheriff was listening and that Elizabeth would give the plan away. "The others feel that it would be best to distance themselves from this town and incident. Do you understand?"

At first, Tom had no idea what Margaret was talking about, but the smile on Elizabeth's face was far from a poker face. She would have to change her expression if the plan was to work. He knew that the two soldiers were coming for him. "I understand. I hope that you'll make it back into town for my trial."

"I don't think so; we're all pulling out for good."

"Goodbye, Elizabeth, tell the others the same." Tom turned, acting sullen, but knowing that there was to be a rescue attempt before two o'clock.

The women turned, thanked the sheriff, and walked out the door and onto the wagon were Dr. Persons waited to drive them to safety. He had placed the horses the men were to use in their escape in the correct spot and was ready to head out of town.

The jail was nothing special. The door was made of fortified wood, and the windows had metal bars in them, both of which were standard. What was surprising was how terrible the jail security seemed to be. *But if they are not guarding the place well they surely don't know we are coming,* Chase thought as he inched his way closer to the street. The jail had only one, at best two guards inside. The building itself was made of red brick and was hastily constructed. Portions of the structure were without mortar to hold the bricks together, making it look as if the building was still under construction. The windows also had reinforced wood covers, but they were not in use. It was only a matter of minutes before the sheriff was to leave Thomas to his date with fate. If the chief and Chase had anything to say about it, fate wouldn't enter into the equation—only their skill would matter. The SEALs crouched behind the post office across the street, waiting, without moving a muscle, for the bribed officials to leave the building. If Elizabeth had done her job, Thomas would know that a rescue was about to start. Just a few more seconds and the fun would start.

Chase looked up just in time to see the door open and the sheriff walk out with his deputy. He went so far as to leave the door open. They eagerly watched as the two men walked out of sight.

Both SEALs stepped out of the corner and slowly walked over to the jail. Upon entering, they found Thomas in the corner preparing for gunfire. He stood with a spring in his step and a smile worthy of Hollywood on his face. He was scared, and despite his best efforts, it showed.

"He put the keys in the top left drawer," Tom quickly pointed out. His two saviors already knew that, however.

Chase opened the desk drawer and reached in, never taking his eyes off the front door, tossing the keys to the chief, who was at the jail cell door. He fumbled with the heavy key chain and had to try three separate keys before he found the right one. The door opened, and Chief James took Thomas by the arm and walked towards Chase.

It was time. Exacting his revenge and taking back his land would all culminate today. Buford and four of his most trusted men moved towards the building with confidence, bantering in a way that only the closest friends could. They had fought together for four years in the war, counting on each other in order to stay alive. Now they would regain what had been lost through all those years of fighting. *Fifteen more feet and this insanity will be over,* was the last thought to go through the mind of Buford's best man outside of Joshua. He was right, but the fight would go on.

Chase moved to the door, waited for the other two to take their positions, and removed the barricade.

"Good to go, Chase." Jesse smiled at him and winked an "I am invincible" wink, the one only SEALs and twenty-year-old star athletes displayed.

The door flew open, and Chase led the way. As he stepped out, he spotted Buford and his men. Chase pointed his 10mm at the first man, the laser sighting pointing at his chest, and pulled the trigger.

Buford watched as his best man and friend hit the ground. He drew his gun and opened fire but was unable to accurately aim in the short amount of time he had to react. The rounds hit the wooden porch well short of his target. The remaining men fired in the direction of the jail, but the smoke from the weapons made it hard to see the men who had what they wanted. With a gust of wind, Buford felt and heard the door of the jail slam shut. One of his men ran to the open window but before Buford could yell, a bullet instantly took his life, making him unrecognizable even to his wife. His lifeless body flopped to the ground, blood pouring from the wound. Buford grabbed his friend and pulled him across the street.

"What the fuck happened?"
"They're early," Chase answered crossly. His anger was directed not at the chief but at the fact that his plan had not worked as he had hoped.
"We need Tom to have a gun. We're going to have the fight of our lives to get out of here, and I'm sure as hell not going to die in this shit hole." Chief James had envisioned twenty men opposing them.
Chase handed Tom the extra 10mm handgun and showed him how to use it.
"What is this? Who are you people?" Tom held the foreign-looking weapon in the air, confused and scared.
"Not now, Tom. If we live, we can talk about it. Just pull the trigger and the gun will fire. When the bolt stays open, remove the clip like this." Chase released the magazine and put in another. "You are ready to fire again. Do you understand?" Tom nodded, but given his confusion and fright, it seemed that he wouldn't be much help.
"Tom, just stay behind me. Everything will be all right." Chief James grabbed Tom on the shoulder, and when he did, Tom seemed to calm down to the point where they could attempt an escape. "That's what a chief is for, commander," he said with a smile, pulling a grenade from his pocket and opening the window.

"What the hell is that," the third of five men yelled from across the street. He ran up to it, inspected it, and picked it up.
"Put it down, you as—"
The explosion shattered the windows of the building behind the target. Buford checked himself for injuries, but the only thing that he found was his brother in law's body torn to pieces by the automatic fire. Buford took cover behind a building when the Gatling gun opened fire. He had never seen a Gatling gun but he had heard that they just keep firing one bullet after another. *What else could it be?*

"Now, Chase!" Jesse yelled from the window as he laid down covering fire with the M 29/ME.
Chase flung open the door and opened fire with his M 29, instantly killing the forth man in Buford's group. With a sweeping motion, he entered the street with Tom and the chief right behind him. Chase led the group down the

alley to the preplanned meeting place, but the horses weren't there.

"Chase, the stables. It's our only choice, our only hope."

"What is your ammo situation?"

"I have one clip left in the 10mm and three for the 29."

"Tom has two and I have one for the 10mm. I'm down to two for the M 29. We had better be fast or we can kiss our asses goodbye. Lead the way, Chief."

Jesse ran back into the eye of the storm, tossing a smoke grenade into the street to mask their escape. They ran alongside of the walls of the buildings, but far enough away that a ricochet would do little damage.

"Targets, two o'clock." Both SEALs turned and opened fire on the sheriff and his deputies. The first set of bullets from Jesse's rifle hit directly in the chest of the farthest deputy. Chase had the other two, hitting the sheriff in the head and his other deputy in the neck, ripping a gaping hole where his windpipe had been.

"Thirty meters, move."

In shock, Buford stepped out from behind the safety of the wall. He cleared his eyes and watched as the men, who had killed four more of his friends, raced for the stables and freedom. He knew now that Thomas hadn't killed those men last night. It had been the other two men, who obviously were soldiers from the war. He picked up the Henry rifle belonging to his best man whom Chase had shot in the beginning of the battle and took aim. The smoke was too much for his eyes and they welled up with tears. He crawled behind the building, which gave him some shelter from the smoke. Only his face and the barrel of the rifle showed around the corner. He waited for his shot. He had no idea who it was, but it would have to be enough. His grip tightened as he pulled the trigger.

"Ahhh, I've been shot! *Ahhh!*" Tom writhed in pain, holding his leg.

Chief James looked behind him to see Thomas lying on the ground, holding his thigh and screaming for help. Running to his rescue, Chief James flung him over his shoulder as Chase laid down covering fire and started on the twenty meters to the stables.

Out of nowhere, Dr. Persons and three extra horses came out of the alley directly in front of the stable. Jesse was on autopilot. He helped Tom onto a horse and hopped on his as if he was a true cowboy, galloping and firing behind him to suppress any advance. With that, the four men rode out of the bullet-riddled town.

Chapter 5

This was a new experience for all three men; though the chief had ridden a horse yesterday for a short time, it hadn't been for as long of a distance. Riding a horse was nothing like driving a car; there was a live animal with a mind of its own underneath you. For both men the experience was exhilarating, being in the outdoors with the wind at their face, and the knowledge that they were the hunted and not the hunter gave the two seasoned soldiers a rush they had never felt before. It was apparent that they would be on the run and that Tom's leg would slow them down. The solution was one that not everyone was going to like: go into hiding until this blew over or try to make it out west-running and hiding every chance they had. Chase would have liked the former, but not everyone was suited for hiding in the shadows, and only he and the chief would have the fortitude to make it. The other option would be to go west and try to outrun the trouble that had plagued them thus far, at the same time trying to figure out what had gone wrong and how they were going to complete their mission. Perhaps they would find the answers they longed for in the wild plains of the Western Territories of the United States. Answers to questions like, why had they traveled to 1865 and what were they supposed to do? How were they going to get home or were they stuck living a lifestyle long dead, filled with daring and heroism? Short lives, mostly ending painfully and often sudden. Perhaps it was a mistake they were in 1865, but they all knew, somehow they had to make it back to 2099.

The group wasn't going to get far with three men who were the antithesis of equestrian genius, and the one person who could ride a horse had a bullet through his leg. Each man had a different degree of difficulty riding a horse, but all three thought that their testicles were permanently part of the hard leather surface of the saddle. The only thing that made it bearable was the utter beauty of the landscape. The remnants of fall's colors clung to the maple and oak trees sprawling clear to the horizon as if somehow finding a way to turn back Mother Nature. The dense, intertwining branches of age-old trees dominated the landscape, and the leaves of seasons past crunched under the weight of their mounts. Each step left a trail, both physical and auditory, a trail the team could ill afford, making a sort of journeyman theme to the ride—man verses nature verses time.

"How far do we have to go before we can rest?" an obviously distressed doctor grunted into the chilly afternoon air. His words mirrored in the condensation of his breath.

"A bit more. We need to make it to the next set of trees." Chase had no idea, but someone had to keep order in the ranks.

The chief pulled side by side with Chase and leaned in, muffling his words with his hand, hiding his thoughts from the rest of the group as he would do during any other mission. "Chase, Tom's losing a lot of blood; we have to have Dr. Persons look at his leg." Jesse observed a slumping Tom, who was barely conscious and becoming pale.

Chase glanced over at his new friend, who slumped over in his saddle, holding onto the horse around its neck. The horse's hair absorbed quit a bit of his blood, but it still dripped slowly from its fur, and his leg looked broken, but the mound of flesh that hung from his leg made it hard to be sure. The chief was right; they needed to attend to his wounds. Hopefully, the doctor, with his advanced knowledge of medicine, could save his leg. If not, they would have to turn and fight—a SEAL never leaves a man behind. If someone from 1865 looked at his leg, most definitely they would have amputated it above the wound.

On the chief's advice, and Chase's order, the group changed direction and headed off the path into the wooded area to the left of their position. The woods would provide some needed cover for the team as the good doctor took care of Tom, but little in the way of sterile conditions usually needed for an operation of this magnitude.

"Chief, maybe one of us should double back and see if we are being followed?"

"I'll go, I have more experience on our furry friends." Jesse smiled at Chase and set out to cover their flank and see if anyone was on their trail.

"Chief." He turned as Chase threw him his last magazine of MP 29 ammunition. "You might need them."

"Thanks." His tone was sarcastic and serious at the same time.

Buford ordered his men to gather what was left of the small detachment sent to kill the Tidwell boy, wondering who was so skilled that they could kill his war-hardened men. The important thing was that he wasn't hurt, the driving force and inspiration of the expedition. Most of the town gathered to witness the carnage of the jailbreak. In the eyes of the town's citizens, there was no doubt that Tom Tidwell had killed those five men, who were now on display at the morticians office, and that his friends were black marks on the town and this renewed country, formed out of the blood and sacrifice of the men of the Civil War.

"These men have to be found and punished."

"Hell yes, they deserve to be hung."

"I say we hunt them down."

A mob was forming and becoming increasingly excitable with every passing second. Some men went so far as to saddle and mount their horses, demanding a posse form, further antagonizing the town. They had no idea that Buford and the late sheriff were conspiring to kill Tom Tidwell, and Buford made damn sure they never would. He had one of his men collect the bodies of the deputies and the sheriff, taking the three hundred dollars from the sheriff's vest pocket. He wasn't even going to share it with his deputies, who had died for nothing, much worse than dying for one hundred dollars.

The crowd became so unruly that the mayor put in a telegraph to the U.S. marshal, who gave his friend the power to form a posse, giving them a temporary rank of deputy U.S. marshal. This wasn't an honor that the mayor was going to take lightly; he had to find the right person to lead the expedition. He was far too old and his sheriff was permanently lobotomized.

"Mr. Mayor," Buford called from across the street. "Please, sir, I would like to speak with you." Buford stopped five feet from him, tipping his hat. "I was wondering if you could inter my friends and give them a decent reading from the good book," he said, handing him a twenty-dollar bill.

"If I might ask, Mr. Buford, where are you going?"

"My men and I have vowed to bring these men to justice."

"By justice you mean...?"

"A trial and, if everything goes as planned, a hanging." Buford knew just what to say to manipulate this old man.

"That, sir, is very noble. I would be proud to bury your men. I sent a telegram to my friend in Washington, and the U.S. marshal's office has agreed to temporarily deputize a posse in order to catch these murderers. I wonder if your men would be interested in the job; it pays fifteen dollars a month, not like that would matter to a man like yourself." Looking down at the crisp twenty-dollar bill Buford held in his hand, he said, "But perhaps your men might benefit from it."

This was exactly what he wanted, but he couldn't look too eager to accept the honor. If he were a U.S. marshal, he could go and do anything that he wanted and get away with it. "I would have to talk it over with my men, but I think that I will be able to persuade them."

"Excellent, I'll be looking forward to your decision. When you decide please bring the names of your men to my office for the records."

The two men shook hands and departed. Buford was just where he wanted to be; his calculating nature had never failed him yet. He wouldn't even ask his men, but rather make them want it. He was a skilled orator and persuasive speaker.

"Sergeant Harden."

"Yes, sir." Harden stood at attention, eyes fixed on Buford's, knowing that he had a plan. "What can I do for you, Captain?"

"Assemble the men. I have an announcement to make."

"Sir." Harden clicked his heals and sharply did an about face. "Listen up, men, the captain wants to speak, let's go—that means you, you fucking, smelly drover. Let's go, move, on the captain. Yesterday, you fuck." He skillfully rounded the men up, intently watching and listening to what their leader had planned.

"Men, starting tomorrow we're all officially U.S. marshals." Laughter erupted among the men, most thinking that Buford was joking. "It's not a joke; we have one job and one job alone: to find and bring to justice the men who killed our brethren." The laughter faded to a silence and then cheering erupted from his men. "We'll go to the ends of the earth to find them and the government will pay us fifteen dollars a month to do it." The laughter returned briefly. "Sergeant, ready the men; we move out before dark."

"Yes, sir," Harden replied with a grin from ear to ear. He was going to enjoy hunting the murderous men; it was going to be just like the war.

"I don't know, Chase, I haven't practiced this type of medicine in years;

what if I mess it up?"

Chase looked up from cleaning his weapons. "Doctor, you're the only one who can do it. You've got to try; we didn't go through all of this shit for nothing."

"The tools are so primitive. I can't work with them"

Chase set down the guns, giving Dr. Persons his full attention. " I've seen a combat medic patch multiple holes in a man's arm, leg and chest with the same fucking med. kit, under extreme conditions, while we were taking heavy fire, so stop making your goddamn excuses and just do your fucking job."

Chase's eyes burned a hole right through Dave; he dipped his head in shame and went to work. Chase was right, God had given him a gift, one that made him useful to these almost super-human men who risked there lives to save complete strangers in a different time and a harsh environment. Persons nodded his agreement with himself and began to stitch the muscle tissue together. Luckily, the bullet had missed his femur bone and his femoral artery, which was on the other side of his leg, and traveled up through his pelvis. If the bullet severed the artery, Tom would already be dead by now. The whole procedure lasted over two hours, finishing just in time for Dave and Chase to watch the sun set in the autumn sky.

"He lost a lot of blood and still isn't out of danger. Most importantly, we have to find some way to immobilize his leg, but he has a seventy-five percent chance of living. The only other thing that I'm worried about is infection. I used the iodine in the pack to sterilize the tools and the area around the wound but I didn't have anything to put on the wound. This isn't exactly hospital sterilization out here."

"Doctor, I'm sorry that I yelled at you. I was out of line; you did a great job." Chase needed the doctor to focus on the plan and not him.

"No, I needed that. I've been afraid to take chances in my life; it felt good to take one. I guess it started with the horses in town; I saw that they were gone, so I stole some from the stables, and then helping this man, I feel invigorated. There aren't many moments in one's life that are so profound that you can single them out, but I think that this is one of them."

Chase laid his hand on his new friend's shoulder; giving Dave some much needed reinforcement. "Will we be able to move him? We can't stay here for long."

"I gave him the morphine in the med. pack, so if we move him we should do it soon before it wears off. The terrain isn't quite freeway quality and most likely bumpy."

"Hopefully the chief will get back soon; he's been gone for a while now." Chase took this opportunity, Tom under the influence of an opiate, to put on the night vision goggles. He scanned the landscape for the chief; more importantly he scanned it for Buford and his men. "What got you into medicine, Dr. Persons?"

"Please call me Dave; I've been taking the liberty of calling you Chase. Family, I guess—my father and mother were doctors. My dad was a vascular surgeon and my mother an OBGYN. They wanted me to be a chip off the block, but I opted for the research route. I enjoyed exploring and discovering new and better techniques not just using someone else's."

"I can understand that. I wanted to be a professor and a wrestling coach. I'm pretty far from that, about 230 years."

"College?"

"Actually, I'm a doctor, too; I have a PhD in history and military science, kind of ironic if you think about it. I studied it and now I get to live it." Chase laughed at his situation, but he knew it was just a defense mechanism.

"How did you end up in the navy?"

Both men were silent; war wasn't something many vets enjoyed discussing. It was an awkward moment; fortunately, a rustling noise in the woods saved them from further embarrassment. Chase took aim at the figure with his laser sight.

"Chief, you scared the shit out of me."

"Christ, Chase, I made enough noise to alarm Buford back in the town. How's our friend?"

The doctor looked down at Tom. "He'll live, I think. Nevertheless, if we are going to move him, I advise that we do it when he is doped up."

"Doped up? Are you sure you are a doctor?" Chief James snickered as he spoke.

"I was trying to put it in laymen's terms for all of the none doctor SEALS present."

"That was a good one, Doctor; I'm going to have to watch you closely from now on." All three men laughed briefly and then collected themselves for the reality of the situation.

"I found the women; they're about five or six miles north of here."

"That's what took you so long?"

The chief nodded. "No one has moved from the town as of yet, but it looked as if they were forming a pos... What do they call it?"

"Posse," Chase answered. He had known that his history degree would come in handy at some time in his life

"Yeah, posse, probably will move out any time now. They may have already. We have about two-and-a-half hours on them, but we have to move out now and move fast, hurt man and all."

"Let's do it," the other two men answered in unison.

Elizabeth and Margaret waited impatiently for the others to return, longing to go home, knowing that it was impossible.

"He said that Tom was hurt; he has to be okay, for I don't think that I can live without him. I love him so much."

"Is it love or is it your baby?" Margaret answered coarsely.

"Love. We will be married soon and no one but you and I will know that I was pregnant before."

"You haven't told him?"

"No, I didn't know how to."

Margaret shook her head in disbelief. "Where does one go to the bathroom around here?"

"You sure are a mean person; you don't care about anybody but yourself. Those men whom you're with risked their lives to save Tom, and you didn't even want to go to the jail because you had to wear one of my summer dresses. I'm sorry all of my winter ones are too short for you." Elizabeth knew that her and Tom's saviors were not of this world, and she was going to find out what was going on, but she wanted to make a point to Margaret, who she liked even less.

Margaret looked over at her young friend in annoyance and asked again, "Where can I go to the bathroom?"

"Anywhere. I don't see an outhouse around here, do you?" Elizabeth turned away from Margaret and pouted.

"You have to be kidding me. I have to pee outside?"

Elizabeth didn't have the energy to argue with this woman anymore. *Where does she think that she is from*? She simply answered, "Yes."

With a huff, Margaret Knox-Harriman, U.S. ambassador to the Arab coalition government, found a peaceful spot and squatted. She heard movement behind her and stood without finishing, spraying her pants with urine. She couldn't stand that dress and had changed back into her now clean 2099 outfit.

Chase had seen her using the tree but opted not to say anything for fear that she would yell at him the whole journey.

"It's about time! We thought that you forgot about us."

"No, we were just making sure that no one was following us," the chief offered in annoyance. "We have to move fast; you're going to have to drive the wagon, Margaret."

"You have to be kidding; I am paid for my brain and not for driving a wagon."

"If you don't get in the fucking wagon, the only thing that you are going to be paying is the piper. Dave has to ride with Tom, and Elizabeth is going to assist him; that leaves you, unless you want to fire the guns."

"No, no, that's okay, I'll drive the wagon." For the first time in quite a while, she felt remorse for her pompous attitude. Chase, Robert, and Dave all looked at her with a stare that could cut through glass.

They were running late and the annoyance showed on Buford's face. The mayor insisted on swearing everybody in personally instead of as a group and insisted that each man have provisions and a blanket, ammunition and in some cases rifles. He didn't seem to understand that time was of the essence and that these trained men were soldiers. Unfortunately, Buford's play tied his hands because he couldn't show this naive mayor what was really up his sleeve. He had to put his best poker face on and play the gentleman, which he did so well.

"Mr. Harden, please send our best trackers out to scout; we will follow shortly."

"Yes." He caught himself. "Okay, Mr. Walton." He motioned to two men who were in dire need of a bath. They each had a beard that reached to the middle of their chest, one continuous eyebrow, and dark brown eyes that were set back in their heads. These two twin brothers had grown up tracking and hunting with their father and had become quite skilled.

"Pick up their trail and we will follow shortly." The men, without saying a word, rode off into the darkening sky. It was going to be much harder picking up the trail in the dark, but they had done it before and were determined to do it once more.

Soon after the men left, the town's mayor finished his politically driven speech. "God bless and God's speed."

Buford still couldn't believe that he had listened to that bumbling idiot for as long as he had, and as his men rode out behind him, he waived goodbye to the man, who, despite his shortcomings, gave him the vehicle to accomplish all of his goals. When he had started this mission, it hadn't been personal, just about getting his land and the land of his men back, but he had lost twelve good, loyal men who had risked their lives every day during the war only to be shot down by a banker, his son and two strangers. Soon he would be rebuilding his house on his land with his wife and daughter.

"Hey, Robert, where's Chase going?"
The chief slowed so that he could see Doctor Persons in the opening in the back of the wagon. "He's going to scout this road and see if there's a better way to travel. Hey, Robert is a bit stodgy. I prefer Bob or my friends call me Jesse."
"Jesse James."
"Ah, I know."
"Your nickname takes on a new meaning now, doesn't it?"
"I don't know, I think that he lived later than this."
"I really don't know. Chase might; I can't believe that he has a PhD, Professor SEAL."
"I've been looking for good nickname for him; I think you found it. Thanks, Doctor Dave." Jesse smiled as he rode up to see how Margaret was doing driving the four-horse wagon.

Time passed slowly for the saddle-sore SEAL, riding ahead of his friends in search of a town or anything that they could use to get better transportation. The odd predicament that Chase found himself in was very taxing and he hadn't had two minutes to relax and think things through, until now. There had to be a reason that they had transported back in time or could it just have been a random act? Regardless, he had to come up with a way to contact home, letting them know what had happened, and complete his mission. Then he remembered the COM gear and retrieval platforms; if he could get them working maybe he could contact earth 2099. Stranger things had definitely happened in the last twenty-four hours.

His mind drifted, thinking of his first day in the navy. He had been so proud, ready to fight for his country, but by the time he had gotten through OCS and BUD/S, an entire year had passed and over fifteen thousand Americans had died. He should have been terrified but he was invincible, unmovable, and so sure of himself that nothing could have detoured him from winning the war single handedly. He couldn't be further from that feeling right now; he was stuck in a world that he had studied, but in real life, it was much different than he had expected. He just wanted to go back to his life as the best SEAL team commander that the U.S. had to offer. He was a proud man, tough, and would focus on the task at hand and repress all of his fears, which was what he had been trained to do.

His eyes pulled him back into the present. "A railroad," Chase said aloud. "We follow the railroad to a terminal and catch a train out West or East, anyplace but here." He turned his now tamed horse around and kicked him into a run. The faster the better; he had to stay ahead of the posse.

"Sir, me and my brother have picked up their trail; it looks like they hid in the woods about four miles north. We found lots of blood and some used bandages. Then they started northwest. My brother sent me here and he is still following them murderers."

"Good work. Keep us informed of your progress; we will have them by morning." Buford yelled for the benefit of his men. That might have been a bit optimistic but moral went a long way in a soldier's performance. He spurred his horse to go a bit faster, his new marshal's badge shining in the light of the full moon.

Chase was gasping for air when he found the rest of the group.

"Rail...railroad about...about seven miles up...up the road."

"Catch your breath." Jesse couldn't understand what Chase had just said.

Chase paused, catching his breath. "If we follow the tracks we'll eventually come to a station, where we can buy tickets. If we can get there soon enough, they won't be able to track us."

"That could work," the chief added with a hint of interest. "What are we waiting for?"

The wagon and horses picked up the pace, giving Dr. Persons fits about Tom's leg, but it was more important to stay ahead of the posse than it was to keep Tom comfortable.

"How's your ass, Chase?" Jesse asked but he already knew the answer.

"It hurts like hell. I can hardly stand it."

"I'm actually getting pretty good at this shit; I found that if you stand up in the leg things that your balls don't get smashed as much."

"They're called stirrups, Jesse, stirrups, but thanks for the tip."

The train station was fifteen miles from where Chase had found the tracks, and the journey took about seven-and-one-half hours in all. Most of the trip was silent, each person reflecting on what was happening and dealing with the realization that they might never make it back home to 2099 AD.

The train station was only a ten-by-thirty shack, which didn't allow for much more than protection from the elements. It was wood, but for some odd reason they had used pine or some other soft wood, probably out of convenience. If they wanted this structure to last more than a few years they should've used a tougher, more durable wood. There were three walls covered by a wood and tin roof. Everyone expected a tall, skinny man with glasses and a lisp to be selling tickets at the window, but they would later find out they purchased tickets on the train. Hopefully the train had a car for hauling horses, or they might be leaving more of a trail than hoped. Tom was awake and coherent by this time, able to move around some, which helped in the preparation for the tip. Elizabeth entertained Margaret and Tom's hand, of which she wouldn't let go, while Dave, Chase, and Jesse packed the equipment left over from the SEAL raid on the Arab compound. They decided the less Tom and Elizabeth knew the better. The three men pushed the wagon as far into the woods as the foliage allowed and camouflaged it. One couldn't see the wagon from the station if one didn't know where to look.

Chase and Jesse took turns patrolling the area on foot while they waited for a train. They began to feel that this was a fruitless effort and that they had better start moving again when the tracks began to rumble and vibrate.

Chief James felt the approaching train in the woods where he was patrolling the landscape for any signs of the posse. He was happy that they had not seen or heard anyone in the three hours and thirty minutes that they had waited for the train.

Shit, was the only thing that came to his mind when he saw a man thirty feet in front of him, hopelessly searching in the pitch-black forest. The treetops shaded the moonlight, which was a distinct advantage for Jesse, who pulled his ten-inch, serrated combat knife from its sheath. He ought not to use his 10mm for several reasons; the first was the desperate supply of ammunition, and the second more important reason was that he might have friends near by that would hear the gunshot and come running. They didn't have enough ammo to fight the posse.

Using the artificial light of the night vision, Chief James glided across the forest floor with the grace and ease of a ballerina. He was the mirror image of the man's every step, writhing and twisting around and through branches and fallen trees. He was close enough to smell his pungent, musty smell, the smell of an outdoorsman. Chief James was right behind him and his target had no idea that he was about to die. He reared up his knife, which was made to kill, plunging it into the base of the unsuspecting man's skull in a downward motion, severing his spinal cord below the neck in the same manner the ancient Romans had used to vanquish their adversary with the gladius. Instantly paralyzed, the tracker fell to the ground; death quickly came to the man, without even a last gasp of air, a look of utter surprise on his face.

Jesse stripped the man of his supplies and covered his body with leaves and dirt. With some luck, no one would find him. Realizing that the train had stopped, Jesse ran to the station, where Chase had negotiated passage for the horses and the group.

"Where have you…" He stopped in mid sentence and motioned to the left side of his face. The chief reached up and wiped the blood from his cheek with the sleeve of his shirt. "Let's get out of here."

Jesse nodded in agreement as they joined the others on the train. Chase had purchased the use of their own cabin, thinking that they would need privacy and knowing he needed to protect their identity.

Buford was frustrated that they hadn't been able to find the murderers; they were more skilled than he had first thought, but they would be found and killed in due time. First, he had to find where they were heading. They were following a wagon trail down some railroad tracks, but there were other tracks going the opposite direction. He had decided that they would have needed the wagon for the woman whom they had and the wounded man. His advance scout hadn't heard from or seen his brother for an unusually long period. Buford ordered Harden to send a patrol down the tracks to see if they could find anything. He looked up to see his men returning with a dead body draped over the lead man's horse.

"What happened?"

"We rightly don't know, Captain; we found an abandoned wagon and him, stabbed in the back, snuck up on, I reckon."

"Snuck up on, he was the best tracker in the company." Buford's rage began to show. "I want to know what kind of man can sneak up on an experienced tracker and kill him without even alarming him to his presence."

"Sir, request permission to bury my brother." His twin gently took the body from the horse and placed him on the ground.

"Yes, yes, you can. Sergeant, form a detail."

"Yes, sir," Harden snapped as the five closest men automatically volunteered for the duty.

"Sergeant, may I have a word with you?" The two friends dismounted and walked a good distance from the others.

"What do you think?"

"Sir, my guess is that they hopped on that train we heard a while back. If we catch the next one we should be able to find where they got off."

"Yes, it's kind of hard to miss four men and two women, one man with a hole in him. We can pick them up on the other side of the tracks. Thank you, Sergeant, tend to your troops."

"Yes, sir."

"Vengeance will be ours, men. The longer it takes the better it will be. We will persevere." Buford's words were hollow; the stress of the encounters with Chase and the chief had taken its toll on Buford and his men's morale. The men, tired from a long day, mounted their horses and made the three-mile ride to the station in silence. They would have to wait until morning for the next train. That was plenty of time for the burial detail to finish and rejoin the company.

Chapter 6

 Chase, David, Jesse, nor Margaret had ever seen a functioning train, seeing as how they had become obsolete before any of them were born. Margaret, however, had seen one in a museum when she was a girl, but it hadn't been as old or magnificent as the one in which she currently found herself. The black body and billowing, thick black smoke signified power in its raw form, gliding across the tracks with authority. Inside one could travel in luxury or in coach, whichever fit one's budget. The coach passengers were herded together in rows, three on one side and three on the other, much like an airplane, combining each passenger's smell together, forming a most unpleasant odor. Luckily, there were windows that allowed the outside air to enter the train. Unfortunately, coal filled the air with smoke from the engine car. Passengers had to pick the lesser of the two evils. In the luxury cars, passengers were waited on and could receive meals—fruit and bread, nothing extravagant—and wet towels with which to wash. It was definitely the preferred way to travel, and thanks to Thomas, they could. Chase had taken the rest of Tom's money from his billfold to use for the train, bargaining with the conductor in order to get the horses on. Because of their lack of money, the conductor had given them the last car before the horse car, adding to the unpleasant smells in the air, but it was better than exposing them to a large amount of prying eyes in coach.

 Every half day the train would stop to load and unload passengers and to take on more coal to use as fuel. This gave the group time to stretch their legs, wash up thoroughly, eat a meal, and find out exactly where they were. The first two stops the group had missed because everyone had been sleeping, but that hadn't seemed to bother anyone, catching up on some much-needed sleep.

Margaret woke to see Chase and Jesse mulling through the equipment quietly in the corner of the cabin. She was in dire need of a bath and she needed to shave her legs, which not many women did in this time. She had gone from a powerful, feared woman to a worthless older lady, and it was hard for her to stomach. She genuinely was sorry for talking to Elizabeth the way that she had; the trauma of transporting two-hundred-and-thirty-four years in the past made her nasty. Margaret considered herself a strong-willed person, having the ability to effectively handle any situation, but now she had little input into the solution and she resented Chase's power over her. Furthermore, she resented Chase and Jesse because they seemed to have it together, always knowing all the correct answers, though it was only her perception and couldn't be further from the truth.

Chase had other things on his mind, like completing his mission, and needed to figure out a way to contact Townsend. "Do you think you can get the COM units working, Jess?"

"Yeah, they need to be switched from satellite to line of sight or UHF, that will give us the ability to talk to each other, but only over short distances, a few miles at best."

"Can you do that? I'll work on the EP450, see if we can get the COM units working, but please be careful not to show too much to our new friends."

"Chase, what about the transport platforms, are they on?" Jesse desperately needed them to be working.

"There's no way to tell; they don't have any switches or buttons on them, but I think we should all keep them on us, just in case." He walked over to Margaret and slipped the platform under the blanket that she had over her legs.

"We need to keep these on our person just in case."

Margaret nodded agreement, grabbing Chase's arm as he turned away. "I'm sorry, I've been unbearable; it's been hard to, I don't know…"

"I understand, it's been hard on all of us, but we'll make it through together."

"I thought that you and the chief had everything worked out; I felt so useless."

"No, not worked out, we're just improvising. We're paid to stay level headed and find solutions to problems."

"That's just it, I'm paid for the same thing."

"When you're being shot at?"

Margaret smiled and slumped further into her seat; she might as well sleep if she couldn't win the argument.

Chase then walked over to Dr. Persons, who was sleeping soundly, and shook him gently, stirring him just enough that he woke from his sleep.

"Tom okay?" he spouted, half asleep.

"Dave, it's Chase. We decided that we need to have the transport platforms on us at all times."

"Good idea, we might get lucky," a fully attentive Dr. Persons answered.

"Do you need anything?" Chase still felt bad about yelling at him in the woods and wanted to make up for it some, but he really wanted Dave to say no.

"Some modern antibiotics would be nice. Tom's leg has the beginnings of an infection, and if I don't stop it now he might loose the leg anyway."

"How about penicillin?"

"It doesn't work on us anymore and it wasn't discovered until 1928. Holy shit, these people have no idea what penicillin is and their bodies will respond. And we can make it; all we need is some mold."

"Dave, go see if they have any bad fruit or bread that we could use."

"Actually, it has to be citrus fruit. They've been serving oranges to us all trip. I would have to cultivate them a bit, but I think that I can make it work." Dave opened the door to the car and jumped to the next, off to find some mold for a medicine long useless, but today he just might get lucky.

Elizabeth quietly listened to every whispered conversation with her eyes closed. She couldn't quite place it, but something was odd about these people. She would wait a few more minutes so as not to arouse any suspicion, then get up and check on Tom.

Buford had the first taste of what a U.S. marshal's badge could do when the train finally stopped at the station. He and his men rode the train at no charge; he simply explained that he was after a group that had murdered nine people the day before. The accommodations weren't as luxurious as his suspects' were, but it would do. He ordered his men to relax and have fun, to a limit. They had been tracking the Tidwells for three months, taking its toll on the group and on Buford, who ordered a brandy and washed up. He paid for himself and Harden to have a private car away from the other men, hoping that the two would catch up and plan a course of action. He had learned long ago that if his men thought that they were involved in the decision-making, they would perform better because they were personally motivated.

"How are the men, Joshua?"

"Tired, sir. This should be what they need to rejuvenate."

"Perhaps having their land back would help more."

"Buford, you do know that many of the men never owned land; they're following you because they love you. There're only five of us who are trying to get land back. You should keep that in mind as we get further away from our home state."

"I know, I'm grateful for their help. I hope they know that they can leave whenever they want."

"They would never leave; the men will follow you until this is done. The first battle at Manassas got ride of all of the cowards. These men are the real deal, the cream of the crop, and you would do well to remember that as you drag them across the country."

Buford ignored his friend's outburst, not really wanting to hear the truth. "I want you to spread some money around to them, maybe find a few bottles. However, they are men of the law now, so each of them has to look, and act, the part. If they need boots, or pants or just a bath and a shave, I want you to take care of it." Buford handed Harden the three hundred dollars that he had used to bribe the town sheriff.

"Yes, sir, but please keep in mind that we're a long way from home and simple pleasures can only go so far."

"Joshua, wait, you always seem to know how to handle me. Why is it that you never took a commission? I always thought you qualified."

"They offered me a commission, but I wanted to be a true leader of men, not a leader because of my rank. I've earned what I have my whole life; I work hard to keep it. War was no different for me."

"You must think me an ass."

"No, sir, I think that you're a man worthy to have me follow him. We just need to stay focused on why we're chasing these men. We're trying to get our land back. Revenge should be secondary. You knew that some men might not make it back."

"Yes, I knew that, but I have a responsibility to each of them and to myself. I will not relent until I fulfill that responsibility. I'm going to get some sleep;

please see to the men, Joshua." Buford's tone changed drastically, showing his anger for the constant bombardment by Joshua, even though Buford knew him to be in the right.

"Yes, sir."

Harden did what he was asked to do even though he knew it wouldn't do much for the men's moral. Every man got what he needed, some quicker than others did, but there wasn't enough time to supply everyone with what they needed in one train stop. In addition, each man got his own bottle of whiskey, a bath, and a shave. This was possible because the mayor had given many of the men supplies when they had left the town.

At each stop, Harden and Buford questioned the station conductor, finding pieces to the puzzle to where the group headed and pieced them together. They hadn't lost them yet; from all accounts the murderers were still on the train and heading west towards St. Louis or Chicago. They were heading west, hoping to get lost in the expansion movement, never bothering anyone ever again.

Buford's men arrived at the end of the line, the junction that took you either to Chicago, Illinois, or to Saint Louis, Missouri. This was the decisive moment for Buford, having to find where Tidwell went; if he decided on the destination incorrectly, they would never find Thomas Tidwell in the vast Western expanse.

Everyone had to exit the train and board a new one depending on which track your wanted to travel. Buford took the opportunity to pay a visit to the station conductor, who hopefully had been working at the station when Tidwell had gone through town.

"Excuse me, sir. My name is Deputy U.S. Marshal Buford Walton," he said, showing him his badge. "I've been chasing a band of murderers who were on one of your trains the last day or so."

"I haven't seen anyone who looks like a killer come through the station the last few days," the conductor replied without looking up from his manifest.

"No, sir, these people don't look like your typical killers; they're traveling with two attractive women and an educated man. The forth man had a leg wound from my rifle."

"I do remember a group with an injured man, but I don't remember any women with them. They passed through yesterday morning going to St. Louis, I think."

"I have to be sure. The two men whom I'm looking for were wearing all black with tan full-length coats, and the leader had a black hat with a silver ring around the base."

"Yes, that was them. Real nice folks, hard to believe that they're murderers. I helped them change their horses over. Mister, I'm sure of it; they went to St. Louis, yesterday morning."

"Great, my men and I need passage on the next train to St. Louis."

"Well, this one here is going there," he said, pointing to a ready train just behind the one that they had just exited.

"Fantastic, can you please make the accommodations?"

"Well, sir, the train is full and I'm not going to bump paying customers in order to let some free ones ride."

"I'm chasing murderers!"

"Company policy, sir: Law men ride free, but not at the expense of the paying customers. The next train leaves tomorrow morning; there's usually space on that one." He turned away and went about his duties.

Buford was irate with the prospect of losing Tidwell's trail; already being one day behind, now he would be two. This was turning into an arduous task, which he regretted, but he had to save face and follow through with the man hunt, avenging the death of his men, who trusted him with their lives, letting them down in the battle.

Jesse and Chase were working on the equipment and trying to come up with a plan. Each man had a different view on how they had gotten to 1865.

"I don't know, Chief, I can't seem to get these EP450s working; they both show power but they're not discharging," Chase mumbled in Jesse's direction.

"Did you field strip it?"

Chase shrugged his shoulders slightly. "I didn't know if I should; there might be some radiation or energy discharge."

"Good point. We'll just need to keep carrying them around with us; we can't let any of these people get their hands on them."

Chase hid the weapon under the environmental suit and went over to see how Tom was doing. "Dave, how is he?" Chase said with the look of concern on his face and pointing at Tom's leg.

"Infected. The penicillin is almost ready though, but I just hope it works. I've never made antibiotics before, just read about it. Like I said, it doesn't work on us, so there really was no need."

"How long until it's ready?"

"Later today, tomorrow at the latest, but we need some kind of syringe to inject it."

"There's adrenaline in the med. packs; empty out one of those syringes and use that."

"Good idea. We should see if it's having any effect in a couple of days, definitely by the time we reach St. Louis."

Chase patted Dr. Persons on the back and flopped into the seat next to him, hoping to relax before they got to St. Louis. He was just dozing off when Margaret tapped his shoulder. He turned with an "I was sleeping" face. "Yes."

"Do you think that the train could get robbed?"

Usually that would have been the stupidest question ever asked, but being 1865, it was a legitimate one and Chase luckily knew the answer. "No, Jesse James, the real Jesse James, was the first known person to rob a train, but he operated out of central and western Missouri; if my dates are right he didn't start his fifteen-year crime wave for a few more months, and that was a bank job."

"Isn't that where we're going, Missouri?"

"St. Louis. He never did more than visit St. Louis, so we should be fine."

"It's not that. I'm finding that I like history, knowing what is going to happen for the next 200 plus years. I could make a bunch of money."

"Possibly, but you would need to pay me royalties," Chase said jokingly.

"Partners then?" Margaret held out her hand and smiled.

Chase shook her hand and turned back around to sleep, thinking that Margaret was acting more civil and he wouldn't have to leave her for dead in the plain states.

The train came to a complete stop, waking everyone except Elizabeth, who had been sleeping quite a bit on this long trip.

"Last stop before St. Louis," the conductor bellowed from outside the car.

Everyone who was able left the train. Normally, Elizabeth wouldn't ever be alone, but she was sound asleep and the group had to plan their next course of action, so the group decided to leave her in the train with Tom.

She waited until she was certain that everyone was gone, knowing that something was odd about her friends and was going to find out exactly what that was. With the dexterity only a woman had, Elizabeth carefully started to root through the SEAL gear hidden under the saddles and extra clothing. At first, all that she found were medical supplies that she easily or conveniently dismissed because of Tom. "Clothing." Some sort of suit made of a spongy, porous material that she had never seen before. "Come on, there has to be something," she mumbled. Before she finished her sentence, she felt a heavy, smooth object between the second and the third suit. She pulled it out, finding a rifle or gun of some sort. It had lights on the side and looked almost like it came from space. Elizabeth shoved the weapon back into its place and stood in the cabin and began to pace in the small cabin, trying to think. *What should I do? No wonder the doctor could fix Tom's leg with some kind of mold, killing off the infection. One man saved Tom and I that night, two men broke him out of jail, and that woman acts like a man. They're from some satanic cult or, even worse, are dammed themselves."*

"We can do two things. We can leave them in St. Louis and avoid the posse or we can stick with them and shoot it out. The only problem with that is that we're low on ammunition."

"Chief, that's a bit cold, isn't it? That man has a wound that might take his leg."

"I thought that you got rid of the infection, Doctor."

"It looks as if I did, but it could come back any time."

Chase and Margaret just watched as the good doctor and Jesse James had it out in the corner of the station, far from prying eyes and ears.

Margaret had had enough. "Hold it. What the hell is going on here? We need to stay together, and if we fight among ourselves, we're never going to get home. First, we need to see if they followed us in the first place. Then we can make that decision. Chase, what do you think?" She always had the ability to control the conversation, which was one of the reasons that she was a good ambassador.

"They followed us; those men are definitely ex-Confederate soldiers, and we killed twelve of their men. They'll come after us regardless of whether we have Tom or not."

"Chief, didn't you hear that Buford character say that Tom and his dad were carpetbaggers? Perhaps we could have Tom give them back their land. That might make them go away."

"No, Doctor, I think that it's too late for that now; we're going to have to either outrun them or find a way to make some ammunition to fight with. If we have to use weapons from this time period, the odds get a whole lot longer that we make it through this in one piece."

It seemed clear to Chase. "We hide Tom in St. Louis and find a way to fight them. Jesse's right; they'll come regardless of whether or not they get their land back. Does anyone have anything else to add?" Everybody shook their heads no and made their way back to the train.

"Tom, Tom." Elizabeth tried to wake her recovering fiancé. Unsuccessful, she decided that she would need to collect more information before she acted. She could steal the gun and show it to the proper authorities, but that might be too difficult. Elizabeth was confused, but she knew that the people she and Tom traveled with didn't belong on her earth, in her reality, and that was all that she needed to know.

She pretended to be asleep when Jesse, Chase, Margaret, and David returned from their impromptu meeting. They were none the wiser about Elizabeth's discovery as they settled in for the last leg of the journey to St. Louis.

Buford heard a knock on his cabin door. "Come in." Harden entered the private car with a smile on his face.

"We should be in St. Louis tomorrow night. All of the men are clean and happy; they send their thanks and have all decided to stay on until this is over. I also visited the marshal's office when we had the layover and got the rest of the men badges; they seemed to like them."

"You did a great job as usual. I've been thinking about our friends on the other train. They had some sort of Gatling gun, but when I went into the sheriff's office after the firefight, there was nothing there. It's been bothering me; these men might have some sort of experimental weapons that we do not know about."

"Buford, they probably just had repeating riles; you know that Winchester has been working on a rival for the Henry."

"Maybe, but they would've had to be fast with them, I mean very fast."

Harden sat across from his friend. "If they were in the war like you think, they would be well trained."

"They're soldiers; they wouldn't have been so skilled if they were just gun fighters." Buford sighed. "Did you get yourself something?"

"No, but I got us a good bottle of whiskey."

Buford couldn't control his joy and he smiled like a child in a candy shop. "What are you waiting for, open it."

They sat in silence and got drunk together for the first time since they had left South Carolina. Both men sat and enjoyed the other's company with an appreciation for each other's skills.

Chapter 7

The train came to a stop on the north end of the Mississippi River overlooking St. Louis, where all of the passengers had to ferry over in a riverboat. No one had undertaken the task of building a bridge, spanning the expanse that was the mighty Mississippi. This fact would later cripple St. Louis and her trade market because travelers and merchants diverted to Chicago, where they didn't have to cross the river. For now at least, St. Louis, Missouri, was a city to behold, a metropolis mixed with wealthy land and plant owners, explorers, and expansionists, hoping to make their mark on history. It was alive with the hustle and the bustle of a great city. The river was cluttered with riverboats, most carrying supplies from one place to another, and others were used as pleasure boats. These exquisite crafts pleased the more affluent, drowning them in decadence.

"How are we going to get across the river; we're broke, aren't we?" Margaret asked in a sullen tone.

"I anticipated this, so I put some money aside for the crossing and our lodging in town, but we're going to have to do something about our money situation quickly. I'll be back soon; I need to find out how we get on the boat."

"Where are we?" Tom looked out at the foreign city and wondered aloud.

"St. Louis, Missouri, honey."

"St. Louis, what are we going here? We were supposed to go home to South Carolina. How did we get to St. Louis?"

"Let's see, Tom, you were almost killed in Virginia, thrown in jail, and shot in the leg by men who are following us—after Chase and I broke you out of jail, of course. We didn't plan to come here; it just happened that way." Jesse was sarcastic to prove a point to his new friend that he couldn't control everything, but really, he enjoyed the banter.

"What's the plan? You have to have a plan if you brought me all the way out here."

"Hopefully, get you back to full strength and then set back East. We had to avoid a battle with Buford and his men."

Chase purchased the tickets for the ferry and called to his friends to join him in line, waiting for the next boat. "I got the tickets; it's first come first serve so we had better get in line," Chase yelled from across the train station, waiving for the others to come over to where he was.

The riverboat was very plain, gutted to accommodate large numbers of people and horses. It had three tiers: the first for livestock, the second and third for passengers. Unlike most other forms of travel, there was no distinction between the rich and the poor, being too short a ride for the trivial. Its white hull and steam wheel reflected the late morning sun, giving the approaching city an ethereal glow about it, almost mystical to Chase, who relished in the glory of history.

People of all race, color, gender, and religious background filed onto the floating melting pot and crossed over into a new life on the other side of the Mississippi. On the other side, they found hope, the hope of prosperity, a fulfillment of dreams long ago forged in the American spirit. There was one exception: They just wanted to go home.

The city was almost entirely made of red brick as far as the eye could see, with homes, shops and office buildings, which were under construction, cascading into the countryside. Along the banks of the Mississippi, the fathers of industry budded and started to take form, placing their mark on what would become modern St. Louis. The main part of the city had a French theme to it, with archways on every doorframe, and large plate-glass windows with wooden ledges on the inside, so one could sit and sun themselves. Fine wood carvings decorated the arches, most painted in blue and red, adding to the ambiance, a mix between French and American culture. Inside the homes, the ceilings, oftentimes vaulted, had beautiful mosaics on them, or in the more modest homes, hand-carved woodwork decorated the surface.

Margaret had never seen something so magnificent in all her life, taking in the entire atmosphere of what later would become the Gateway City—what now was the gateway to the West. She had started her life on a mission to right the wrong, but along the way, she had lost her way in the political way of life. The knowledge that her ancestors, and now her, had shared the colossal task of taming the West, left her with the longing to see more, know more, to live again.

Chase had other thoughts, scanning the landscape for a suitable hiding spot, one that would afford Tom the luxury of rest and relaxation, not knowing that Buford was less than two days out and still hunting the boy. He suspected as much, but deep down inside he hoped that they had lost the motley group of Civil War bandits.

"Jesse, we need to find a place for Tom to rest and then we need to scout the city. We need to find a few things as well," he said, motioning to the sidearm holstered on his hip.

"Perhaps we should split up in order to cover more of the city; that way we can cover the ground more quickly." Jesse knew that they had to keep moving so they would be less conspicuous.

"Sounds good, but where will we meet?"

The chief started to tug on his ear. "That's the best part: We don't have to prearrange a spot."

"You got the COM working," Chase said with the knowledge that they had just repaired a very large tactical advantage. The chief handed Chase a set and motioned Dr. Persons to come and get the last.

"Doctor, if you and Margaret can stay with Tom and Elizabeth and look for a place to put the horses up while we scout the area and find some supplies, that would be very helpful."

"No problem," Dave answered in disappointment, wanting to go with Chase or the chief because they had the most fun. He had come to like the dangerous life somewhat, at least how his body felt afterward, a life that he had never dared to live in their time. He was always playing it safe and doing the prudent thing. The thought of going back to his regular life made him even more disappointed with how he had lived his life to this point.

All three men fixed the small earpiece into place and hooked the receivers under their shirts. The system was wireless and the receivers flat as a quarter so they had no problem hiding them from the now visibly nosey Elizabeth.

"Jesse, you look for some cheap housing, I'll look for a gunsmith," Chase said, handing him the remnants of Tom's money.

The two men split up, walking down the same street in opposite directions. Chase went east along the river, Jesse west, and Dave and Margaret, with Tom and Elizabeth in tow, north away from the river, each of the groups searching for a different necessity.

"Can everyone hear me?" Chase said into the COM unit, hoping that it worked.

"Yes," Jesse answered quickly.

"Dave, are you there?"

Jesse paused for an answer. "Chase, I don't think that his unit is working." Both operators were silent, waiting for an answer from the third COM unit and Dave, who manned the equipment.

"So, Tom, how is the leg feeling today?...Good, when we are settled, I want to look at it to make sure that you didn't rip the stitches out."

"Clever, Doctor." Chase was impressed. "We read you loud and clear. In fact, I have a joke for you. A man who just got a new sports car took it out for a test drive. He was taking corners, weaving in and out of traffic, having a great time. He decided to take it on the highway to see what she could do. He punched the pedal to the floor, going 180 miles an hour. A cop saw him and started to chase him. The guy put the hammer into eighth, bringing his speed to 250 miles an hour, trying to outrun the cop. After about two minutes of this, the guy was like 'What am I doing trying to outrun the cop?' so he pulled over to the shoulder. The cop got out of the car, gun drawn.

"'What the fuck do you think that you're doing trying to outrun me?'

"'I don't know, Officer, I just got this car and I got carried away.'

"The cop put his gun away and said, 'Okay, sir, it's five-fifteen and I was supposed to get off fifteen minutes ago and I need to get home, so if you can tell me a really good reason that I should let you go, I will. Otherwise I am going to take you to jail.'

"The man thought for a bit and answered the cop. 'Sir, about a week ago my wife left me for a state trooper.'

"The cop was stunned; not knowing what to say, he just looked at the man. Thinking that the cop wanted more, the driver replied, 'I thought you were trying to give her back.'"

There was no noise on the COM set until Jesse put his two cents in. "Do you think that joke would work with horses because it doesn't with cars?"

Everyone who was privy to the joke laughed uncontrollably.

"Doctor, what's so funny?"

"Nothing, Margaret. I'll tell you later." Dr. Persons gained control of himself. "Perhaps we should get the paper to see if anyone is renting spaces for the horses."

They walked down the street towards the main intersection three blocks up. The street was overflowing with ornate carriages, decorated with silver and brass fittings, giving the accurate impression of money. On the outside of the road, individual horses trotted up and down the street. When they came to the main street, they noticed it was twice as large as the other streets they had explored, with shops and businesses sprawled down from one end to the other.

This is going to be fun, Margaret thought as they went into the closest hardware store to ask directions.

Jesse had other things on his mind, slated with the task of finding a place to stay, but all he could focus on was finding two things. The first, an escape route out of town, and the second, if push came to shove, a tactically sound location for the last stand. He scanned the buildings on the outskirts of the city proper, trying to locate a suitable hideout. Nothing was even close to what he needed: an open, easily defended building with at least one side covered by a natural obstruction, or an elevated landmass so they could cover the high ground. He didn't even see the boy coming out of the building, slamming into him and knocking the boy to the ground with a thud.

"I'm sorry, are you alright?" The encounter startled Jesse more than the boy he knocked down

"Sir, I've been thrown from my horse harder than that." He grabbed the chief's hand and vaulted to his feet with one forceful motion.

"Hey, watch the arm, mister. I need that still."

"I'm sorry again; sometimes I don't know my own strength. Hey, do you know the city very well, because I just got here and need to find a place to stay."

"Sure, I come to these parts six or seven times a year. My name is Tom Truman." He extended his hand and almost immediately, Jesse took it.

"I'm looking for an out-of-the-way place for myself and five of my friends."

"That's a bunch of people, mister, but I might just have a good place. Let's go. I'll take you there."

Jesse followed the boy down the street, wondering where he had heard the name Truman before; he would have to ask Chase when he had a chance to reach him on the COM unit. *It will wait,* he thought, disappearing around the corner where the street turned to gravel and headed out away from the city.

Chase walked from street to street, looking for a gunsmith, but he wasn't really looking very hard; he was taking in the atmosphere of the famed gateway to the West. People filled the street despite the cold, overcast day, and it looked as if it were going to snow. Where Chase was from, western New York, there would already be a few inches of snow on the ground and that was with a degree of global warming. *The climate is definitely milder here,* he thought as he remembered how he had liked to play in the snow as a boy, wishing that it would snow right then. *There's nothing more beautiful than the first snowfall of the year. There's something about it that just makes one stop and appreciate nature and its power.* His thoughts rang true in his mind, knowing the changing of the seasons set the world's life cycle, and if this held true for Chase, winter was death. He put the morose thoughts out of his head and focused on finding the gunsmith.

Scanning the different stores for his target, he passed a wrestling ring with a few curious people standing and waiting for the next match. He had read that wrestling would be big in this period until the turn of the century, before baseball took over.

"Hey you, want to try and beat the champ?"

Chase looked up to see a thin man, almost a midget, staring back at him. "What?"

"Five dollars gets you a try; if you last four rounds without giving up or getting pinned, you win one hundred dollars. If you can beat the champion, you win the whole pot."

"How much is the pot?"

"We have a taker, huh? You think that you can beat the champ?" The volume of the ringmaster's voice increased as he tried to play to the crowd.

"I just asked what the pot was, I wasn't offering to wrestle," Chase snapped back quickly.

"The pot is seven hundred dollars; you could buy some land with that much. Come on, what do you say? You just have to last four rounds to get the hundred."

Chase knew that they needed money and this might be their best bet. "I'll do it. What are the rules?"

The man smiled at Chase, thinking that he had another sucker he was going to take for five dollars. "No punching, kicking, biting or grabbing in the privates; if you do, you'll be disqualified, understand?"

Chase nodded his head yes. He striped off his jacket, shirt, and gun, revealing his war-hardened body complete with scars from three bullets and a knife. He began to stretch and warm up when the champion entered the ring. He was six feet four inches tall, a very large man for the time, and built similar to Chases, but on a larger scale. He had a bald head, probably by choice, and looked as if he could chew a hole in a chain-link fence if he had to. Chase shook his head as he climbed into the ring, hopping up and down to try to break a sweat in the cold air. He had seen this type of wrestler when he had been in college, thinking that strength was everything, relying on the fact that he would intimidate his opponent. A weak-willed man who needed a sideshow to make money didn't intimidate Chase. The reality probably was that the wrestler got a daily wage from the man who had approached him, who was obviously the brains behind the operation. Chase appreciated free enterprise, but he needed the money and would have to embarrass this champion, breaking his manager in the process.

A crowed gathered to see the challenger wrestle the champion, who had already beaten all of the ambitious men in town. He put on a spectacle as he entered the ring, throwing his hands in the air and grunting profanity at the crowd that would make him look even more idiotic at the hands of Chase, who was ready to wrestle.

The ringmaster rang the bell, starting the match, and Chase circled to his right, trying to size up the man's speed and agility. He was in a wrestling stance, knees over feet, shoulders over knees, keeping his butt down and back straight. His right foot was in front of his left and shoulder width apart, arms and elbows in, both tucked safely against his body, limiting the champion's options. The champion circled the same direction as Chase, trying to find an opening, failing. He grabbed Chase in a collar tie, pulling him forward slightly. Both men tested each other's strength, vying for a dominant position. Chase knew that he was the weaker of the two, but had the benefit of an extra two-hundred-and-thirty-four years of wrestling technique to draw from. The champion pushed into Chase, which in wrestling wasn't a good idea, trying to bully him into submission. Chase put his arm under the champion's extended elbow, throwing it by, off his own head, creating an opening. With lightning quickness, Chase dropped to his left knee, allowing the champion's whole body to flop over his back. He grabbed the thick, muscular leg that was in front of his face, immediately changed direction, coming to his feet in a wrestling stance outside the champ's view or reaction and driving across the champ's body, catching his opposite knee with his left hand. With a thud, the champion hit the canvas mat, temporarily knocking the wind out of him. On his side and in danger, he scrambled to his stomach where he wasn't in any danger of being pinned. The champion, using his strength, stood, Chase on top of his back and escaping the grasp of the national champion, who had little else he could do except let go.

Chase was certain that a takedown pinning combination wasn't going to work; he had to take the man down feet to back and pin him that way. They circled once again, the champion being more cautious than last time, knowing that he was wrestling a man worthy of his talents. Chase could throw the man, but most likely, in the process of throwing a larger man, he would be pinned. They locked up once again, but this time it was Chase who initiated the tie. This tie was different than the last in that each man had one of his hands on the inside of the other's biceps and not in the other's collar, controlling that side of the body.

In a situation like this, a skilled wrestler would have the leg on the side of the arm that you controlled forward, protecting the other one. The champion had his leg forward on the same side that Chase controlled, creating an opportunity for his adversary, who, unlike the other challengers, was a skilled wrestler. Chase pulled the champion's arm tight to his shoulder, the unsuspecting man's elbow resting firmly on Chase's chest. Dropping to both knees ninety degrees to the right and pulling the man over his shoulder like a fireman's carry, which was the name of the move, he rolled and dropped the champ to his back in one effortless motion. Chase jumped on the man carelessly, getting their legs tangled, but was able to stabilize the champion on his back, pinned to the mat.

The ringmaster stared at Chase in surprise, unwilling to call his man pinned. Ten or twelve seconds passed with no call. Losing his grip, Chase decided to shift his weight; when he did, the champion, using his locked leg, reversed Chase. Without warning Chase found himself on his back; knowing that the dirty ringmaster would call a quick pin, he arched his back, slamming his free arm onto the mat, pushing himself into a high bridge. He twisted his body first towards, creating space, and then away form the champion, who held Chase in an unfamiliar place. Using the space created by the shifting of his weight, he was able to belly out, staving off the pin. The champion used his leg to keep Chase down by placing it through the opening in the center of his body, locking around the other side of the leg. Chase had seen the cross body ride many times before, knowing just what to do. He had to make the champion submit because his friend wasn't going to call the pin. He jackknifed his body, putting his ass high in the air. He then ducked under the arch that he created towards his opposite foot, rolling into a ball, kicking the champ over with his legs, using his momentum to catch the champ with his head up. It worked; the champion hit the mat face first, knocking himself unconscious. Chase climbed on top of the ex-champ's limp body, giving the ringmaster no choice but to call the pin.

He had defeated the champion; Chase had known he would, but the crowd, whom Chase realized was cheering him on, was surprised. Chase helped the stunned man to his feet shook his hand and went to collect his prize.

"You cheated, and I'm disqualifying you," the ringmaster yelled as he hoisted the defeated man's hand in the air. Boos filled the air as the crowd demanded Chase be declared the winner, slamming their hands onto the canvas and chanting "Bullshit, bullshit."

"That's my money. I earned it and you will pay me." Chase put on his shirt, jacket, and gun belt as he glared in at the ringmaster, who was becoming uncomfortable.

"You used unnecessary roughness to win and that's against the rules."

"What do you think this is, billiards? Give me my fucking money before I get pissed off," Chase retorted with a matter-of-fact manner that sent chills up the spine of the ringmaster. Chase took his 10mm from its holster, grabbed the man around the neck, and put the gun up to his forehead. "You'll give me my money." Before he finished his sentence, Chase felt something warm and wet hit his leg; looking down, he saw that the ringmaster had urinated on his pants. Chase reached over and took the box that had his winnings and let the man go, who scurried into his tent, scared and broke.

Jesse and his new friend, Thomas Truman, came to a large white house with three ionic pillars in front supporting a second-story veranda. The home looked weathered and old, but had a mystique to it that Jesse found irresistible.

"Is this where we're going?"

"Yes, the old woman who owns the place lives alone, her husband died quit a few years ago and her two boys died in the Mexican War. She's always looking for boarders and the place is cheap. This is where my father and I stay when we come to St. Louis. Right now I'm staying in the city with friends while my parents are traveling, but I enjoy visiting the old lady; she doesn't have many visitors."

"It looks great, but I'll have to talk to my friends." He knew that was a lie, but he wanted to scout the area to find out if the home was defendable.

"I'll go and negotiate it out with the old lady; wait here, I'll be right back."

"Good, I be around, but I want to walk a bit." Jesse wandered off, looking at the land. The front of the house was about three miles outside of town and had no defendable structures, but the back of the place was situated on a hill that could have been a cliff if it had been a bit longer of a drop. If they only had to defend three sides of the structure, they could handle an attack much easier. Another good aspect of the house was the land directly in front of the place, which was mostly open until you came to a wooded area about three hundred yards out. That would give them an advantage if they decided on a frontal assault, which they would have to because of the cliff.

"Mister," Truman yelled from the house, "she agreed to take you in but she said it would be a little more than normal because she would have to cook for so many of you."

"How much is she charging?"

"Two dollars a week each, and another dollar total for the horses. If that's too much we can go to another place that I know."

"No, this place will do. Give this to her for the first week." The chief handed the boy eleven dollars, and he hurried to pay the woman.

"Chase, Dr. Persons, do you copy?" He initiated the radio COM set.

"This is Chase, copy."

"Yes, I read you, Jesse," Dave added quietly.

"I've found the perfect place to stay; it's about three miles out of town to the west. A huge white house with pillars. I've already paid and we can put our horses here as well."

"That solves my problem, then," the doctor was quick to point out.

"Not mine. I haven't been able to find anyone who can make us any ammo, but I got us some money."

"How did you do that?" Jesse asked with genuine curiosity in his voice.

"It's a long story; I'll have to tell you later. I'll try and make it to the house before dark; I want to look around a bit more. Chase out."

"Jesse, we're coming now. These horses want to eat and need water and I have to look at Tom's leg."

"Copy. See you in a bit."

Chase had gone to every smith in town after his exhibition with the ex-champ, trying desperately to find someone who could make the ammunition needed for use in the 10mm. He was out of luck with the M 29 because of the case-less ammunition, but the 10mm might be enough to hold off the bandits. Nobody even wanted to attempt to make it, leaving his group without a way to defend themselves when it came to a fight with Buford Walton. Chase walked down the road to the house that Jesse said was a suitable location to hide when his foot kicked something, sending what looked to be a ball down the street. Curious, he ran after it, finding it near a tree that had stopped the ball from rolling down a small hill. *It's a brand new baseball*, was Chase's first thought, but then he doubted himself, thinking the sport wouldn't begin to become popular for a few years. He picked it up, turning it to the writing on the side.

"World Series 2098. What the fuck?"

He didn't know what was going on, but realized that someone from his time had sent the ball to them. *But how*? He put the ball in his pocket and started to run. This was too good to keep everyone waiting.

"We should be in St. Louis tomorrow sometime; how do you propose that we find Tidwell?"

"We'll have to split up. St. Louis is a big city; we look around and ask questions, and hopefully we get lucky."

"Lucky, sir!" Harden snapped back to his friend. This was the first time that he had ever seen Buford not come up with a plan. He understood that this was hard, if not impossible, with the delays that they'd endured, but giving up wasn't Buford's style. "Buford, what about the men? They've followed you halfway across the country for our cause, not theirs." His voice was becoming louder and agitated. "After all of these years of service, you owe it to them to finish this and let them go home in peace, while they can."

"They don't have to do this. Who do they think that I am, God? I couldn't win the war and now I can't get my land back."

"Is that what this is about, you're feeling sorry for yourself? Do you know what I would do to one of the men if they started whining like you are? I would start hitting him until he decided to fight back. If he didn't fight, I'd beat him within an inch of his life."

"How dare you talk to me like that? I am an officer."

"We lost the war, remember? Just get your head on straight and stay focused on the mission. You have twenty-three hours." Harden left the room to be with his men; they would need the same pep talk.

Buford sat in silence, searching for a plan in his rattled head. Whatever the solution to his problem was, he wasn't going to find it in the bottle or his tears. "Harden's a hell of a sergeant."

The four time travelers gathered in a small room in the corner of the house that they had rented. Everyone was confused and excited at the same time. They all wanted to go home and Chase's discovery gave them all hope.

"Where do you think it came from?" Margaret knew that it was a stupid question, but couldn't stop in the middle of it.

Chase saw that she was embarrassed that she had asked the question and ignored it. "What we need to focus on is finding out how they sent the baseball and use that to get back home."

"What about Tom? He's still hurt and he has a group of killers after him."

Jesse interrupted Chase before he could answer Dave. "Personally, I would rather get home than defend him. For all we know, we could've changed history by saving him. We should concentrate our energy on getting home.

Chase chose his words carefully, pausing momentarily before speaking. "I think so as well, but I'm not going to throw him to the wolves. We can do both, but Jesse and I are going to have to rely on both of you; I think that it would be a good idea if you both learn how to use a gun."

Margaret looked petrified. "Chase, I am fifty-four years old and I've never fired a gun; it's against everything that I've worked for my entire life. I work to keep countries from going to war and I can't. I just can't."

"You might feel differently when you're dead." Chase laughed at Jesse's remark but stopped short when no one else was laughing.

Chase cleared his throat and got back to business. "We have to draw up a defense plan and an escape plan—both need to be perfect—and we'll need to practice them. The first thing that we need to do is decide what we're going to use as weapons. We only have one-hundred-twelve rounds for the M 29s and thirteen for the 10mms. That's only four per gun."

"Couldn't we make our own, Chase?" The doctor was doing whatever he could to help.

"If we had the cartridges from the jail break, maybe, but the problem we face is that anything resembling the munitions that we use in the handguns were not invented until 1873, so we're shit out of luck.

"We also have some C40 high explosives and some grenades that we could use, but that will only get us so far."

Margaret wasn't going to be silent anymore. "Let's just leave town before they get here and avoid the trouble. We could even talk to them, try and get this straight."

"We could leave, but we would have no idea where to go and how to get there. We're just strangers here; there are only a few places that we would classify as civilization from here to California. How do you feel about running, Jesse?"

"I don't know, I think that we should stay and see if home sends us instructions." Everyone thought that was the best idea yet.

"That brings us back to square one. We need to get to work on our plans." Dave and Margaret left the room, leaving the two SEALs to discuss the plans. The task that they had was a difficult one, but that was no problem for these battle-tested problem solvers.

Chapter 8

Elizabeth didn't know what she was going to find, but she knew that it was going to be big, giving her the evidence that she needed to bring to the authorities. Everyone was outside, creating what seemed to be a war base, giving her the opportunity to conduct a thorough search. She sat on the fence playing both sides, always looking the innocent. Unfortunately, the fence was a double-edged sword. These people were protecting Tom, giving him the opportunity to heal; on the other side, she vowed to bring these imposters to justice. Elizabeth had to play this just right.

She rooted through the equipment once again, finding nothing that she could use. She flopped on the bed and stared out the window, pouting over her failure when she saw something outside of the window appear out of nowhere. It was a black, rectangular, metal box, which was three feet long and one-and-a-half feet high with the words "U.S. Navy" on the top and side. She wasn't as surprised as she would have been before she had met Chase and Jesse. They seemed to defy conventional limits and rules.

She popped up off the bed and opened the window, looking around to see if anyone else had spotted the black box. Convinced that she was the only one, she climbed out of the window, running to the box. She looked around one more time and opened the box. *Bullets*, she thought. Disappointed, she put the cover down, but it wouldn't close properly. Elizabeth opened the box once again, investigating why the lid failed to close with greater scrutiny. Finding a removable shelf, she promptly removed the top, using every ounce of strength she had and placing the shelf on the side of the box. Inside the box, she found more ammunition and a cylindrical stone that took up half of the space in the bottom of the box. What seemed odd to her was that the stone had a removable top on it, which she could not remove for the life of her. Using great caution, the type that a nuclear scientist might use when handling uranium 235, Elizabeth removed the stone, carrying it to the window and placing it on the bed. *I will remove the top when I have more time*, she thought and returned the shelf to its proper place in the box, closing the top. She had what she wanted, so she thought; now it was time to play the game that she had seen Tom and George Tidwell play for so long. She would use her discovery to ruin the group of extra terrestrial beings, but only after Tom was safe. Elizabeth had no idea what this dangerous game of intrigue would cost her and Tom, but she had no other choice in her eyes.

Outside, Chase, Jesse, and Dave directed the building of a fortress hideout, which could hopefully withstand a direct assault. The men were filling burlap sacks they had gotten in town with dirt, using them as sandbags. The nearly frozen ground made digging difficult, but all three men in the makeshift unit were fully aware of the importance of the improvements. The odd person out, Margaret, was moving the bags, using a wheelbarrow, to their correct locations. Even in the cold weather, the men were sweating through their shirts, which needed washing. They placed the sacks in five locations around and inside the house. The first two were directly outside the white structure, fifty feet from the door and twenty feet wide of it, creating cover for the lookouts and a forward firing post to direct the battle. The third place Chase decided to use the sacks was on the veranda overlooking the countryside, allowing someone to cover the high ground and snipe the targets as they approached. Fourth, the burlap bags filled with dirt were placed around the front door, which was located in the center of a small porch, creating a collapsible firing position if the team had to fall back to the house. Lastly, they fortified the second-story windows, facing the sides of the house, covering what became their flanks because of the cliff, which made it very unlikely that an attack would come from the rear. The only problem left was the right flank, covered by trees one hundred feet from the house, which the bandits could use for cover unlike the front. One person couldn't cover an assault from that side because the natural cover the trees provided would take the tactical advantage away from the defenders.

"Chase, what do you think we should do with the right flank? It's open even with the good firing location on the second floor; it could bog us down and create an opening for a frontal assault."

"Yeah." Chase paused in thought. "Have you ever seen those old movies where the heroes use pikes to defeat horses? We could use the same thing on humans."

"What do you mean?"

"We can build a revetment with wood from the forest, a series of interlocking pikes that force the attackers into our line of fire, either from the second-story side window or the veranda in front. It would at least give them pause enough for us to get into position to repel boarders."

"Chase, that'll take time and I don't know how much we have, not to mention we still need to go into the city and get guns and ammunition."

"Okay, we start now and work as long as we can tonight. Tomorrow you go into town for ammunition and rifles. Dave, Margaret, and I will finish whatever revetments we can't finish tonight. Here's the money; it's all we have so be frugal."

"How did you get all of this money? There has to be five hundred dollars here; that's a shitload of money for this time."

"Five hundred fifty-four to be exact. I won it in a wrestling match. That short motherfucker tried to keep the money, he even lied to me about the amount; it's supposed to be seven hundred."

"What are you talking about?"

"I don't know, I got cheated. I'm just pissed about it."

"By the way, on a totally different subject, I've been meaning to ask you, but I forgot about it when you brought that damn baseball home. Have you ever heard the name Truman? That boy who showed me the house and hung around earlier, his name is Thomas Truman; he said that his dad guides wagon trains out West."

"Are you sure that it's Truman?"

"Yeah, he said that his name was Tom Truman. Why?"

"Thomas Truman is the name of the father of President Harry S. Truman of Missouri. If that's him, we could be in some serious shit. Buford can never know he was here. How did you hook up with him? He could only be thirteen or maybe even younger; I think that Harry was born in 1884, so he couldn't be very old. What is he doing here alone? This is all we need right now, Jesse. We have to get him the fuck out of here; if he dies we could really fuck up history even worse than we already have. Harry Truman was the president who ushered in the Atomic Age by dropping the first atomic bomb on Japan in World War II in 1945."

"I don't even know where he is, but if I don't get those guns we could be fucked even worse; we can't worry about the boy. If he shows up we just send him away."

"When you are in town try to look for him and tell him to stay the hell away from here, but for now, we need to start on the pikes. If you see him in town you need to have him leave town immediately." The SEALs continued to work after their break; they still had a lot of work to do. It was going to be a long, grueling night.

Buford and his men arrived in St. Louis at 12:23 p.m., setting the stage. His 125 men were determined to find the Tidwell boy and his guardians and kill them. His plan called for the St. Louis authorities to help them locate the group, who he reasoned had to be in the town, letting Tom Tidwell heal from Buford's rifle wound. The only problem was that St. Louis was a melting pot of people, all fusing together to form a metropolis. He would have to be vigilant in his search, keeping watch even in his sleep.

"Men, listen up. Sergeant Harden is going to lead you on the search while I inform the local authorities we're here and see if they can help us. We can see the end and have to stay focused on the goal. In a week, your first pay will come in and you'll be able to let loose, but for now discipline is important. Sergeant."

"Listen up. We'll split into three groups, each looking in a different third of the city; remember, we need to talk to people and find out what they know. We're all lawmen, so it's important that you are courteous to everyone. They'll tell you what you want to know if you are nice to them. Platoon one and two, the left third, platoon three and five with me on the middle third, and platoon four and six on the last third. Does everyone understand who we are looking for and where you are to look?" The group of men shouted a resounding yes and separated on a quest to find Tidwell and his new friends.

Harden knew the task was gong to be difficult, but if they were going to find them, it would be because someone was pissed off at the murderers. The land was the most important thing to Harden, whose family had owned it since the British had ruled the states. He also saw Buford's point that the mysterious soldiers had to pay for killing the men. They would prevail and make everything right again, as it had been before the war.

Harden's group went from street to street, looking for any sign of the men.

They filed down the red brick streets in a single line, looking as if they were still fighting the war, marching in a column. No one was in the streets, making his job even more difficult.

Jesse was frustrated, wanting only to get home, not play babysitter to history. If Truman died then another person would step up and take his son's place, but Chase was still his commanding officer, no matter how close they were; he knew that if they returned home he would face disciplinary action, so he did what he was asked to do. Chase was a good commanding officer because he asked for and used the men's advice, knowing that they were the ones who had to complete the tasks at risk to their lives. Jesse respected that, many of his COs never bothered, and men lost their lives unnecessarily.

The streets of St. Louis were barren. Jesse had no idea what day of the week it was, but he would have thought that a large city like this would have more people in it. He looked at his navy issue combat diving watch, reading the date. He would not be able to tell the day, but the date would be sufficient. 3:13 December 25, 2099. Jesse laughed, saying aloud, "No wonder no one's out in the streets; it's Christmas. That meant that he was not going to be able to get the weapons, but he would try anyway, it was of vital importance.

He pulled on the reins of his horse, turning down Laclede Avenue on his way to Main Street, which ran parallel to the Mississippi River three blocks up. He had decided to change into his environmental stabilizing suit earlier in the day and it had turned into a good idea; the wind had picked up, giving the air a bit of a nip to it. He had also borrowed one of Tom's business suits to cover the futuristic all-weather garb. No one had ever seen his face clearly and he hoped that a change of clothing would allow him to blend in better.

Just as Jesse reached Main Street, it started to snow heavily, covering the ground and Jesse's hat quickly. He made his way up the street to the gun shop, finding it closed. They were in big trouble without ammunition; dejected he turned his horse about and started back to the hideout.

Margaret was helping Elizabeth and the old woman who had taken them in cook in the kitchen, making Christmas dinner for the whole group. She had never really cooked Christmas dinner before, always having servants to prepare the meals. Margaret found cooking relaxing; chopping and dicing in the kitchen was very different from doing the same to a foreign country. They weren't going to eat until about six-thirty, so she had time to relax. She walked to the small doorway, leading out of the kitchen and into the dining room where Chase ran into her, knocking her to the ground. Before she landed, Chase reached out and broke her fall, saving her a large bruise on her behind.

"Sorry, Margaret. I've been looking for you and Elizabeth."

"We've been cooking Christmas dinner; I'm actually having fun."

"Good, I'm looking for that boy who has been hanging around with us. Have you seen him?"

"Yesterday, he went into town, something about seeing a friend."

"I don't know how he does it. When I was his age, all I was concerned with was if my hover bike was in style."

As usual, Elizabeth was listening to their conversation, convinced even more that they were not from this earth. *They made an army instillation out of a house in two days, boxes appear out of nowhere and what is a hover bike?* She knew that they were her and Tom's protectors but she refused to get too close to them. The question now was when to tell Chase about the box in the back of the house by the cliff, if at all. She focused in on the ongoing conversation between Chase and Margaret.

"If the chief doesn't come back with any ammunition, it might be all over for all of us including Tom and Elizabeth, who seem to be the primary targets. We have to hope he gets creative because I didn't know it was Christmas until you said something. Everything is probably closed for the day."

Elizabeth had to tell him about the bullets now; she had to protect Tom. She walked to the doorway; noticing that Chase and Margaret stopped talking as she approached.

"Chase, when I was outside I found a box with bullets in it, but I thought that you had put it there so I haven't said anything about it. I overheard you talking about ammunition; perhaps that is what you are looking for."

Chase's eyes lit up with relief and thankfulness. "Show me, can you show me?" Elizabeth led the way through the dining room and out the side door, around the side of the house and to the box. Chase wiped the snow from the box, reading the U.S. Navy insignia on the top. He picked up the box and cumbersomely struggled to bring it inside. It was just what they needed; now if they only could find the Truman boy, everything might work out.

Harden had come on a bad day; everyone was inside. He had no idea that it was Christmas day just like everyone else who had been thrust into this situation. He decided to make one more lap of the city before stopping for the day. He turned onto Laclede Avenue towards Main Street, motioning his men to take the other direction, meeting on Third Avenue, five blocks down. He had to think, and the tranquility of being alone in the snow gave him that opportunity, making a wide turn onto Main. Out of the corner of his eye, he noticed a solitary man walking his horse in the same direction that he was, but back about three hundred feet. He turned his horse around, heading towards the man.

Jesse knew that he was in trouble; he took his pistol in his hand, gripping it firmly. He walked slowly, his horse in tow, up to the mystery man, tipping his hat, as Buford had done in the sheriff's office, passing the man who had a U.S. marshal's badge on his lapel.

"Excuse me, sir," Harden let out as if rehearsed.

Jesse played it cool; if this was one of Buford's men, Jesse had the upper hand. He loosened his holster's grip on his gun before he turned. "Yes, sir."

"The streets are quite deserted this afternoon. Where is everyone?"

"It's Christmas day today; everyone's with their families, eating dinner."

"Christmas, really? My men and I have been on a train for a few weeks; we just got here today. Excuse me, my name is Joshua Harden, U.S. marshal."

"Bob James, it's nice to meet you."

"You too. What brings you out today?"

"I'm on my way to my sister's house; she is having me over for dinner. My wife died, God rest her soul, last winter, and I'm not much of a cook."

"That's nice. I'll let you get on your way, but first I would like to ask you a question."

"Sure." Jesse moved his hand closer to his 10mm, near the vest pocket of his suit.

"My men and I have been following a group of murderers and have tracked them to St. Louis. You haven't seen any new people come into town? Specifically, four men, one with a bullet through his leg, and two women."

"Mister, more people come every day; most head out West. I haven't noticed anything out of the ordinary. I'm sorry."

"That's okay, tomorrow is another day. Have a nice Christmas."

"You too, Marshal."

Jesse turned his back to the man, taking a calculated risk, walking to the corner of the street and mounting his horse, hoping that he had fooled the man. Taking his time as not to tip the marshal, he rode down the street to First Street, turning left. He kicked his horse, prodding the beast to trot and looked behind him, making sure that Harden was not following him. Convinced that he wasn't, Jesse slowed and resumed his ride back to the hideout.

Harden resumed his search, knowing that it was futile, or was it? He went over every word and detail of the conversation he had just had. That man had a black handle on his gun; Buford had mentioned that the men who had broken Tom out of jail had black-handled handguns. At the time Buford and Harden had tried to think of any handguns that had black handles—most were made of ivory or wood—but came up blank. *That was one of the men we're looking for,* he realized. Harden violently pulled the reins of his horse, stopping almost immediately, turning around, and spurring the animal to a full gallop.

Chapter 9

Home free, he thought as he turned onto Third Street. *Shit* was his next thought, seeing fifty men in the distance coming towards him. He decided to avoid the extra aggravation and turned around only to see Harden, on a full gallop, coming towards his position, yelling for help. All fifty men responded at once, shooting in Jesse's direction. He turned down an alley between two houses, drawing his gun from its holster. He decided to stay in the alley, kicking his horse to run faster, but it was running as fast as it could. He looked over his shoulder at the oncoming group that was gaining on him. He had a slow horse, which was par for the course to this point. Jesse smiled, thinking of all the things that had gone wrong on this mission. As the group of deputized bandits closed on Jesse, rounds from their handguns came closer to hitting him, bouncing off the walls and brick alley and jumping by his head. He was almost to the opening, where the next road was, putting his head down and concentrating on making that point.

The bullets ricocheted off the walls all around him as he looked up before reaching the next street to see where he was going. Greeting him was the other half of Harden's men. Jesse's horse reared up, frightened by the appearance of the other men, throwing Jesse from the saddle. He landed on his side, watching as his horse took three rounds center mass, the rounds intended for him. He planted his feet firm on the ground, pushing away from the falling animal. His feet slipped on the snow, but caught on a raised brick in the alley, moving him just enough to avoid his falling mount.

He raised his gun, targeting the first man in front of him; he pulled the trigger, and dead on, the shot entered the head an unsuspecting man. He didn't bother to aim at his next target as he didn't have the time. He emptied his first clip, scaring most of the other men into taking cover, with a remaining fourteen rounds of his 10mm. He looked behind him. *Harden is going to be on top of me in a matter of seconds,* he thought, his training taking over his actions. Jesse jumped over his slain horse, dropping the empty cartridge from the gun, not realizing that he was leaving it on the ground in 1885. He loaded the weapon and fired four rounds in the direction of Harden, hitting the man riding next to him. Harden stopped and dismounted, dropping to the ground in an attempt to avoid Jesse's fire. Harden had men on both sides of Jesse, who was hard pressed to find a way out of the alley. He looked around, locating a door leading into a building. He put two rounds into the lock and kicked it in.

Running, he saw a family huddled under the dinner table, hiding from the violence that had erupted during Christmas dinner. He ran to the front of the house, knowing that Harden's men were on the other side of the wall. Jesse slowly opened the door just enough that he could see the men hiding, still taking cover from his last volley of bullets. He took aim, killing all seven of them without warning, each shot ringing out in slow motion as Jesse could see the expression on the face of each man he killed. *Clear.* He ran into the street and away from Harden, who was fast approaching the mouth of the ally.

Jesse was halfway down the street when Harden came out of the alley. Unfortunately, Harden was on horseback, quickly leading his men closer to catching Jesse. He decided to cut through a house, kicking another door in, running through the empty house, slamming into and knocking down furniture as he made his was through the dark house faster than the light would allow. He came to the back of the house, both his legs hurting from the furniture, but there was no door. He looked around in the dark for an exit with little luck, until he turned the corner to a room that looked like a parlor, where a gleam of light reflected off the snow and lit up the room. *A window.* He fumbled with the locking mechanism until he unlatched it and opened the window, diving head first outside, finding himself in another alley. Jesse stopped for a moment to catch his breath, knowing that he had to press on quickly. He drew in a deep breath and started to run down the alley. He stopped again to catch his breath with his back to a door. He checked the street for Harden's men but it was clear. Suddenly, the door opened and Jesse fell backward into the building. Scrambling to his feet, he grabbed the person at the door and hip tossed him to the ground, pointing the 10mm in his face.

"You, what are you doing here, Truman?"

"Helping you, mister; you look like you need it. Follow me." He ran to the back door, checked to see if it was empty and removed a primitive manhole cover, motioning Jesse to enter the alien hole in the ground. He hesitated but decided that it might be his best bet. He held onto the lip and dropped into the whole, landing in liquid. Truman followed, falling face first as he landed.

"This is a fucking sewer; the smell is awful."

"They just put these in here last year; some of the rich people go to the bathroom in their houses, can you believe it?"

"No, it's hard," Jesse answered sarcastically. He put the cover back on the hole and started down the sewer, drugging his way to freedom.

Harden desperately looked for Jesse in and around the houses, interrupting quite a few dinners. He couldn't believe that he had gotten away once again; Buford had said that these men were highly trained, but he hadn't really believed him until now. He recalled his men and decided to look on the west end of town. *They were probably preparing to move west,* he thought, motioning for his group to move out.

Jesse and Tom Truman walked west through the sewer towards the river, where it emptied. They moved as quickly as they could in the sludge, completely covering themselves in it. After quite a while, Jesse could see a light at the end of the tunnel.

"Here, right here." Tom looked up at a manhole cover. "We get out here, it is the last one before the river and only two miles from the house."

Jesse pushed the cover off the hole, poking his head out, checking to see if Harden had somehow followed him. He didn't see any danger so he pulled himself out of the hole and reached down to help Tom. He covered the hole and started to run in the direction of the road, which was fifty feet to the left of his position. Reaching the road, Jesse stripped his wet, smelly suit, revealing the environmental suit. Tom stood in silence and wondered what Jesse was wearing. Deciding that it was not important, he concentrated on trying to keep up with Jesse, who was running too fast for Tom's short legs.

"Wait up, Mister, I can't run that fast."

Frustrated, Jesse squatted down, waiving his hand for Tom to hurry up. "Get on my back; we have to hurry. Harden is bound to find our trail in the snow." Tom climbed on Jesse's back, securing himself around Jesse's neck. They had to make it back to the house and warn Chase with all possible haste.

Chase and Dave just completed the revetment on the left side of the house; it was nothing special but would buy them enough time to thwart an attack if one ever came.

"Dave, I need to talk to you," Chase said, leaving him the sandbags to pick up an M 29/ME. "You're going to be using one of these if the shit hits the fan." He showed Dave how to load, fire, and reload the weapon, paying close attention to the single shot option on the rifle.

"I want you to use the single shot, one bullet at a time. You press the trigger halfway down and the laser sight comes on. What you see is what you get." He handed the gun and a bag of ammunition to Dave. "I want you on the veranda, looking out. You put that environmental suit on and the battle armor that Rodriguez was wearing and keep a close look out."

"No problem, Chase, I can do it." Dave was unsure but he wasn't about to show that to Chase.

"I know that you can. Good luck."

Harden set out on the road west out of the city; he had already sent a reconnaissance rider to see if there was a trail. Not expecting much, Harden beat himself up over losing Jesse after having him in his grasp. He looked up from his anger to see his rider approaching.

"Sergeant Harden, I found these up the road about a mile or so; this looks like a suit but they have been in shit."

"Thank you, Corporal, rejoin your men." *I have him; this man was careless for being such a tenacious fighter.* Harden raised his hand, signaling to his men. "To the gallop, hoe." He lowered his hand, pointing west in the afternoon sun.

Jesse ran towards the house, mumbling something about the posse; nobody understood him until he stopped in front of the house at the right sandbags, where Chase put the final touches on the barricade. Soiled with excrement, he carried the young Tom Truman on his back. Tired and smelling of a sewer, he struggled to speak.

"Catch your breadth. Jess, what happened to you?"

"I had to crawl through a sewer to escape. Buford's righthand man, Joshua Harden, is coming with a shit-load of men; we've got to get out of here now."

"How do you know that it's his righthand man?"

"I spoke to him in the city; he has about fifty men on their way here to kill us. We need to get the horses and get on the move."

Jesse had barely finished his sentence when three bullets slammed into the sandbags just to the left of where Chase was standing. The two friends ducked behind the sandbags where Chase had stashed the M 29/MEs with their new supply of ammunition.

"Where did all of this come from?" Jesse was relieved and upset at the same time. Happy they had something to fight with, he also knew they could have avoided all of this if Chase had called him on the COM unit.

"They sent it to us from home. Tom, get in the house and keep an eye on the woman." Tom knew what was coming so he ran to the house, slamming the door on the way in.

Jesse grabbed an M 29 and a bag filled with ammunition for both the M 29 and the 10mm guns. He ran across the way to the other set of sandbags and loaded his machine gun. It was daylight so the night vision goggles that were in the bag would be of no use, but it was nice to know that he had them just in case.

Chase yelled across to Jesse, who was taking a sight on the other side. "Jesse, everybody is in place; I have a COM unit, Dave has one, and Margaret has the last. Dave is on the veranda and Margaret is on the second floor where the barricade is; she is going to be our spotter." Master Chief Robert James just nodded as he mentally prepared for battle, a battle that did not favor victory.

"Dave, this is Chase, do you copy?"

"Copy, Chase."

"When you see them crest the hill, take aim, just like I showed you, and shoot them as they bare. Follow the laser sight; whatever it's on it kills except when the target is moving horizontal to you, and then you have to lead them. Do you understand?"

"Copy, Chase. I'm scared though."

"Everything is going to be fine, just like back in the Arab compound. You did an excellent job there and you'll do the same in this situation."

Margaret listened to Chase's pep talk and felt a relief that he and Chief James were there to lead the defense. She felt relieved until she saw the first of the men come out of the woods. "Chase, seven men just came out of the woods like you said they would. They've just seen the revetment and are coming your way."

"Jess, the left flank, you cover the front." The chief waived his acknowledgment without taking his eyes off the road. If they were on the left flank, they were going to charge over the hill at the first shot.

Chase popped his head up over the bags just enough to see his targets. He had his laser sight searching for a target, but none were coming around the corner.

"Margaret, where are they? I haven't picked them up yet."

"They're hiding behind the house, trying to get through the barricades. What should I do?"

"How far along are they? Have they broken through yet?"

"No, but they are almost through the corner joint."

"If they get through, they could flank us and we'll be in trouble; you have to kill them."

"No, I will not kill anyone. I told you that I wouldn't and that has not changed."

"Goddamn it," Chase yelled into the COM set. He had to get to the raiders before they got through the wire. Seven was a good number of people to kill at close range, especially experienced gunmen. He would have to use a grenade. He left his cover at the sandbags and crawled on his belly to the house, where he inched to the corner of the structure. Risking detection, he called Margaret on the Com.

"Where are they in relation to the corner of the house?"

"About thirty feet out and about fifteen feet in from the corner; they are trying to dismantle the joint."

That was a good distance. Chase would have to stand and throw from plain sight. *They're going to run towards so I'll have to lead them just like with a rifle,* he thought just before he acted. Chase pulled the pin on the grenade and stood; he heard gunfire so he turned for a brief second, looking towards Jesse as twenty-five men crested the hill. He immediately started taking fire as he predicted. It was no mistake, these men were good, and Chase was in real danger. He turned the corner, looking the lead bandit right in the eyes and tossing the grenade right on top of him. The party scattered but it wasn't enough; the blast radius form the grenade would get all of them. The explosion shook the ground, killing all seven of the men save one, who was crawling to the safety of the woods. Chase aimed at him with his rifle and pulled the trigger. The bullet entered the base of the man's skull, stopping him in his tracks.

Dave had never fired a gun before, except for the time in the compound, but this was different; he could actually see the men he killed. The problem was that he couldn't hit anything. He aimed but the gun would kick, throwing the trajectory of the projectile off.

"Chase, I can't hit anything." There was no answer, just a huge explosion on the side of the house. "Chase, do you copy?"

"Copy, say again."

"I can't hit anything," Dave yelled into the COM set as if he were trying to reach Chase from around the house.

"Dave, listen up, we are being overrun. Switch the guns to auto. The bullets are going to come out very fast, and the clip will only last a few seconds; when you fire, the gun will kick up and to the left, so you will have to compensate."

"Roger."

Dave open fired on automatic, aiming low and to the right. The first volley startled him, missing everyone, shooting over everyone's heads. He reloaded and open fired a second time, knowing just what to expect. To his surprise, he saw four men fall from the belch his rifle made. He had the best seat in the house. He yelled, discharging his next cartridge as the adrenaline pumped through is body.

Jesse heard the explosion, taking the shock with ease, and continued to find and hit targets. There were too many of the raiders, and he was going to be overrun if he didn't get help fast. He looked in Chase's direction, only to see an empty instillation. Switching his machine gun to full automatic, he opened fire with a spraying motion. It wasn't very efficient or effective, but the spread of the bullets might afford him some more time, he had so little. Jesse's peripheral vision caught a man to his left, twenty feet from him. He turned, looking directly into the man's gun barrel. Jesse was without reaction; he stood there for what seemed to be an eternity. *How did this man get so close? After twenty-seven years in the navy, twenty-five as a SEAL, this vagabond of a soldier is my end.* He closed his eyes, bracing for the impact, but nothing happened. He opened his eyes to Chase and the dead body of the man who was going to be his end. He turned to the oncoming men, opening fire. With both Jesse and Chase firing on full automatic, the men dispersed and retreated back over the hill.

Harden had taken it upon himself to raid the house. Buford was nowhere to be found, and with the murderers knowing that he was on to them, it seemed to be a good idea. However, now half of his men lay dead outside St. Louis, Missouri.

"Form up. We hit them again in five minutes. Call up the reserves and form two companies; the first will assault straight on, and the second will flank them left. The explosion blew a hole in the barricade. I think that we can get through if we can occupy the two lead soldiers. We need the frontal assault to be better organized in order to be an adequate feint for the flanking maneuver."

Harden was taking a gamble, but the firepower that the two soldiers had gave him few choices. He had to hit them hard and fast, closing in on the barricade before anyone on the other side could react and overwhelm them with his numbers. Most likely, all of the men assaulting the front would die, but that was the curse of a commander; good men had to die to obtain a worthy objective.

Perhaps we could wait until dark, giving my men the upper hand, he thought. Most battles happened in the light; at night, the armies retreated to the safety of their encampment, but his men had performed numerous raids at night. *Yes, we will go at night.*

"Listen up, men, we wait for dark; it will give us a better chance." Harden knew that this was going to work; he had more men and experience in night operations.

"Chase, what's taking them so long? They should be reformed and ready by now."

"I know, maybe they had enough."

"They followed us almost a thousand miles; they'll come again. They're probably waiting for reinforcements."

"Speaking of which, I need you in the second floor window; the grenade blew a hole in the revetment. They'll try to hit it, and it's our weakest point. If we get you up there, we can make it a much harder fight for them."

"Dave, this is Chase, copy."

"This is Dave, go ahead."

"I need you to come down here and take Jesse's spot."

"Margaret, copy," Chase called up to relieve her.

"This is Margaret. Go, Chase."

"Jesse is coming up to relieve you. You did a great job, but I need someone to check on Elizabeth, Tom and the Truman boy."

"Okay, Margaret, out." She was calm and collected in her response, but she was relieved that she didn't have to deal with another attack

What does my adversary have in mind for the second installment? Chase racked his brain for the answer. *They wouldn't come at night. I have night vision...but they have no idea what night vision is.* The bandits were going to attack at night, out of the woods and the front of the house. *Whichever attack creates an opening, they'll exploit it.*

War was like a good chess game; if one knew his opponent's moves before they did then he would win. This was an absolute in war, except for this instance—three against a heavy company— but Chase had radios, night vision equipment, and automatic weapons. It was going to be a good fight.

The minutes and hours passed slowly as they waited for the second attack, which afforded everyone the opportunity to reflect on the gravity of the situation in which they found themselves. The sun was almost under the horizon and the battle was nearly at hand. Everything was in place on both sides; it was time to kill their adversary or die trying. Chase reflected on what the government had done to him; he was a stone-cold killer, but when it was done in the name of one's country they were called patriots. He wondered, *Which one am I, a killer, or a patriot?* when the shooting started. The remainder of the men crested the hill, firing as they came.

"Here we go, Dave; remember, the gun will kick up and to the left." Chase fired into the night, lit up with the help of the artificial light from the night vision. "Twenty, maybe twenty-five men. Chief, this is the diversion. Get ready."

"Roger that."

Chase keyed in on a group running together; he aimed low and fired into the group, killing three of them. The others separated and hit the ground. A second group of bandits appeared further left; he couldn't keep up with all of the men coming his way, so Chase aimed and fired in a long burst, making sure that the men couldn't advance. He looked over to his right at his partner for this battle. Dave was doing the best that he could, but Chase didn't expect much of him. He was spraying his fire erratically, not killing, but slowing the advancing Confederate raiders. Some groups of brave men were able to get through Dave's gunfire and immediately charged Chase, trying to kill the experienced, rather than the novice, killer, making their job of overrunning the compound much easier. Chase swivelled around to his right to see three men right on top of the bunker, where Dave was supposedly guarding. He fired at the men but was not able to aim; the bullets harmlessly firing into the air. The first man fired his handgun, hitting Chase right in the chest, knocking him back but not down. The second man's bullet grazed Chase's arm, taking a gouge out of the flesh but not penetrating the muscle. He finally got his rifle around and fired, hitting the first man before this rifle clicked empty. The last man's bullet hit Chase in the chest once again, but knocked him to the ground. Using his momentum, he pushed his body clear of the sandbags, drawing his handgun in mid flight; he shot the second man in the groin and the third in the chest. The second man writhed in pain on the ground, his blood covering the melting snow. *A beautiful contrast of color*, Chase thought as he maneuvered to kill the last of the men. Chase took aim and shot the man in the top of the head, putting him out of his misery.

"Chase is hit, he's down. Chase is down!" Dave yelled into the COM set.

Jesse stood with alarm, but the sound of Chase's voice on the COM unit reassured him.

"I'm okay, the vest stopped them. I'm okay." He popped to his feet, ignoring the pain in his chest and arm, and fired into oncoming men, who massed for one last attempt at the frontal assault. The men on the flank would attack at the same time, trying to overwhelm their target.

Jesse had his first taste of the second wave as the remainder of Harden's men came out of the forest. Jesse waited until they moved far enough away from the woods that they were unable to use them for cover and opened fire. His goggles clearly picked up the oncoming men. He used single shots to dispense the group. One by one, he killed, just as a good soldier was trained to do. The raiders didn't know what hit them, falling on the frozen ground, dead. Some of the men triangulated the sound of the firing machine gun but couldn't see very well through the falling snow and the darkness. They simply fired into the house, harmlessly giving the old woman who lived there some extra ventilation. Jesse sighted Harden, one of the last five men alive. Faltering, Jesse picked up one of the other men, killing him. The other three followed; with precision and ease, Jesse killed everyone but Harden, who stood in the middle of all his dead men.

Jesse showed himself in the window and yelled out to Harden, who was standing, stunned, halfway from the woods to the house.

"You best get back on your horse and tell your commanding officer to stop hunting us. You have seen firsthand what we can do. Harden, we are both soldiers fighting a battle that we don't want to fight. I have no problem with you, you seem like a good man, but you will die if you don't get Buford Walton to stop. Do you understand?"

There was no answer, so Jesse took aim at Harden's head, squeezing the trigger, shooting his hat off his head. Harden dove to the ground, yelling, "I understand, I understand." He got up and ran back into the woods, vanishing into the brush.

"Clear, all clear on the left flank."

"Clear in front, we did it!" Chase knew that they had to leave quickly and quietly; they couldn't handle many more men at one time. He gathered the remaining ammunition and followed Dave into the house.

"Let me see that arm, Chase." Dave inspected his bullet wound. "Man, you're lucky that it just grazed you."

"Doctor, this is the forth time that I have been shot, and this is definitely the least severe. We need to gather everyone up and leave now."

"Everyone has to get their belongings together; we pull out in thirty minutes." This was not what Chase wanted, but he couldn't change the fact they had to keep running, trying to figure what had happened and why they were in 1865, soon to be 1866. Chase stopped in the doorway, viewing the horror that he had just created. Man after man lay face down in the snow; bright red bloodstains littered the landscape as if they were a modern art painting. This was much more serious and morose than a painting. He looked to the sky as if to ask God why. *How many more people have to die by my hand in name of country and liberty?* He stepped outside and pulled himself together, out of the way from prying eyes. *Or is it just my vanity I'm fighting for?*

Chapter 10

The snowfall had picked up substantially since Harden had run away from the house; he slowly walked the three miles to town without looking up from his feet. He was ashamed that he had left all his men lying on the frozen ground, bleeding, dying so far from their loved ones. The war was over; they should have been preparing for the spring planting and making love to their wives. That wasn't the case; they had followed Buford Walton on this fool's errand, losing the only thing that most of these men had ever had: their lives.

He was in no hurry to report his error in judgment to Buford and stood outside the outskirts of the city for almost an hour, freezing in the snow, which had begun to blow and drift. The temperature had fallen fifteen degrees in the time that it took to walk to the city, making the cold and snow even more unbearable. Harden reluctantly swallowed his pride and ventured into the city, trying to find Buford and the rest of the men, which he had unwisely split up, sending them in different directions to look, unsuccessfully, for James and his men.

The best place to start would be the police station, where Buford had gone to gather some help, a ploy that he should have heeded. Harden walked the streets, obstructed by the blowing snow, feeling his way from building to building. He came to the police station and entered, finding Buford sitting and talking to the police chief, drinking coffee and laughing. He would not be laughing when he found out what had happened to his men, killed by the soldiers whom Harden in his conceit had dismissed earlier, not knowing how talented they really were.

"Joshua, where have you been? The rest of the men were looking for you before this storm set in; the police chief has been so kind as to put them up in the hotel for the night, in account of the storm outside."

"I need to talk to you outside, Buford." Harden looked at his friend, trying to keep his composure in front of the police chief; feeling like a ton of rock had just hit him square in the chest, he started to weep in front of the chief, Buford, and the three prisoners, who did not much care, being so drunk.

"What happened?" Buford got up to tend to his friend, giving him a fresh cup of coffee and showing him to a seat.

"I found the murderers near the city in a house about three miles from the edge of the town. They knew that I was on to them so I confronted them."

"Confronted?"

"Attacked them. They had made some sort of military installation out of the house, complete with revetments, but I thought it best to attack instead of letting them run again."

"What happened?" Buford's voice became agitated, grinding his teeth together, knowing what was coming next.

"They're dead, all of them, every single one of them, dead. We hit the complex as soon as we arrived, thinking that we could catch them by surprise, but they were ready for us. We had to retreat."

"How many?"

"Sir?"

"How many men?" Buford was having a hard time containing himself and his body language showed it.

"Sixty-five. Sixty-five men killed by three people. The closest we got was fifty-five feet from the house. I decided to reform and hit them at night, when we would have the upper hand; the snow started to fall and they couldn't have known where we were, but they killed every last man. I was the last one standing, and the only reason that he let me live was to tell you to stop hunting them or you'll end up just like the rest of the men—dead."

"Stop hunting them! They have my land and you let them go, you took sixty-five men and could not kill three people." Buford Walton, a Southern gentleman from South Carolina and member of a prestigious southern family, ranted and feverishly paced from corner to corner of the station, yelling at Joshua but not looking at him, everyone watching and wondering what was going through his head.

"Buford, it was a well-planned assault, they just had some kind of portable Gatling gun or something; it cut us to pieces. I thought that I was doing the right thing, but they were well trained and prepared for us; I couldn't do anything about it."

"Goddamn it, you could have waited for more men, for me."

"Then we would all be dead; they are nothing like any soldier that I have ever seen. They move and fire and kill with a skill that has never been known, at least in my experience."

Buford knew what Harden was talking about, having seen the men in action outside the jailhouse. He also knew that his longtime friend had done the right thing, thinking that he could overrun the murderers with his numbers. The only problem was that he could not admit it to anyone; Harden had acted without orders, without him, and that was not tolerable. The fact that the men were still at large gave Buford more concern than his dead men lying on the ground, covered in pure white snow as they spoke.

"Joshua, you are relieved of your duties. Please hand over the badge. I don't want to ever see you again." In one monotone sentence, Buford was throwing twenty-two years of friendship out the window and into the snow.

Harden threw the badge onto the floor of the station and walked out the door, trying to keep a better composure than when he had entered. *Buford has gone over the edge, and he has no regard for his men, the same men that he pampered in the war with money from his family,* Harden thought as he exited the jail house. They had the best equipment, having everything necessary to fight a war and they did it in style. Now he had discarded his oldest friend and sixty-five of his men with one sentence.

In a way, Harden was glad that, at least for him, it was over; he would go back home and start a new life, trying to repent his sins, the sins of war. He walked to the hotel where his former men were staying and gathered up his belongings, which his comrades had carried to the hotel for him. Without saying a word about the battle or about Buford, Harden said his goodbyes, saying that he had received a telegram from home and that he had to attend to his sick mother.

He had expected to leave before Buford arrived, but his luck was not as good as normal today to say the least. Buford entered the hotel as if nothing had happened at all. He gathered the men into a room that gave them some privacy, wanting to address them. Harden stood in the back by the door, curious to hear what Buford was going to say about what had happened.

"Today is a sad day for all of us..."

He is going to blame the attack on the dead men and on me, Harden theorized.

"Today over sixty of our men, including Sergeant Harden, decided to leave us and go back home."

"That bastard," Harden mumbled so no one could hear. *He isn't even going to tell them about the attack, he is going to keep them happy and content.*

"They've abandoned us in our time of need…" Dozens of men filing to the back where Harden was standing interrupted Buford as if to say that they were going with Harden and not staying. In a matter of a minute, ninety-five percent of the men sided with their sergeant against their commanding officer.

One brave soul stood up and declared his loyalty to Harden. "If the sarg doesn't go we ain't going; we have families and homes to tend to and most of us just want to go home."

Buford was in shock; he had made the worst error in judgment in his life at the most inopportune time. *How could things have come to this?* He had to think fast. Harden had to stay.

Persuasive speech was Buford's talent; he had always been able to convince people that he was right, even if he was dead wrong. "Sergeant, I ask you to reconsider your decision."

"My decision?" He was Buford's best and oldest friend; he knew what he was going to do before he did.

"I was mistaken, upset and I made those comments in haste. Please, old friend, reconsider; we can make this right together."

"Buford, only you can make it right." Loyalty was Harden's gift and curse all in one. He would do anything for a friend, even kill a boy and his woman. He would continue on this pilgrimage, but needed Buford to set the record straight first.

Buford was a proud man, but he needed Harden and would have to pay his price, a steep price, one of humility.

"That's not the whole story; the men that I spoke of attacked the murderers' hideout and were killed in action. I didn't know how to tell you that your comrades in arms are dead. I was wrong, Sergeant Harden called me on it, and I ask you to avenge their deaths. No land, no money, just let your friends rest in peace, knowing that they died for a reason, an end, unlike all of those men in the war. I'm going to fight on, hopefully with the help of my friend, Josh Harden, and hopefully with your help."

The men looked to Harden, who was not convinced, but satisfied with the speech. "Men, I have a hard time seeing my troops die, but I have a harder time letting a friend down." *The sins will have to wait for another day,* Harden thought. Buford still needed him. He walked to the front of the room and stood next to Buford, who grabbed his hand and lifted it to the ceiling.

One by one the men filed back into the room, disappointed in Buford, but understanding his motives. They would go on; many of them had no reason to go home. Even the man who had spoken up had nothing. His wife had thought he was dead and had remarried, leaving him to roam the countryside until Buford had called for him to help. It gave him and many of his comrades a sense of belonging, one that would not end in defeat.

The plan was to go to the battlefield, see if anyone was still alive, and start after the murderers when the weather cleared. None of the men had any idea what they were in store for when they arrived at the house outside the city. Most of the men had been raiders during the war, never witnessing the horrors of a major battle. That would all change.

The blizzard took the running time travelers and their new friends by surprise, slowing the group to a crawl along the trail towards the Missouri River. It was thirty miles from the city to the river, but they were lucky if they were two miles from the house when the weather forced them to take cover. The white snow cascaded from the sky, blowing from north to south. Chase, Jesse, and David put on the accessories of their environmental suit, gloves and a headpiece that covered everything including a clear plastic cover for their eyes. Unfortunately, the three suits did no good for Tom Tidwell, Elizabeth, Margaret, and Tom Truman, who was Chase's main concern. He had to keep him alive at all costs, knowing how important his son would be to the United States.

Tom Tidwell was doing all he could to keep Elizabeth and him warm, riding together on a horse. They had every piece of clothing on that they could possibly get onto their bodies. Elizabeth was even wearing a pair of Tom's pants, giving Margaret a sense of retribution. They were both frozen to the bone and miserable, wondering why the others didn't seem bothered by the cold, especially Elizabeth, who took a mental note of Chase and Jesse, riding effortlessly in the cold and added to her conspiracy theory. Margaret smiled and kept to herself, trying to will the cold to go away and doing a decent job at it.

The trees were bowing from the snow's weight, and ice was forming on the tips of the branches, falling, making it even more difficult to travel. In addition to the ice, visibility was only two feet, giving the weary travelers no choice but to stop and seek shelter from the snow, ice, and wind. Thick, lanky trees surrounded both sides of the dirt road, which was only detectable by the lack of such trees because of the snow. The group stopped on Chase's orders and waited while Jesse, Chase, and Dave foraged the forest for branches and anything that they could use to construct shelters.

Dave appeared twenty yards from the group and was unable to see the others, who were just to his right. He yelled to them, following their response to where they waited.

"Chase and Jesse are waiting for us; we have found some material to make shelters for everyone." They all trudged through the now knee-high snow into the woods and relative safety.

Jesse had made the first shelter for Tom Truman by digging a pit in the snow just big enough for one person to sit in a ball, packing the remaining snow hard, forming a bowl, which would help shelter the person from the wind. He then took fallen branches and made an enclosure, insulating it with snow and the leaves on the forest floor. He handed Truman a blanket and squeezed him into the shelter, covering the exit with more branches and snow. The premise of the shelter was to keep the person alive, but in no way was it going to make them comfortable or happy. He started on the next shelter for Tom Tidwell in the same manner that he had made Truman's, though Tidwell's wound made the construction a bit more difficult as Tidwell couldn't bend his leg very well and was just in the beginning of the healing process after the infection had cleared up. Any sudden movement could tear the sutures and his chances at life.

Chase did the same for Margaret and Elizabeth, keeping them alive for another day. Everyone was in a shelter that needed one and the three men of 2099 watched the group, making sure no one panicked or succumbed to the cold. They propped themselves up on a tree just far enough from the shelters that they could talk without any problems.

"Jess, how many men have you killed?" Chase could feel the post-battle depression setting in and could not fight the urge to ask.

"Why do you ask?"

"I've been trying to count them the past few hours and I think that the list will never end. I'm at 567 and I'm still counting the men I killed in the war. I can remember every one of them vividly; they haunt me at night sometimes. What do you think would happen to us if we killed that many men, say, being a serial killer?"

"We would be hunted and executed. You can't think about it. Chase, we do it for our country. We do what has to be done, what other people can't do."

"Yeah, because they're normal; they've never smelled someone's blood on them because they killed them face to face. They don't slit unsuspecting people's throats, or put a round in someone's head at three hundred yards. We've been in 1865 for over a month and we're living the same life that we left in 2099: kill or die. I was just wondering when it stopped."

"It never will. Chase, we are what we are. I know that it sounds like a cliché, but it's true. You and I are predators in the employ of our government. We kill for them and die for them, mostly without recognition. I know how you're feeling, I went through the same thing; you just have to come to peace with what and who you are."

"That's the problem. I am navy through and through and it scars me."

"It scars me, too, but you have to come to terms with it; we need your leadership out here, and you are the only commanding officer who could get the job done right and I respect you for that. By the way, I can remember everyone that I have killed too. 1,765 people dead by my hand."

Both men fell silent. Chase was fighting the same demons that Jesse had wrestled with long ago. They were from the same mold, Jesse knew, fighting the first losing battle of their lives.

Harden led the way to the house where his men lay dead, battling the snow and wind every step of the way. He was in no hurry to return, but needed to see if anyone had survived the attack. He welled up with emotion when he crested the hill, but unlike in the police station, he kept his composure, stiffening his back and holding his head high. He focused on the area in front of the house, but was surprised to find that there were no bodies on the ground. His first instinct was that the snow had covered the bodies, but there would be some indication of where the men rested. He approached the sandbag installations slowly, using caution, but not letting the rest of his men know that he was scared. He knew that his adversaries were gone, but dreaded seeing what the men had done to his dead friends.

His line of sight topped the sandbags and he saw them, lined up in three rows from behind each set of the bags to the house. The blood, frozen and unsuccessfully covered by the falling snow, told the tale of the battle. Many of the brave men still had their eyes open, displaying an expression of fear and pain. Harden closed his eyes and said a prayer for the men and for forgiveness for leaving them to die. He opened his eyes and counted the group.

"Fifty-four." Harden counted one more time, coming up with the same number.

He looked behind him for Buford, finding him to his left surveying the death, remembering what they had gone through together.

"Buford, there are only fifty-four of them, and that means that ten men are alive." Harden was the eleventh man that had survived the battle. "They are probably inside the house."

Harden showed a glimmer of hope on his face for the first time all day. They dismounted and entered the house without knocking, pistols drawn. They saw the old woman, taking care of the wounded, some cognitive and talking, others near death, but all of the men seemed comfortable.

"These men must belong to you?" the old woman asked Buford.

"Yes, they do. How did they get inside?"

"The other men brought them in and the doctor took care of their wounds before they left."

"How long ago was that?" Buford had to find out where they had gone.

"A few hours, but this storm moved in so quickly that I doubt that the got very far. They told me to tell you that all of these men should live, but those two over in the corner only has a 60/40 chance."

"Did they say where they were going?" Buford had tunnel vision; he had injured men and fifty-four men to bury, and all he could think about was catching and killing the Tidwell boy and his talented protectors.

"They went west to the Missouri River and over to St. Charles; they had a guide with them, a boy who stays here occasionally. Like I said, they could not have gotten very far, but neither can you. Your men can ride the storm out here."

"Thank you, we're grateful." Harden looked into the old woman's eyes, which showed her years and her experience. He focused out and took in the whole picture. He found a woman who had seen her share of death, pain and tears, but he also saw a kind and battle-scarred woman; the battle that was her life had taken its toll. He nodded to the woman and walked out to address the men and attend to the dead. He knew there was nothing he could do, but he felt obliged to try.

Harden looked over his dead soldiers and realized that the men whom he had hated just a few minutes before had taken the time to take care of his injured men and collected the dead; perhaps they were not as evil as Buford made them out to be, though they were still the enemy. He had met the leader, Jesse, so he thought; he seemed to be a decent fellow. He knew that it took two people to tango, and without Buford chasing the men, none of this would have ever happened. He felt a small amount of solace in that thought, but he still felt partly responsible for fifty-four deaths. Regardless of his personal feelings, he needed to avenge the death of his men.

Chapter 11

The storm lasted the night, giving Chase and Jesse a chance to sleep in shifts, both men trained to sleep in the most difficult of environments, and with the environmental stabilizing suits, they were rather comfortable in the blizzard. They were still concerned about Buford following them, but the storm would stop Buford from looking, knowing that when it was over, he would hunt them once again. Every hour the man on watch checked the shelters and their inhabitance, looking to see if they were alive and free from frostbite.

Chase was on watch when the storm let up, looking at his navy diving watch. *5:45 a.m. December 26, 1865. Buford will be on the move and we don't have much of a head start,* he thought, looking over at his chief, soundly sleeping and propped against a tree. He reached down and woke Jesse, who was not sleeping very soundly and went to gather the gear and group members, preparing for a race to the Missouri river, where they could defend from across the riverbank using their highly accurate weapons to snipe Buford's men from out of range of their own relatively primitive weapons. Alternatively, they would disappear into the countryside, avoiding any additional killing, leaving their troubles behind them and concentrating on getting back to 2099, soon to be 2100. The second option would have suited Chase just fine in his present state of mind, but he had a mission to attend to first, and no matter how stressful the situation, he needed to be on his toes.

The temperature outside was still well below zero, but the snowfall gave way to drifting and blowing, allowing them to travel, but not quickly. The snow covered the road with three-foot drifts, hampering the horses' ability to drudge through it easily.

Tom Truman led the way, only because he knew exactly where he was and the best route to the river. He looked over his shoulder at the two soldiers riding side by side on the snow-covered dirt road. He had never seen anything like the display of soldiery at the white house and was enamored by his new friends, wondering exactly where they came from, hoping that they would travel with his dad's wagon train west, protecting the group as they went through Indian country. First, he would have to lead them away from danger, theorizing the further west that the group got the safer that it would be, both weather-wise and posse-wise. Truman turned around and concentrated on getting to the river

Jesse had more than just one problem; he had Chase to deal with as well as Buford and Harden. Chase had begun to question his life as a SEAL and felt that he was nothing more than a killer. Good operators reached that phase in their career when the killing began to outweigh the duty. Chase was a good officer, earmarked for admiral before he had found himself in his present situation. *Getting through this will be difficult. I'll have to help him to overcome his fears.* He picked up his pace, moving up to keep stride with Chase's horse, patting him on the back, giving him the encouragement that he desperately needed.

"How are you doing, boss? I was worried about you last night; you seemed to come down with some kind of pussy bug."

"Real funny, Master Chief. I just had the down effects of adrenaline. My mind was working overtime to compensate for the lack of adrenaline; it made me get a bit emotional." Chase was making an excuse and he knew it.

"Where I come from we call it pussy, but that's just me." Jesse knew that support came in many ways; he was not the warm and fuzzy type of person, he was tough love.

Chase smiled at him, knowing that his chief was razzing him; he felt better, for the moment, but it would take time, and that was one thing that they had plenty of: time. He kept telling himself that he loved his country, his navy, and being a SEAL was what he was good at, but it wasn't working; he still felt sorrow about killing all of those people. He resorted to something that in the past had relieved tension especially before big missions. Chase unbuttoned his coat and flung it behind his gun belt, revealing the environmental suit and the 10mm handguns to the rest of the group. Chase drew his gun, quick-draw style, pointed the laser sight at his target, and returned the weapon to its holster. He had become quite proficient at it over the years, having such a love for the Old West. He never had the opportunity to use his skill in the late twenty-first century; perhaps now he would. Repeatedly he drew, pointed, and returned the gun, until he had forgotten all about the white house and his pain.

The twenty-five miles that the group traveled after the snowstorm seemed to pass by quickly, each person pondering their own involvement in the group's situation, all except Jesse, who decided it best if he doubled back. He knew Buford was coming, it was just a mater of when, and he wanted to be prepared.

Tom Truman decided to use a little-known path to the river; he went downstream to where the Missouri River ran east to west and not west to east in the heart of St. Charles, Missouri, the first capital of Missouri and the beginning point of the Lewis and Clark expedition. The town had a floating pontoon bridge constructed, spanning the river, which looked rather unmaintained. It was just wide enough for one wagon to pass over, and most people crossed one at a time, limiting any accidents.

Chase was the first to cross the rickety-looking structure, demanding that he test the bridge before anyone else crossed. He had the environmental suit on, keeping him from freezing to death if he fell in the river. He would know how to handle the pressure of being in icy waters, where someone else might panic. Jesse was the other option, but he was covering their flank and tracks behind the group. The plan was to cross the river and then wait for Jesse from behind the safety of a quarter mile of water. One by one the party crossed the river, slowly and with a great deal of caution, keeping their eyes fixed on the other side and not the ice-filled water moving swiftly towards its meeting with the Mississippi a few miles downstream.

The snow began to fall once more, further covering their tracks, but at the same time hampering their plans to move further west. Jesse appeared from the wooded area on the other side of the river about thirty minutes after everyone else in the group had braved the pontoon bridge, the snow driving to the ground with a greater volume than the night before, and by the time Jesse got to the bridge crossing, it was covered in snow. He spurred his horse to start slowly moving across, but not knowing much about horses, his mount started on a dead run to the other side. Startled, he pulled back on the reins without remorse, jerking the horse's head hard right. She stopped running, but started sliding across the width of the bridge on the snow-covered ice, hitting the railing on Jesse's right. The rail was waist high for a human but only came to the top of a horse's leg, and being made of wood was just as old and rickety as the rest of the bridge. It gave way with a loud snap, like a tree falling in a forest, tossing Jesse, the horse and half of their supplies into the ice-filled river.

The water was cold, like putting your ankle in a bucket of ice water, but the only parts of Jesse's body that felt the sting of the river were his face and hands, the only parts exposed to the river. He looked down at his horse, which had righted itself and Jesse with it, still attached to her, trying to swim to the bank, quickly succumbing to the ice-filled water. She stopped swimming and began to sink to the bottom of the river with Jesse frantically trying to detach himself, tangled in the stirrups and the harness. He took a deep breath before going under, hoping to free himself before he got too far below the surface.

With every jerk of his body, the now dead horse's rigging ensnared Jesse like a mouse in a trap. He had little air left and was not close to freeing himself from the horse. His automatic pilot kicked in, the one that never let him down in a time of danger; swiveling to where his equipment was, he pulled out his MBA, loosing the two EP450s he carried in the process. He placed it on his head and turned on the startup air tank, the size of a CO_2 cartridge for a paintball gun, gaining much needed air. Knowing that he had more time, he put the gloves of the environmental suit on and pulled his combat knife from its sheath, cutting the leather straps that held him on the bottom of the river and starting to drag him downstream. Piece by piece the harness loosened its grip, allowing Jesse to get free. He cut his supplies free and took a quick look for the two lost pulse rifles; with no luck he started for the surface with what he could salvage.

Chase watched in horror as his closest friend and mentor skidded through the sidewall of the bridge and into the river, splashing, still attached onto his horse, into the icy river. Chase had no idea if Jesse had his environmental suit on and could not ask him because he had sunk below the surface of the water. Chase did not hesitate. *SEALs never leave a man behind* rang out in his head over and over, realizing he was reacting when he felt himself slip his MBA over his head, put his environmental suit's head cover and gloves on and bounded towards the river, risking detection by Elizabeth. He calculated the current speed to mass ratio in his head and sprinted to the point that he calculated Jesse would hit the bottom. Jumping in the river, Chase swam out to where Jesse had sunk beneath the surface of the water, looking for his friend as he splashed into the ice-filled river. He decided to dive under the water, searching, desperately, for Jesse, who had just cut himself free. He was three feet from the bottom when he saw Jesse, fifteen feet straight in front of him. He had calculated the distance correctly, finding his friend swimming towards him. He reached out and tucked his arm underneath Jesse's, quickly starting to the surface.

When they came to the surface, each man helped the other swim to the bank of the river, where Dr. Persons was ready with blankets. To the untrained eye, it seemed as if Chase had saved Jesse's life, but they knew that it was not the case. Nonetheless, Jesse appreciated Chase coming to his rescue and realized that he had a friend who would give up his own life to save him, something that was reconfirmed almost every day.

From a distance Julia Hudson watched as Chase jumped into the freezing river after Jesse, risking his life for a friend; to her there was no greater sacrifice, no greater show of character. Julia attended Lindenwood Equestrian College for woman in town, and was out exercising her horse when the snow had started, prompting her to turn around, catching Chase and his rescue attempt. She trotted to where the rest of the group stood, amazed that both men were all right. Julia was a beautiful woman by any time's standards, with long black hair and green eyes. She stood five feet six inches tall and had all the right curves, the apple in every man's eye. She jumped from her horse and ran to Chase, beating everyone except Dr. Persons, wanting to meet her brave man. Chase stood in the snow, dripping wet with a blanket around him when his eyes met hers. She was majestic, breathtaking to behold. To Chase, she was Helen of Troy; having never felt such an attraction for a woman at first sight, he stumbled on a rock as he passed her, not being able to take his eyes off her, swiveling as he passed, letting a smile creep onto his face.

She took his arm and wrapped the blanked around him, patting him dry, looking into his eyes and smiling.

"Are you alright?" Her voice was soft and elegant, educated.

"Yes, I seem to be. My friend took quite a fall; perhaps you might want to ask him."

The rest of the group cut Julia short, deciding it best to see how their protectors—and only hope of getting what every individual person wanted—were doing. This was the case for everyone except Elizabeth, who watched and thought, *How can two men jump into a frozen river, stay under water for over five minutes and come to the surface without drowning? They are not human, rather something grotesque, and they need to be put in their place: under humanity.* She would have what she wanted soon, and these men would become expendable, learning long ago from George Tidwell that people were just a vehicle for your own personal gain. She would gain from turning these two men into Buford and Harden, and her and Tom would live happily ever after, together.

"You need to rest and get out of this snow. I have the best place for that." Julia was determined to keep Chase close to her so that she could find out more about him.

"Where?" Dr. Persons knew that he should check Jesse and Chase, and the snow was coming down so thick that one couldn't see at all.

"Up at the college, there are quarters for the employees, and I know the headmistress will allow you to stay there when I tell her what happened."

"Show us, we need to get these two warmed up quickly and I need to examine them."

Julia was off, her horse traveling on muscle memory because the snow created white-out conditions. She had gotten her way, but would she like the outcome, having no idea whom she was helping and what they were capable of doing?

"Goddamn it, what do you mean we need to turn back? I don't care about the storm; we need to push on, we need to find them."

"Buford, there is no way we can travel in this weather, but the good news is neither can they. We're only a few miles from the white house, but we are twenty-five miles from the next town. If we go back to the house we can send a rider out to find them but we can't go any further in this storm."

"Bullshit. Harden, if we stop we lose them for good and that cannot happen; it will not happen to me."

"Buford, I'm going to turn the men around and you're going to come with them; you need to sleep. I'll go forward and try and find James and his men, but my men are going back to the house." He held up his hand and pulled on the reins, stopping his horse. There was no complaint from the men about turning around; they all pulled an about face and double-timed it to the white house.

Harden continued on, knowing he shouldn't push his luck; he did it for his friend, who seemed to be coming apart after all the years they had served together in all the battles that he had gotten them through. He had to try and help his friend keep his sanity. He bundled up and pressed on, not knowing if he was going to make it, or die, frozen in the snow.

Chase and Jesse entered the gates of Lindenwood College for Women on Chase's horse, trotting down a long brick path, two hundred yards long to the main campus, which consisted of two buildings and a vast acreage of land for running and training horses. The main building where the women lived, eat, and attended class was a three-story Southern plantation-style house with three floors and a basement level. The outside of the building was brick, as everything in the St. Louis area was, and wood, which was painted white. There was a second floor veranda, held up with two pillars, much like the white house. The veranda hung over a porch that extended the whole width of the structure. The other building was more modest in its scope and housed the servants and horse trainers.

The campus had over two hundred trees on it, sheltering the group from the snow and winds just enough to be able to see. Many of the trees were very old and could tell many stories if they could talk. The stables were on the bottom of the campus, down a gradually sloping hill that stopped at a large rectangular building used for a training area, and the stables were behind that.

"Lindenwood is the second oldest college west of the Mississippi River and the oldest west of the Missouri River; over the years it has grown into a coed university with over fifteen thousand students and close to one hundred fifty acres."

"Chase, how in the world do you know anything about this place? This probably was not in your history curriculum."

"No, they have a good wrestling program and wrestling is a small community. They had an open tournament that we brought our team to when I was in school. That building with the pillars is still standing in 2099; it's a historical landmark in Missouri."

Jesse took his handgun from its holster and put it in Chase's side. "No more talking until we get settled." He jokingly jabbed the gun in Chase's ribs. Chase settled into his saddle with a smile, the first genuine smile he had had in some time.

The team was allowed to stay in the employees' quarters until the weather cleared and they were able to move on, which was just fine with Jesse and Chase, who knew that Buford and Harden would not be far behind. They settled into the rooms assigned to their use and went about their business as if nothing had happened. Chase and Jesse cleaned their weapons and did an ammunition check, Tom Truman had to stay with Margaret and Dave in the larger of the three rooms, and Mr. and Mrs. Tom Tidwell, so they had introduced themselves to the headmistress, had there own room.

Harden braved the snow and wind for his friend Buford, coming to the river crossing; finding it impassable, he made a makeshift shelter from the cold and snow, nowhere near the quality of Jesse's, but it kept him from freezing to death. Periodically he exited the shelter to examine the surroundings and keep an eye out for anything abnormal, which, with the events of the past few weeks, would take quite an ordeal. He had been in the shelter for three hours when he decided to venture out for his third time, finding a rider at the base of the bridge on the other side. He squinted to examine the mystery person, who obviously wanted to talk to him, taking a double look at the figure who appeared to be a woman. Curious, he motioned the rider to come closer as he began to walk, pulling his horse to the middle of the bridge, ignoring the danger. As the person got closer, Harden realized that the mystery person was a woman; he drew his gun and placed it out of sight under his wool Confederate gray coat, thinking that it was a trap, but he was overwhelmed with curiosity.

He stopped in the middle of the bridge, forcing the woman to come to him, lessening the chance of an ambush. He watched her approach; she was pretty, but not stunning, with a dark blue coat and a matching hat. Her figure was nice and she acted the part of a proper lady. She tentatively approached, obviously scared, knowing that she could die by Harden's hands, stopping three feet from him and smiling a very provocative, alluring smile.

"My name is Elizabeth Thompson, Thomas Tidwell's fiancée. Are you one of the men following us?"

Harden didn't answer her; he couldn't believe the audacity and bravery of this woman, who was undoubtedly going to try to play both sides. He remembered to whom she was engaged and snapped out of his fog of disbelief. "Perhaps. What can I do for you?"

"Well, I have a proposition for your leader." She paused, trying to get Harden to give up some information about who he was. Disappointed, she continued. "As you know we have been traveling with strangers who have protected us from your attacks. These men are not normal. I even doubt that they are human."

"You want to give up the men who are keeping Tom alive? That sounds like a poor idea to me."

"No, I want to trade Tom's life and mine for the lives of the men with whom we have been traveling."

"Who's to say that we don't kill all of you?" Josh Harden was going to play hardball.

"The sixty dead men back at the house? Three people did that."

"Three, who's the third?"

"He is a doctor, a very skilled one; he did just enough in the fight to get by. Mostly, it was Chase O'Sullivan, the commander, and Robert James, his sergeant or something. Chase calls him Chief, whatever that means. They have weapons that I have never heard of before and seem to enjoy killing."

"How can you help us if we take you up on your offer?" He was curious to hear her plan.

"Everywhere we go they make sure that they have an escape route and that they can defend the structure, so you will never be able to get to them, but with me on the inside, you can plan a surprise attack when their guard is down. If they think that you are not following them, they'll let their guard down, and then we can come up with a place that your men can lay a trap."

"That sounds good, but how do I know if I can trust you? This could be a ploy."

"You need to figure that out for yourself. I'm concerned for Tom and I, not those men, and I'll do what it takes to complete my task." She was taking her second gamble of the day and for some reason she was confident that this man would accept her offer. She hadn't worked out the details of her plan, but she knew that it would work if she could convince Harden it was a good plan.

Harden looked at her intensely, trying to find out if she was lying to him, knowing that she was not. "Where are you staying now?"

"We are at a woman's college down the road about a mile and a half; we are going to stay there until the weather clears and then we go west towards the Kansas territory."

"We need to have another meeting with you; my commander will want to talk to you. Meet us here two days from now at nightfall. That is the only way that we will do this, and I want some details and some proof that you will do what you say you will." He turned and walked to his horse; he would ride in the snow to the white house. This information was too promising to wait until it cleared. He would have his land and his friend back very soon.

Chapter 12

Dr. Cormier sat at his computer terminal calculating possible mathematical solutions to the mass-energy problem that his transport system had now created. He tried to send supplies to the time travelers, but had no idea if they received them. He theorized that the electromagnetic pulse that the EP450 emitted when fired polarized the transport's electrical field, creating a shortcut to the energy problem that breaking the light barrier inherently possessed. Cormier's staff discharged the same amount of electromagnetic pulses from the rifle that the SEAL team had fired in the battle at the Arab compound, theorizing that the transport platforms that each team member wore would reacquire the platform signal, creating the same tear in the fabric of time, and giving the travelers much-needed supplies in addition to the magnet needed to repair the pulse rifle. After testing the rifle, it became apparent the new rifle wouldn't fire after the time travel because the portal de-magnetized the extremely powerful electromagnet that the weapon used to discharge its phosphorous rounds.

If the team replaced the magnet, which had to be transported in a stone enclosure, protecting it from the same fate as the first magnet, and fired the same amount of volleys, the transport platform would activate the retrieval portal, which NASA and the navy maintained at all times. It was a plausible theory, but he had no way to prove it until the group reactivated the portal and traveled home. The problem he foresaw with the SEAL team initiating the transport was that they might not be intelligent enough to figure out the solution to their problem, leaving them wherever they were, forever.

"Doctor Cormier." Cormier turned his head to the door where Admiral Townsend was standing in the doorway to his office.

"Admiral, how are you doing this morning?"

"I'm doing better, thanks; the base physician prescribed a sleeping pill. I'm getting more sleep than at our last meeting."

"I'm glad to hear it." Cormier really couldn't care less, but he reported to this man and had to remain cordial. Over the past few weeks, he had pushed himself and Admiral Townsend to the limits of sanity, and it took its toll on their relationship.

"Do you have anything new for me today, Doctor? I have to make my weekly report to the president today." Christopher Townsend needed something new to tell his boss, who was becoming impatient at the slow progress that Cormier and his team of NASA scientists had. It was difficult for him and the president to sit and wait for results; they were both used to their orders being completed quickly, but the scientists were used to the opposite: slow, tedious clinical trials and experimentation. It wasn't that Townsend disliked Cormier, but he didn't accept his methods, wanting speed, not science.

"We sent the ammunition and the magnet a few days ago; if my theory is correct, they should've received it instantly. However, on your orders, we didn't send actual weapons or instructions on repairing the EP450 because of your concerns for the historical ramifications. We're in a holding pattern, waiting to see if your men are smart enough to figure everything out."

"Commander O'Sullivan has a PhD, just like yourself, and David Persons has a PhD and an MD, so it's not a matter of intelligence, it's a matter of your equipment and theories working as you say they'll work."

Cormier was used to exchanging insults with Townsend and decided to give him what he wanted: a clear, no bullshit theory. He would get the last word today, but tomorrow was another day and another argument. "I do have something that might be of some use to you when you see the president. As you know, Chase and his group don't belong wherever they ended up. I've been working on a theory that basically says because they don't really exist where they are, their matter is in a type of stasis or hibernation."

"What the fuck does that mean, Doctor?" Townsend had played right into Dr. Cormier's cleverly laid trap, and was annoyed with his constant bombshell theories.

"When the transport system malfunctioned and sent your team back in time, it created a tear, or rip in the fabric of time, that I believe can never be fully repaired. I think that there is no doubt that they've interacted with individuals from the time to which we accidentally sent them. Frankly, it's been over a month since they disappeared, and I don't think your people, or anybody for that matter, could hide out that long without going into a town for supplies or running into someone on the street."

"What's your point, Doctor?"

"With every person that the team interacts with, the rip in time becomes larger. Now it might or might not change history, but as the rip grows and the number of people with whom they come into contact grows, the more likely it is that the time continuum will change."

"Exactly. That's the reason that the president's science advisors didn't want anything else sent through the portal."

"I understand that, but my theory goes further. Your team created the riff, making them the starting point, and focal point of the shift in the continuum. Because they were never meant to interact with the individuals in that time, or even be in that time, the tear in the fabric will protect them from changing."

"Do you mean to say that they can't die?"

"No, their physical bodies can die from blunt force trauma, but if I'm correct, your people will never age or even change the slightest little bit until their matter realigns with the correct time period. I think the most likely time for the realignment is when they're born."

"Doctor, you need to give me things that I can use, not this science-fiction shit. There is no way that I can present that theory to the president of the United States." Admiral Christopher Townsend walked to the door, upset that he hadn't seen the trap sooner. He couldn't let Cormier have the last word, but after that performance, the only way he could get the last word was to give him an order. "Don't send any more supplies through that portal; we feel that it might mess the space-time continuum up, just as you yourself predicted. Do you understand, Dr. Cormier?"

Doctor Cormier went back to his calculations, ignoring Townsend, who got the picture and left without saying another word. *Townsend is correct,* he thought, *my theories aren't proven and my methods are unorthodox to say the least, but I am doing everything I can to bring the group back.* If he didn't bring them home, Cormier would be the cause of their death, a fact he couldn't handle.

Cormier turned the computer off and went to the transport terminal, making sure that the calibrations were correct. Satisfied, he decided to get some sleep; he had been up all night and would need his sleep for tomorrow when he presented his theories to the other NASA scientists.

Sleeping was a good idea, but unfortunately for Cormier, just like his boss, he didn't sleep much these days, being more concerned with finding Chase and his group than maintaining his health. He was lucky if he slept three hours per night, and the sleep that he did get was listless. One had only look into his eyes and they would understand the physical and emotional pain he felt at the loss of the team. In this respect, he and Townsend were similar, but in every other way, they were polar opposites. He had never met Chase and his men, only observed them use his system at the onset of the mission. He had no way to gage whether Chase was capable of coming to the correct solution to the problem and couldn't afford to take that chance emotionally or mentally. His reputation was at stake as well, though taking second chair to finding the group. However, to Cormier, they went hand in hand: find the group and further his career. To him there was only one choice: keep sending items of use through the portal, guaranteeing the team's success.

He tried to sleep, but only counted the seconds until it was time to go back to the base. He decided that sleep would have to wait and started his day by taking a cold shower and drinking three quarters of a pot of coffee. It only marginally helped, masking the exhaustion that was mounting; later he would see that same physician that Townsend had mentioned and get the same sleeping pills, but first he had a classified mission of his own to complete.

The base was almost empty, except for the guard, who paid little attention to Cormier because he hardly ever left the transport area and was virtually a permanent fixture at the base. He waited until the current guard's watch changed, and made his way to the transport room, placing a black box filled with the necessary equipment onto the platform and activated the terminal. In a fraction of a second, the equipment was gone and the guards were none the wiser. If his plan worked, he could afford to lie down and take a short nap, and wait for results that were sure to be positive.

Cormier staggered back to his office, wanting to lie down on his couch; thankfully, he felt as if he could finally sleep. He sat on his couch, preparing to kick off his shoes, when out of the corner of his eye, the other half of his message, lying on his desk, flattened his aspirations of positive results. He didn't have enough energy to get upset at himself. He picked up the letter and made his way back to the platform room, dropping the envelope in the pod and sending it to the group. He acted as if he were performing tests on the transport system; it was something he did often enough and wouldn't raise any suspicions from the guards, who all knew about Townsend's order not to send anything else to the team. He stayed a while longer, keeping up the charade, and then went directly back to his office and his couch, which would be his bed for the next three hours. Cormier wondered if his theory was correct or if he was just crazy. His mind almost didn't finish the thought before he was fast asleep.

Townsend didn't exactly know what to tell the president about the status of the classified operation unfolding at his Norfolk, Virginia, base. His only concern was keeping the president from terminating the operation. The White House and many of the joint chiefs considered the operation a waste of valuable resources. The last meeting he'd had with the president hadn't been positive, and all indications pointed to a change in the classifying agency from the navy to the Central Intelligence Agency. It was a safe bet that the CIA was not going to be concerned with two Navy SEALs and a no-name doctor. His only trump card was Margaret Knox-Harriman, a U.S. ambassador whom the last presidential administration had appointed, where the current president had served as vice president. It wasn't much, but all of his hopes were pinned on a woman, who after the war might have outlived her usefulness.

The military transport plane rumbled as it hit the runway at Andrews Air Force base, jarring Admiral Townsend from his thoughts. The plane, with its lone passenger, came to a stop on the tarmac, pulling close to a parked military car, which the Pentagon had sent to pick up Townsend and take him directly to the White House. Townsend returned the salute of the petty officer second-class assigned as his drive and entered the car on his way to stave off the CIA and penny-pinchers from ending his operation.

Townsend cleared security and made his way inside, stopping at the entrance to the briefing room to straighten his uniform and clear his head. Satisfied with his state of mind and appearance, he entered the large room, which featured a circular table in the middle. The table, made of oak, was the centerpiece of one of the White House smart rooms. Every place at the table was equipped with a complete computer terminal, video teleconferencing equipment, and an overly comfortable chair. At the head of the room, a thirty-foot video screen dominated the wall, completed by a state-of-the-art projection system hanging from the ceiling.

"Thank you for coming. Admiral Townsend, I know it's a long way to come for an hour briefing."

"It's my pleasure, Mr. President, I just hope that it wasn't all for nothing." Townsend took his seat and waited his turn to make the case for continuing the project. He requested he be the last to speak, hoping to be able to counter many of the objections raised by the other principles.

The opponents to continuing the operation looked to Army General Eric Mathews Jr. to make their case. Two years ago, Chase had landed on the bad side of General Mathews when his team had received orders to rescue five marines, seven army rangers, and a CIA operative from a captured U.S. base in Pakistan over an Army Delta Force unit. It hadn't been enough that a navy unit had been chosen over an army unit to conduct the rescue, but Chase had added fuel to the fire when he had refused to relinquish command of the operation to an army lieutenant colonel, who was senior to Chase by eighteen months.

The team and the rescued hostages had found themselves pinned down by hostile fire while trying to extract by helicopter. The extraction unit had retired due to extremely heavy fire and the group had been forced to fight their way into the mountains and safety, prompting the lieutenant colonel to demand command of the unit. Because of the leadership and tactical superiority of Commander O'Sullivan, the group had been able to cover the ground to the mountains and extract without any casualties. One person had received wounds in the operation, his injuries forcing him out of the army. Lieutenant Colonel Eric Mathews III had received wounds under fire while disobeying an order from the operational commander to fall back to a more defensible location, scouted by Master Chief James. The general never forgot the black mark and possibly tried to exact a measure of revenge on Chase and on Townsend.

"Gentlemen, what we have here is wishful thinking; there is no reason to believe that the SEAL team and the rescued hostages are alive. There is no scientific proof that time travel is possible. In fact, it's easier to believe that the group didn't survive rather than that they are trapped in some unknown time. It is unfortunate that the armed forces are spending millions of much needed dollars to continue an operation that will never bear fruit. We have supported funding for this operation for over a month, and I would think that a group of talented operators would be able to use the supplies sent to them to phone home, if you will. The cost and the bleak outlook for success leaves me no choice but to recommend a suspension of this operation, and that the classifying agency change from the navy to the CIA."

Admiral Townsend stood, adjusted his uniform, and pointed to the junior officer operating the AV equipment. The room went dark and exploded with the sounds of battle. The satellite replay of the firefight in the Arab compound startled the group; they had all seen the feed before, but none of them could seem to look away from the heroics shown by the SEAL team. On Townsend's command, the junior officer lowered the audio, letting the video play in the background while Townsend began his plea.

"Sirs, I have the honor to know and the pleasure to have served with the men in that video. They put their lives on the line every day, doing things that only a handful of people can even dream of doing. They kill, capture, infiltrate, rescue, and yes, die at your orders. In return, they ask for the support of their country and the knowledge that no one would leave them behind during a mission. They defend this country silently; no one ever hears about the bravery and sacrifice of this group of extraordinary men. The general would have you believe that Dr. Cormier's theory on time travel is nothing more than a dream. People said the same thing about breaking the sound barrier, or traveling into space, or finding unlimited energy from cold fusion—impossible. It's easy to dismiss what we don't understand as impossible, but I think we need to embrace the change that comes with the acquisition of knowledge. Sirs, please remember that you put these men into harm's way and told them they had to use your rifle and your transporting system. All I ask is that they be given a chance to return home."

The video feed ended in perfect synchronization with the end of the presentation as the transport system transported the team into nowhere. It was an emotional plea, but Townsend didn't have any real facts to support his position.

The president stood in front of the group and rendered his decision. "I think that these brave soldiers deserve the benefit of the doubt, but I cannot dismiss the recommendation of the joint chiefs of staff. Therefore, this operation will continue until our next briefing in one month. At that time, if nothing new is known about the team, it will be terminated and the transport system turned over to the Central Intelligence Agency to be classified."

Townsend had bought some time; he would have to move quickly and get some results, or his friend would be lost forever. He exited the White House and quickly ran to his car.

This driver snapped him a salute and opened the door to the car. Townsend entered the car without returning the salute.

"Sir, to the airport?"

"No, Petty Officer, I need to go to the CIA."

Chapter 13

Tom Tidwell was feeling much better and decided to test his leg by walking to the stables and back. The leg ached, but the sharp pain was gone; Dr. Persons had told him that he was going to take the sutures out at the end of the week, giving them an extra week to make sure the wound healed properly. He had warned Tom about atrophy and the need to rehabilitate the muscles in his leg, so he took it upon himself to start ahead of schedule. The snow was still falling, but it felt good to get out of the house. He had felt stir crazy the last few weeks and was sick of the injections that Dr. Persons had given him, which made him sleep constantly.

He slowly walked down the sloping hill to the building where the school housed the horses. The door was much like a barn door, but slid on a track instead of opening out like a regular door. He walked in, finding Elizabeth, soaking wet, and putting up her horse.

"There you are. I've been looking for you for over an hour. Where have you been hiding yourself?"

"Tom, you startled me." She put her hand over her heart, giving the impression that she was startled; rather she was frightened that someone had seen her with Harden. "That nice woman from the river was kind enough to show me around the campus; it is quite beautiful. I could see myself coming to school here."

Tom had seen Julia with Chase before he went on his walk, but he decided to let it slide; he had not had much time to be with Elizabeth the past few weeks and longed for her touch. He hobbled over to her and firmly grabbed her shoulders, forcing her, without much resistance, into the hay. He kissed her passionately, planning to have her in the stables.

"Chase you seem to have a new friend; you give a new meaning to a woman in every port." Chief James was a bit jealous; he was a handsome man, but a Marlboro man of sorts, rough and tumble, while Chase was the pretty-boy type. *They always get the most attractive women; it just isn't fair to the ordinary-looking men,* he added to himself.

"No, she is just being nice to us, being guests and all." He had to hide his true feelings.

"You keep telling yourself that; she wants you and you know it. I've seen you with women before, you know when to go in for the kill."

"I wonder how Dave and Margaret are doing, staying in the same room? They'll probably kill each other before we leave." Chase had to change the subject; this Julia Hudson beguiled him, but he could never have her, not in 1865, which meant not ever.

Margaret and Dave had their own problems; each was an adult and had seen naked people before, but they were both modest and staying together, indefinitely, in one room. To add insult to injury, they were not fond of each other, but not as hostile. Dave had had to tolerate Margaret in their previous life, working for her at the embassy. Fortunately, he didn't have that problem anymore and could say and do as he pleased. Unfortunately, he was a complete gentleman at all times.

"Margaret, I've decided that I'll stay on the floor for the time being and let you have the bed. However, from time to time, I want to sleep in the bed. I think that's fair."

"Yes, that's very descent of you; it shouldn't be a problem." Dave had taken her by surprise with his sense of chivalry; he had been fighting alongside Chase and Jesse, and she had felt that he looked down on her because she would not kill someone, but perhaps it was all in her head. He had given her the bed and rigged a privacy barrier between them, so she was wrong about him; he was a nice man, one with whom she could get along.

Tom's head was on Elizabeth's breasts, feeling content and happy, but he was thinking of home and what he had given up. "Honey, let's stay out West;

we could get some land and make a life for ourselves out here."

She ignored his idiotic statement. "Tom, what do you think of the people with whom we are traveling? Do they seem odd to you in any way?"

"Sure they do, but they saved our lives, we owe them everything, they could have left us to die, and instead they took us in and defended us from those men. I couldn't care less what they act like or how they dress."

I cannot risk telling him of my plan, but he will appreciate it in the end; we'll be alive and back East, achieving all of the things that we talked about, having money, land, and power, she thought. She desperately wanted to include Tom in her plans but she knew this was not the proper time. Completing her mission would be harder without Tom, but she would persevere in the end, getting everything that she wanted. For now she agreed with Tom and snuggled him closer to her bare breasts; she would need him on her side and she knew just how to do that.

At first, Tom Truman was going to stay with Dave and Margaret, but they kicked him out into Chase's room; he had never seen a woman naked before and had no desire for his first experience to be with an older woman. He knocked on the door to his new room, wanting desperately to get to know these super soldiers who had killed all of those men at the white house.

"Who is it?"

"Tom Truman, sir. I have to stay with you guys; they kicked me out of the other room."

"Just a second." Chase and Chief James had to put their weapons away, which they were cleaning. After a moment, the door opened and he entered the room with a huge smile on his face.

"Come in and put your things in the corner. Actually, I need to ask you a favor. Chase and I need to finish a personal conversation. Could you come back in a little while?"

"I've already seen your weapons in use; there's no need for you to hide them. We all know that you have them." Jesse looked at Chase and shrugged his shoulders in indifference.

"Okay, sit down, but this is classified information; you cannot tell anyone about this." Tom Truman nodded and sat on the corner of the bed, watching, learning, and wondering where these men came from.

Truman watched as both men dismantled and cleaned their weapons. Jesse paid especially close attention to his, being plunged into the river. Neither man spoke a word to Tom; rather they just worked on their task at hand. Tom had never seen two more focused men in his life; they were undaunting in their task, in everything that they did, in the construction of the fort at the white house, the battle, the shelters, the list was probably endless. They could do no wrong. He looked out at his two new friends in awe. *This is the same work ethic, the same drive, and heart, I want my children to have. It has served these men well and will serve me well.*

It took Harden all night to get to the house through the falling snow, fighting the cold the whole way, arriving near dawn, knowing that his day was just starting and he would have little sleep in the near future. He stumbled into the front door and immediately made his way to the fireplace and the smoldering coals, putting a few logs on the fire, restarting the flames. A few of the men, who were already awake when Harden had come in, put a blanket around him and went about their business. He had to warm up before he did anything else. Through the night, he had contemplated whether to continue the mission. He had seen what Chase and Robert could do firsthand, and they could be setting him up for an ambush. *Why would this Elizabeth want to trade, unless she has a trick up her sleeve? I'll let Buford make the final decision.* He knew his loyalty to his childhood friend was overshadowing the longing to go home and start a new life. *I'll see the task through as promised; it's my duty.* His mind re-focused on his condition and on getting warm. In his thoughts, he contemplated whether he would ever warm up. To his pleasant surprise, it only took him a bit over an hour to warm up; by that time many of the men were up and moving around the house. With his decision made, he started upstairs to inform Buford of his meeting with the woman.

He walked the once-grand spiraling staircase to the second floor and stood in front of Buford's door, contemplating knocking, but too many things had happened on this trip to be courteous. "Buford!" he yelled as he violently opened the door, finding his friend finishing dressing. He looked refreshed and ready to go, which was a good sign.

"Joshua, I'm glad that you are safe. What did you find out?" He had every faith in his best soldier, and his best friend; he had to have something that they could use, for he had to have his revenge, and nothing more mattered at this point.

"They are held up in a college in St. Charles, just across the Missouri River. I have something else." He paused, heightening Buford's interest.

"What? What did you find?" Buford was interested and he smiled at his friend as he inquired about his trip.

"A woman approached me in town, Tom Tidwell's woman. She wanted to trade her life and the life of Tom for the group of people that killed all of the men. She seemed genuine enough, but I would be cautious."

"What did you tell her?" Buford didn't look up from putting his boots on.

"I told her to meet us tomorrow at dark on the bridge that spans the river. She's to come alone and have the details of her plan."

"What is her plan, or is she not telling us until tomorrow?"

Harden could tell that Buford had made up his mind. "She confirmed that they are army, perhaps navy, nonetheless trained, and that they are very organized."

"We already knew that, Josh. What else did she tell you?"

"She spoke of a setting a trap when they lapse into the false sense of security. She also gave us their destination. They are going to go west to the Kansas territory, when the weather breaks, of course. That could give us enough time to form a plan. Like I said, I told her to have some details tomorrow."

"I knew that I could count on you. Have you had any sleep?"

"No, I got in about an hour ago, but I had to warm up, and I thought that you needed your sleep."

"Good, good. Get some sleep and be ready to pull out at dark. I want to scout the position before we commit to meeting this Elizabeth woman."

Thank God, Buford has his faculties back, Harden thought as he flopped on the bed that Buford had just vacated. He was going sleep like a baby, one that had a long, hard day.

Morning came quickly for Tom Tidwell, waking to the wonderful smell of the woman he loved lying next to him all warm and funky. He had decided to start early on his rehab, against doctor's orders, and then making love to Elizabeth yesterday had made him feel alive again. *I have been off my feet for far too long.* He decided to continue with his walks today, but found his leg was stiff and hard to move, figuring, correctly, that it was just his muscles getting back into shape. He gently stretched it and went outside on a quick walk before everyone woke for the day.

The campus was beautiful with many different varieties of trees covering the place, with a few building nestled in between. The snow covered the branches of the trees as if they were in bloom with a beautiful white flower. The extremely high volume of foliage, and the proximity of the trees to each other, combined with the clinging snow, gave the effect that he was walking inside a huge white cave. *It is breathtaking*, he thought. *I could make a life out here, perhaps not in Missouri, but somewhere out west.* He had come to the realization that he was a spoiled brat, getting everything that he ever wanted or everything that other people wanted. *The only reason that people like me is because I am rich. I want to be a real man, not one to whom people act nice, but a genuine, hardworking man, one accountable for his actions.* Jesse and Chase had showed him what real friendship was and he wanted to have that for himself, realizing that he would never come close to having that type of friend if he didn't change.

The bandits want the land that my father stole from them; they can have it back. He had no use for it anymore. *If they have their land back, they will stop following my new friends and me.* The question that he had no answer for was how to inform the bandits of his decision. He walked down past the stables, finding Chase and that woman, Julia, riding in the snow. It surprised him that someone was up before him. She seemed to be teaching Chase how to ride a horse. He would go the opposite direction, giving them some privacy. A decision made more for him—he wanted his privacy, not the other way around. He frowned at himself as he realized he was continuing in his selfish ways; breaking that trend would be difficult.

"I can't believe you don't know how to ride a horse well at your age." Julia smiled at Chase as she prodded him for information

"I lived in the city my whole life and never had the need to ride a horse." In a way, Chase was telling the truth, but if he had explained cars and airplanes, she would burn him at the stake for witchcraft, a fate that he almost wouldn't mind at this point.

"Speaking of age, what's yours, Chase?"

"Is there a correct answer to the question?"

Julia batted her green eyes at Chase and laughed at his poor attempt at humor. "No, I was just curious."

"Thirty-three." *Negative two hundred.* he thought. He could tell that she liked him. *She is so very beautiful, the most beautiful woman I have ever seen, but I have to be strong and stay away; bedding her would only cause her heartache in the end, or even worse, screw up the gene pool.*

"I'm only twenty, but I'm old enough." She reached over and touched Chase's thigh, nothing vulgar, just an inviting touch that Chase ignored.

"We had better get back; my friends are probably wondering where I went." He could tell that she was disappointed as she let go of his leg. Chase looked into her green eyes and lost control of himself. He took her horse's reins in his hand, leaning over and stealing a kiss from her. Her lips were like rose petals on his skin; then he remembered the thorns and rode off to the stables. She trotted alongside of him, relishing in her victory.

Chase was a few lengths ahead of Julia when they arrived at the stables, looking at the snow-covered ground, contemplating his incredibly stupid act a moment ago when he saw an envelope appear just like the baseball on the trail to the white house. He would have never found it if he had not watched it appear. He knew exactly what it was and dismounted his horse, quickly picking the envelope up before Julia had a chance to see what happened.

"Chase, what are you doing?" She really wanted to get him alone, but couldn't think of anything else to say to him

"Nothing, something fell out of my pocket."

"Hurry up, they're serving breakfast soon."

Chase entered the stable and put the horse up; he would have to open the letter later.

Everyone gathered in the dinning hall for breakfast; girls surrounded them, all talking about the men who were staying on the campus. They all envied Julia and her newfound love, which she was eager to share with all of her friends.

"All I have to say is don't do it, Chase, it will only screw things up worse than they are now." Dave had to add his two cents in; he felt their equal, though he knew that was not the reality, but they made him feel that way.

"For once I agree with the good doctor, but she's quite beautiful, yes?"

"Jesse, that's not going to help, you're just going to encourage him. He has to keep it in his pants."

"Leave it to a woman to say that. Margaret, you need to get your head out of the gutter." Everyone laughed at David's comment, but they all knew that she was correct. Chase had to say no.

They ate their meal, the first of three in the day, a convenience that everyone had come to respect again, not having meals for days on this supernatural trip. No one even missed Elizabeth and Tom. Tom walking and Elizabeth plotting.

Elizabeth set out for the bridge and her meeting with the head of the Confederate soldiers following them. She exited the stable, her horse in tow, turned to close the door, and saw it on the side of the stable, flush against the wall. It was a fluke that she saw the box; it would have been quite difficult to see otherwise. The box was similar to the one that she had found at the white house, only smaller. She looked to see if anyone was watching and picked up the box. She would have liked to examine the contents, but only had a small window that she could meet Buford. She mounted the horse and rode towards the meeting with the box in her hand.

Buford and Harden waited for Elizabeth to come, wary of an ambush, making sure that there was no one near the bridge. They scanned the area for her, using a looking glass. *The sun is setting and she ought to be coming soon,* Buford thought. Just then Elizabeth showed herself from behind the trees, moved towards the bridge, letting them see her hands at all times. She again stopped in the middle of the bridge, using Harden's idea against him, if he had planed an ambush.
"My name is Buford Walton. You are?"
"Elizabeth Thompson. I have a proposition for you."
"I know of your proposition, what I want to know are the details."
"I want to set a trap for them; you get them and I get Tom. When we move out, I will tie a red ribbon on the bridge. I have already told you our destination. You can follow us until they let their guard down and then you can ride ahead of us, setting a trap."
Buford was intrigued. "How will we know where to set the trap?"
"I'll leave the destination and a signal; we have women and a child traveling with us so we will not be able to move fast, and it wouldn't be a problem getting ahead of us. The deal is Tom and I go free, and you get your land back. However, only you and the man whom I met earlier; we keep the rest. Tom did not steal your land; George, his father, did, and you have already killed him. The men you want are in your grasp, but you need to make the deal; otherwise you will never be able to get the upper hand on them."
Buford listened to her deal; it sounded like a sound plan and a fair deal. If they got their land back and killed the other men, who cared about Tom Tidwell and his woman? Certainly not him. He put out his hand to seal the deal. Elizabeth grabbed it in triumph, feeling that she had saved Tom and herself. "If you double-cross us I will hunt you down like a dog and kill you slowly, do you understand me?"
Elizabeth didn't even flinch; she had no reason to, for she was going to keep her end of the deal. "I understand, but there will be no need for that. I'll provide the location, but it'll be up to you to plan the attack. I'm not

responsible for that part." Buford shook his head yes and let her hand go, setting the roulette ball rolling, rolling to black.

"By the way, what's in the box?"

Elizabeth was silent; she didn't want to give up the box, but she would have no choice in the matter now. "I found it in the stable; there was another one like it that I found at the white house. The other one had ammunition in it. I have no idea what's in this one."

Buford held out his hand and took the box from Elizabeth's grip. She hadn't even had time to see what was in it. "Thank you. We'll be waiting for you signal." The two men backed off the bridge and out of sight with the box that Cormier had sent through time.

Chapter 14

It snowed for ten days straight, blocking any plans for Chase and Jesse moving on; it was the dead of winter and both men were used to being able to move from place to place in the snow. Their inability to complete the mission made each man uneasy, though Chief James was able to control it better than Chase, who was also fighting his inner demons. Because it was impossible to travel, they made an arrangement with the head of the school to work for their rent, keeping busy in the process and helping the school at the same time. The only bad thing, if one could call it bad, was that Chase had to spend more and more time with Julia, who was openly smitten with him. Chase tried the stave off her advances, but became more interested every day, complicating matters immensely.

Jesse and Chase secretly patrolled for Buford and Harden daily, knowing that when the weather broke and the snow started to melt that they would come looking for them, figuring that they had already scouted their position and were just waiting, the same as their group was. Once again, they made fortifications using snow, moving it into piles in strategic locations; each pile had a thick piece of wood inside in order to deflect oncoming bullets, blocking any attacks, but not giving themselves away as the sandbags had. In addition, Chase, Dave, and Jesse carried their assault rifles hidden under their jackets, allowing protection from a surprise attack.

All in all the SEALs felt as if they were safe until the snow started to subside, allowing for easier travel, and killing, if necessary. Chase desperately hoped he didn't have to kill anymore; he'd had enough of the senseless killing and wanted a different life. Julia could be that life, but he had a responsibility to Jesse and the navy; completing his last mission had to come first regardless of his feelings.

Tom Tidwell gradually began to walk without a limp, but had a ways to go before he was one hundred percent healthy, working out every day, getting stronger and having more confidence in himself. He and Elizabeth were content in the little room, so he thought. He liked having her sleeping in the same bed at night; it gave him a comfort level that he hadn't had since he was a child, when his mother had tucked him in at bedtime. Tom had changed drastically since he was shot; he had thought that he was going to lose his leg, but Dr. Persons was one hell of a doctor. He had to find a way to pay the doctor back for what he did for him.

Tom went out on his nightly walk down by the stables and back acreage of the school, giving Elizabeth the opportunity to meet Buford and Harden for the second time; they would want an update and perhaps some more information. She made sure that no one was watching her and slipped out the side door of the building, where her horse was already tied up. For the first time in over a week, it wasn't snowing, but the standing snow was still too high for the team to pull out, prolonging the inevitable, which in her mind was the death of Jesse and Chase. She moved south to the river and their meeting place on the bridge, crossing the river and arriving before the other two men. She didn't have much time for the meeting and hoped her fellow conspirators were on time. She had to return before Tom got back from his walk, not to raise any suspicions. Tom had changed, but Elizabeth felt she knew what was best for the two and was going to continue with her plan. Besides Buford's threat gave her little choice in the matter; she had to follow through despite Tom's feelings.

The evening air was cold but not blowing, as was the normal the last few weeks; hopefully no new weather front would come in and ruin her chances to end this insanity soon. Only one man approached her from the other side; squinting, she saw that it was Harden. She liked him better than Buford; he wasn't as bossy.

"Elizabeth, it's nice to see you again." Buford would have never said that, proving her point to herself.

"Thank you, you too. There's not much to tell; we're still stuck at the school."

"I know, we've been watching periodically." That meant constantly to Elizabeth, who didn't much care.

"The plan is to move as soon as the snow subsides a bit, so if it warms up at all, we'll be moving. Apparently, we are escorting a boy named Tom Truman home to the western part of the state; when I find out where I'll tell you. After that, they have no idea what they're going to do. Things keep getting weirder. I heard them talk about a machine they called a four-wheel truck; apparently, it would move through the snow. Have you heard anything like that before?"

Harden thought that she was rambling and just wanted to start back on the long trip to the house. "No, I can't say that I have." He trailed off his sentence as two people approached them from Elizabeth's side of the bridge. Elizabeth turned to see who it was and jumped on Harden, kissing him quite passionately.

"Don't look. Josh, it's Chase and his girlfriend." Elizabeth talked out of the corner of her mouth as she kissed Harden. She was sure that she was going to be found out and killed by either Chase or Harden, whomever shot first, being directly in the middle of the firing path. Her only hope was to act as if Harden and her were lovers.

Chase and Julia turned the corner onto the bridge, holding hands with one set and steering the horses with the other. Chase had become a competent rider under Julia's tutelage and almost enjoyed riding, but he still would rather have his truck.

"That's nice, Chase, two lovers under the moonlight on the bridge over the river. I should be so lucky."

"Do you want to make out on the bridge? We can stop." Chase pulled on his reins just past Elizabeth and Harden, prompting Harden to pull his gun. Elizabeth grabbed his hand and folded into his crotch where Chase couldn't see the weapon.

"No, leave those two people alone, they were here first." Julia tugged using their intertwined hands to pull Chase in her direction. The two soon-to-be lovers moved on to their destination.

Elizabeth made sure that Chase had gone before she stopped kissing Harden, who was enjoying the attention. Her heart was pounding in her chest so hard that she thought that it was going to come out and fall onto the snowy ground. Without saying a word, she ran to her horse, slipping in the snow on the way there, falling on her hip. She didn't even feel the pain shoot up her side as she mounted her horse, having to get back to the college quickly. Harden decided to follow her, waiting until Chase returned before he started back to the white house.

Elizabeth and Harden rode in silence together until overwhelming curiosity filled Elizabeth and couldn't hold out any longer.

"Josh, what was in the black box?"

Harden looked over at her and smiled, not wanting to reveal what they had taken from her. "Books, plain old books."

Elizabeth watched as Harden went left when the road split off. Elizabeth stayed straight on her way back to the stables; she would have to sneak in. She went the front way, knowing Tom's nightly route, having walked with him a few times, passing a few of the college girls on the way. She made it to the stables on time, but Tom was early and had just passed on his way back to the room. She put her horse in the stable without removing the saddle or harness and ran to the door, finding Tom about thirty feet in front of her; she would never make it back before him. Thinking quickly, she fixed her dress and stepped out from the barn.

"Tom," she called to him with her best seductive voice; she was getting good at using her talents to manipulate Tom.

"What are you doing here?" He was surprised to see her, but didn't think anything of her appearance in the barn for a second time.

"I remembered how much you liked the barn a few weeks ago, so I decided to surprise you." She used her finger to pull him over to her, realizing that she had a power over men, one that would come in handy.

She pulled Tom into the barn and over to their familiar spot, kissing him. "All I want to know, Tom, is do you want me?"

"You know I do."

She pulled his shirt over his head, trying to be provocative; she had no need, she had him completely. As he lay on top of her, Tom noticed that the saddle was on her horse; thinking nothing of the saddled horse, which was convenient, he was more concerned with making love to Elizabeth than asking stupid questions. He went about the task, one that he would enjoy.

Dave and Margaret took the time to relax, which they had not really had the chance to do since before their kidnapping; each had separate goals in life, which were totally opposite, but they found that they had a lot in common and spent the days talking about home and the things they took for granted. The biggest one was indoor plumbing, but others were high on their list, like central air and heat, cars, planes, basically all of the conveniences of modern life.

For Margaret it was a treat to be able to speak to an educated person who was not trying to get something from her; she usually spent her days bickering with other foreign dignitaries and not talking about the pleasant things in life. She enjoyed and looked forward to her and Dave's conversations each day.

It was about time for Dave to get off work and Margaret wanted to be in the room when he arrived. She hurried up the stairwell to the door, collecting herself before she entered. Opening the door, she was greeted by Dave, who had beat her home again; they had a running bet on who was going to get in first. She seldom won.

"Shit, you're always here before me, I don't understand it, and I even left work early."

"I'll never tell, you'll have to torture me." Dave was making fun of her, but he did have a secret, allowing him to beat her home even if he had to work late. He had discovered tunnels under the buildings, connecting each from underground. There was even an entrance by the school's main roadway. Each day, after working off his rent, he would use the tunnels to beat Margaret home.

"How much do I owe you now?"

"One thousand U.S. 2099 dollars. I don't accept checks either. But we can work out a trade." He laughed at Margaret, knowing that he might have just crossed the line, hoping that his subtle advances would not be rebuked.

"Trade, give me another month and I might take you up on your offer, but as of now, I'm not that hard up." *Take that,* she thought. He wasn't the only witty person. She thought that she might even enjoy being with Dave; he was handsome, intelligent and liked to take baths unlike men from 1866. He was probably just kidding and she wouldn't make a fool of herself by coming on to him when he wasn't interested in her romantically.

Chase and Julia had been riding for some time and he was becoming edgy, not having protection from an ambush. He had brought his 10mm but only had two clips, hardly enough to defend against an attack. Chase shook his head in disbelief; he was alone in the wilderness with the most beautiful woman who was ever created, and he was thinking about an ambush. *I've got to get a grip on my emotions.*

"Where are you taking me? We've been riding forever."

"It's right there in front of you." Julia pointed to a cabin in the woods, which looked like it had been there for a hundred years.

"Why are we going to that old thing?" That was a stupid question; she was taking him to a deserted cabin in the woods, and he doubted she just wanted to talk. He wanted her so badly, but ever time that he contemplated it he came up with the same answer: no.

Julia didn't answer him; she just dismounted her horse and went inside the cabin, turning on a lantern, conveniently stashed there. She came to the doorway, having taken off her winter coat and made herself comfortable. He knew what came next; women always made themselves comfortable before they seduced you, in turn, throwing the whole human race a curve ball.

"I don't think that I should go inside. Julia, it's getting late and we need to be getting back to the school." He knew that if he went inside with her that he wouldn't be able to control himself. *What man could, with her green eyes staring at you and her long black hair sweeping over your face?* "Shit." Chase entered the cabin, finding that it was warm and cozy, having a fire already burning in the stove, and it had a made bed in the corner and nothing else in the one-room cabin.

"What do you think?"

"I think that you planned this well, and that you used trickery to get me out here." He had to try to stay away from her because if she got too close he would revert to his primal urges, not using the one power that man had over animals: the power of self will.

"Well, you wouldn't have come if I just asked you and I really needed to get you here; we need to talk."

"If you just wanted to talk, we could've done it at school or when we were ridi—"

She kissed him with a passion only a person in deep love could have, grabbing the back of his hair and guiding him to the bed, where the edge tripped him, Julia landing on top of him, moaning her longing to Chase.

Chase flipped her onto her back and tried to unbutton her blouse; unsuccessful, he ripped her shirt off, not thinking of the ride home. *She is exquisite. I definitely could love this woman.* Which was something that he had never thought about any woman. *I could not afford to fall in love before and I cannot now.* But she was too powerful, like she put a spell on him. He unbuttoned her pants, finding that she was already ready for him; she moaned at his touch, gripping his arms tightly in passion.

She looked deep into Chase's eyes with her beautiful, green, glazed-over eyes. "I have never done this before, be gentle."

Jesse and Tom Truman were the only men who didn't have the company of a woman; one of them did not much care, not having been through puberty. It would have been nice for Jesse to snag one of those historic coeds like Chase, but he was too old and too ornery for them; besides, they wouldn't know what to do with him, being quite the lover, so he thought. He never knew when he would get a return engagement so he always gave it his all. Unfortunately, he was babysitting Truman, who wasn't the best of company, wanting to know how many men that he had killed and talking about the army every ten seconds.

"Hold it. Chase and I are in the navy, so stop talking about the army; they give me gout." He thought that he was making a joke but Truman took him seriously.

"The navy, how could you be in the navy? Both of you are so good with guns, I could have sworn that you were in the army."

"They teach you how to use a gun in the navy, they use very big guns, in fact. Who cares about that. What about you? Your parents must be worried sick about you."

"Actually, I was staying with friends in St. Louis. Where you fell in the door, that's where I was staying while my parents lead a wagon train west. They scheduled to be home already and I was to meet them to go on the next trip. My father said that I am old enough to go this year. I was hoping that you and Chase would help protect the wagon train in Indian country."

"I don't know what we're doing, those men are still following us I'd imagine, and we'll have to keep moving."

"That's what you would be doing, helping settlers go west, moving west. What I don't understand is why you just don't kill all the men and be done with it."

"Tom, killing someone is not something to be taken lightly, and it's not a life that you want to lead; it's a hard life, always looking over your shoulder. If I could, I would leave it in a heartbeat, but it's all I know, it's what I'm good at."

"You're crazy, I want to do what you and Chase do—the adventure, moving from town to town, like my father."

"Not like your father. He makes a living helping people move west, not moving from town to town, killing people. I don't want to talk about it anymore. Get that deck of cards. Let's play a card game." He was getting angry with Tom and had said more than he had wanted, but Tom Truman seemed to be more in tune with the situation than Elizabeth or Tom Tidwell and he had a child's propensity to ask questions.

The full moon lit the night sky as Harden made his way back to the white house where Buford was waiting for a report from his sergeant. He should have just killed Chase and been done with it, but he knew that James would have wanted and probably gotten revenge on him and his men, so he decided to let him live. He respected both men, but they had to pay the price for killing his men, a price that he wanted to exact. Earlier in the journey he had been skeptical of killing the men, but after the massacre at the house he could not let it slide; he had to let his men rest in peace, and killing their murderers would do just that.

His horse struggled with the snow, so he traveled slowly; he would have no sleep once again, taking all night to get back. The more that he thought about Elizabeth's plan, the more he liked their chances for victory. They would follow from a distance, giving the group a false security. When they were complacent, his men would pick a spot ahead of the group and hit them when they least expected it, hitting them in the open with sharp shooters. *It could, no, it will work*, he thought as he passed the halfway point of his journey. For the first time since the massacre, he was happy, as happy as one could be who had lost half of his men and planned on killing more. It was unavoidable; even in an ambush these men were too skilled to not kill any more of his men. It was part of war, they all knew, and accepted that fact.

Harden and Buford had to plan everything perfectly, something that Buford was excellent at. Chase and that James man whom he had met had no chance when Buford had his wits about him, which he seemed to have the last week. Harden could hardly wait for that day, but he would have to wait for quite a while, a fact that he did not know yet.

Chase spent every free second with Julia; she was so beautiful, young, and innocent, giving Chase an alternate world in which to live. He stopped going to his room and stayed with her. They spent most of the time in bed together, making love.

Chase was free when he was with her, free of the demons that haunted him in his sleep. Chase was struggling with his past and future, coming to grips with his life and his lack of it, socially. He lay on her bosoms and contemplated everything.

"Chase, why don't you just stay here with me? I'm graduating in the spring, and we can get a place together."

"You mean get married, don't you?"

"I thought that you loved me. I shared myself with you."

Chase didn't know if he loved Julia or not, but he wasn't about to ruin a good thing by saying no. "Of course I love you, but my friends are counting on me. I can't just leave them, can I?"

"No, you shouldn't, but perhaps they would let you stay."

Chase didn't answer her; he just turned his face to her breasts and decided to distract her. What he was really doing was distracting himself.

"Dave, are you cold?" Margaret was just like any other woman in the world; she was cold in seventy degrees.

"No, why?" He had grown fond of Margaret when she wasn't being the ambassador, and should've played along.

"I'm freezing, can you turn up the heat?" She had forgotten where she was.

"I'll just go over to the thermostat and turn it up." Dave laughed at her briefly, but was met by a playful smack in the chest, and stopped for fear of a real left hook. Margaret felt stupid for forgetting where she was, but it still didn't solve her problem of being cold.

"Dave." She was taking a calculated chance but thought that she could try and kill two birds with one stone. "Do you want the bed tonight?"

"It's colder down here on the floor."

"I meant share the bed; we're both adults, we can share the bed." Dave didn't know what to say; he wanted to share more than the bed, and he had to be in the kitchen if he wanted to cook.

"I can do that; we can share our body heat." Dave climbed into the bed on the opposite side of Margaret and they both pretended to sleep. Neither could bring themselves to tell the other how they felt.

The morning came quickly for Chase; he was supposed to meet Jesse to patrol the area for signs of Buford's men, but Julia had other plans. She was so powerful; one touch and he forgot all about his duty and the inner demons that had plagued him thus far. *Why should I care about what happens to these people? We probably already changed history when we saved Tom and Elizabeth. I should just let them go their own way and stay with Julia; besides we are never going to make it back to 2099.* Chase had to stay focused, but it was extremely difficult nestled in Julia's arms. His thoughts drifted back to Julia and her beautiful body.

Chase went to work when Julia went to class; he would have to avoid Jesse for a few days, having no desire to hear him bitch about not doing his duty to God and country. He would have to face him eventually, preferably when he was not as upset with him.

Chapter 15

The room that Chase, Jesse, and Tom shared was hardly big enough for one, let alone three people; two of the three had to stay on the floor, rotating every few nights. The system was fair, giving each person three days on and six days off the comfort of a bed. The only one who even seemed to care was Tom who wasn't used to living in such close quarters. However, the two navy men felt right at home, living together in a barracks style atmosphere. Jesse and Tom had had more than their share of the bed the last few weeks. Chase was spending more and more time with Julia, giving Jesse fits, making Chase miss patrol on more than one occasion.

Jesse had never seen Chase like this in the years that he had known him and was concerned that he was getting soft and frankly pussy whipped, a disease that Jesse purposefully avoided in his life, which was probably the reason that he was single. The fact that Chase wasn't going to be born for another one hundred ninety-eight years prompted Jesse to plan an attack, not at Buford or Harden, but one directed at Chase, who was making an ass of himself and his profession. Now, all he had to do was to see him long enough to strike, which was the difficult part, knowing that Chase would come to his senses with a swift kick in the ass. That was what chiefs were for: attitude adjustments.

He had almost given up for the night when the door slowly opened, so as not disturb the sleeping people in the room, but Jesse wasn't sleeping; he was hardly ever sleeping. The time was now, but he would have to do it quietly. Tom Truman was sleeping in the bed that Chase had hoped to occupy, being his turn in the rotation.

Chase stealthily entered the room, softly closing the door behind him and removing his winter coat.

"Chase." Jesse was low in tone but loud on authority.

"You scared the shit out of me. I thought that you were sleeping."

"No such luck. We need to talk about some things."

"What do you mean?" Chase was well aware of what Jesse wanted, but decided to play dumb, a tactic at which he didn't have much practice.

"You now damn well what I want to talk about. I want to talk about you taking your head out of your ass long enough to remember our situation. You've been fucking that Julia girl and not tending to your duties, Commander O'Sullivan, sir, a fact that would land your ass in hot water back home, and probably get a few people killed."

"We aren't home, are we, Jess? We're in bumble fuck Missouri babysitting people who can't wipe their own asses, and it's bullshit."

"No, you're bullshit, sir. What happened to the Chase O'Sullivan who never let any of his men down, who stormed an Arab compound to rescue a chief whom he had just met three days before? Do you remember that?"

Chase nodded his head yes, leaving it hung in shame for what he had just said to his friend and his only confidante in this mess.

"You were just a JG but you commanded the respect of everyone, even admirals. You kicked in the door to the room in which they were interrogating the prisoner, killing five men singlehandedly. You flung the man over your shoulder and marched him right out of that place. If I remember correctly, you were shot twice but still managed to get me out. Chase, the navy gave you the Navy Cross for that, but the men and I gave you so much more: We gave you our confidence, and you never fucked it up, never. All those missions we went on, you were always there, and I need that man back right now."

Chase looked at Jesse, tears running down his face; his voice was shaky, but he understood what had to be done. "I've always known what to do, in battle, in life. I had the answers, but I don't have one now; I can't get us back home, I can't complete my mission. I've no idea why we're here, if we're fucking history up, or if the things that we do, the decisions that we make, are already part of history and unavoidable…They haunt me. Every night, they're all there, hundreds of them and they want answers, too. I don't have them, not for us and certainly not for them. When I'm with her, Julia, they don't visit; the men that I killed, they stay out of my dreams when I'm with her."

"Chase." Jesse put his hand on Chase's shoulder, and the pain seemed to leave his body all at once. " I told you that we are what we are, and that I went through the same thing, but what I never told you or anyone for that matter was that I left the navy for a short time when the demons came for me. I drank and beat the shit out of anyone who would let me; most nights I ended up in jail. I wasn't out a month when my master chief found me. I was bloody, beaten by the cops, had the worst hangover that any person could stand, but he touched me, and I was all right. We talked all night. He never put the paperwork in, and the Navy thought that I was on hardship leave; he had said that my mother died, saving my career, my life. From that day forward, I vowed that I would help someone like he helped me, and I'm honored that it's you."

"Honored?"

"It sounds fucked up, but you are one of the precious few who get it, you get what it's all about."

"Jess, that's what I'm trying to tell you. I don't."

"Yes, you do, you know without realizing. You lead by example, you lead with a soft hand and big head and most importantly, you never let the men down. When they look to you, you're a pillar of light guiding the way. You and I know that it's bullshit, but the men don't." Both men laughed at Jesse's attempt at humor.

"I have no idea how this is going to end, but I'm glad that it happened with you; you've always been there for me as well and I can't even dream of doing this macho shit without you." Jesse smiled at Chase and wiped the tears from Chase's face with his sleeve.

"Stop that shit, I thought you were a man, but that chick has whipped your ass and now you cry like a little girl who scraped her knee. I think that I'm going to have a chick-to-master-chief talk with her." He started to half get up and Chase grabbed his shirt right on cue.

"You have such a way with words, every woman in the world would be demanding that you be dipped in honey and placed on an ant hill if they heard you say that shit. But I'll make a deal with you: Keep this to yourself and I'll make sure no woman ever hears your beautiful philosophy."

Jesse punched Chase in the chest, knocking him onto his back. "Get some sleep, we have a lot of work to do tomorrow. The snow's been melting and I think that we can start west to meet up with Truman's parents."

Sleep was not Elizabeth's problem, sleeping soundly every night, having a clear conscious. She had to sneak to the bridge and give Harden the signal; they were leaving in the morning and had to keep her end of the bargain. The snow had melted just enough that the group could travel; Chase insisted on escorting Tom Truman home, though she had no idea why. He was just a boy and didn't matter in the scheme of things, just one more person for Buford to kill. She had to tolerate Chase and Jesse for a few more weeks; they were so odd and seemed to keep so many secrets, like the stone that she had found, which she still couldn't open. Elizabeth had thought about having Tom look at it, but he respected Chase and Jesse too much to trust him with the stone. She knew that it was important, being sent with the weird-looking bullets, but she had no idea what it was or what they would use it for, deciding to keep it just in case she had to use it for leverage.

She was sure that Tom was sleeping and crawled out of bed, getting dressed for her journey as quietly as she could. She would have to walk to the bridge because she could not risk being spotted at the stables. She had done this many times in the month that they had been encamped at the school, finding that the hardest part of the sneaking around was not leaving but getting back in; on more then one occasion she had been caught by Tom or one of the schoolgirls. Luckily, Chase or Jesse had never found her sneaking around, though Chase had come close last month; they would have killed her for sure.

For the last few days Harden and Buford had been gathering their men and preparing to move out; they assumed that because the snow was melting that Chase would be moving his men. Just to make sure, he had men, advance scouts if you will, watching the campus for any sign of movement. They were not going to count on Elizabeth one hundred percent and were never going to tell her their plans, which did not include letting her and Tom Tidwell live. Harden argued against it, but Buford made him realize that if they lived they could be arrested and tried for murder, with Elizabeth and Tom testifying against them, a consideration that Harden had never thought of; he had been treating this like a war, and in a war you killed people without ramifications.

Harden was in charge of getting supplies for all of the men, which was much easier than before, being half as many men to supply. Food, tents, blankets, ammunition, powder, and water, each man carrying their own equipment, they could not afford the diminished speed of wagons. When the word came from Elizabeth, each man would have to move quickly and quietly to the ambush sight, and pulling wagons would give the men away.

The team of U.S. marshals would move out for St. Charles tonight, riding half of the way and setting up camp, waiting for the signal from Elizabeth or their lookouts, whichever came first. Harden planned to leave before the rest and meet with his contact, who he needed to meet at the bridge tomorrow night. He wanted to take some time to scout the school and make sure that they were still there. Elizabeth was affable enough, but he didn't trust her completely. He had come to like Elizabeth and didn't want to see her killed, but it was unavoidable if he was going to go back to his home in peace, but first he had to avenge the death of his men by killing three more.

He was very used to the twenty-five mile ride to St. Charles and could do it quickly, planning how he was going to kill each member of the opposing team on the way. It was a game to him and he seldom lost any game. Even as a child he had been the one who had usually won; that all changed in the war, but he would have his victory, for himself, Buford and all the men whom he had lost in the war and over the past few months.

Elizabeth made sure that no other person was around from behind a store about one hundred feet from her destination before she walked the last few feet to the bridge. She tied a red ribbon to the bridge with a note that was rolled into a cylinder shape, tucked underneath the tie of the bow, giving Harden the direction and time of the trip. She stared at the ribbon, wondering if she was doing the right thing, but that was short lived and she made her way back to the college with a clear conscious.

For the first time she had no problem getting inside the dormitory that her and Tom shared; she didn't even wake Tom up, which was a good thing. She didn't feel like having sex, she was too tired. She fell asleep almost immediately upon hitting the bed; she would sleep soundly for four hours before Jesse woke them up.

Harden was about two hours out when Elizabeth put the ribbon on the bridge, but the few people who used the bridge even noticed the decoration. He had wanted to scout the college but would not have a chance seeing the ribbon tied to the bridge in the middle, the usual meeting place. He approached the signal with caution bordering on paranoia, grabbing the note from it without even stopping. He rode down the street and made the same turn as he had when Chase had caught Elizabeth and him on the bridge. He rode to the end of the street, which dead ended at the river, looping back around the town further downstream, righting its flow from east to west to

west to east.
He slowed and stopped at the river to read the message.

>At first light.
>West on the trail towards the Kansas territory.
>Greenville, Missouri.

He would have to start back to Buford without scouting their position, which didn't matter since he had the destination and route; besides, he still had his lookouts posted at the school. He trotted down the riverbank to the bridge and made the trip to meet Buford quicker than he ever had over the past month.

Four in the morning came quickly for Jesse and Chase, who had stayed up later than they should have correcting Chase's attitude. Both men had a bath, thinking that it might be the last chance for one for a few weeks. They woke Dave and Margaret, who oddly enough were sleeping in the same bed, but fully clothed; both men had a chuckle at that as they stood over them, poised to scare the shit out of the unsuspecting duo.

Both Jesse and Chase grabbed the frame at the end of the bed and shook the two until they fell out of the bed. The two flopped on the floor, obviously disturbed at the two SEALs' attempt at humor, until Chase spoke up.

"You two looked so cozy together snuggling, Jesse and I were jealous."

"It's not what it looks like; we were just sharing the bed, not sleeping together."

Jesse had to get in on the conversation, getting his cracks in at the doctor, who he had come to respect after his performance in the battle. "I thought that you were gay, Dave; if I had known that you liked women I would have picked a professional up from the brothel in town."

"Very funny. Jess, perhaps you and I could cuddle later. I really would like that." He was sarcastic in his tone, just enough to be funny, not making his statement seem out of anger.

"We need to get ready to go; meet in our room in fifteen." Chase was serious and both Margaret and Dave were glad to see it, hopping to their feet and preparing to go.

Jesse meanwhile went to wake Tom Tidwell and Elizabeth, who had only been sleeping for a short time. He was a bit more considerate, knocking on the door before he went in.

"Time to leave. Meet in our room in fifteen." He made sure they were up before he left; neither person seemed to want to get up, which didn't surprise Jesse. He swiftly moved down the hall to his room where Chase already had Tom Truman up and packing his things.

"Jesse, we should try and leave before the sun comes up. I would put money on it that Buford has men posted to watch our every move, and if we can get a good jump on them we might be able to lose them."

"That's what I like to here from you. Chase, you're back to the man whom I love."

"It doesn't mean we're going to hold hands on the trail, I'm just focused and ready to move on."

"Does she know yet?"

"No, I'm going to leave her a note. I can't risk the emotion before we go into harm's way." Just as Chase finished swallowing any resemblance of human decency, all four of the people they were waiting on came through the door, groggy, but ready to go.

Chase and Jesse continued to discuss the best way to get to the stables and on the move without Buford's men spotting them. Dave, who was paying close attention to them, was going to save the day.

"Chase, I might have the perfect way to get out of here without anybody seeing us."

"How?" both curious SEALs said in unison.

"There are tunnels under the school that connect all of the buildings, steam or pluming tunnels. They must have had a bit of foresight when they built the place."

"Why are we just hearing about them now?"

"Because I used them to beat Margaret in a game that we played; it's a long story. I guess that I didn't think that they were important before."

"Does this building have a tunnel under it?" Chase replied enthusiastically.

"Yes, it's on the bottom story in the southwest corner, behind the large table." Everyone filed down to the bottom level where the table was; Dave shoved it out of the way and removed the board, which he had rigged to easily detach, from over the hole. The opening was small, making it hard for a larger person, like Chase, to wiggle his way down, but he found a way, squeezing through the opening into a larger tunnel. It was dark and they had to pass two lanterns down so that the group could see where they were going, avoiding being hurt before they left town.

Dave led the way down the tunnel, which was four feet wide and five feet tall, allowing for travel but not comfortably. Everyone in the group, with the exception of Tom Truman, who was exactly five feet tall, had to hunch over in order to avoid the cobweb-filled ceiling. Dave came to a crossroad in the tunnel and stopped, trying to get his bearings. He pointed down the left tunnel, quickly moving further down the well-placed tunnel system. They came to a dead end, where the ceiling of the tunnel became high enough to stand. Dave reached up and punched the cover made of wood off the hole in the floor of the stable. They had traveled undetected; now they had to get from the stable to the woods without being found, definitely the harder of the two, seeing as how there was no tunnel in which to travel.

Dave made way for Jesse, who was the first to exit the hole, finding that he was alone in the stable; he had expected to be, but had learned long ago to always be prepared for anything. He motioned to Chase all clear with a hand signal and came out of the hole, making a straight line to where their horses were housed, finding the saddles nicely lined up, ready to go, obviously the work of his master chief. He prepared the mounts for departure one by one with a speed and accuracy that had not been possible a month ago. Julia had taught him well; she had even showed Chase how to do some stunt riding, though he probably would never need to use it. Within ten minutes, every member of the group was on their horse and ready to leave, again waiting for Jesse to make sure the coast was clear.

The forest was about five hundred feet from the stable, making the team very visible to anybody who was trained to look for cavalry riding in the dark. Jesse knew that he was taking a calculated risk, but he had to find out if anyone was watching them, so he put his night vision equipment on and magnified the picture, scanning the pre-dawn horizon for any sign of Buford or his men. Satisfied that they were safe he motioned Chase to lead the riders out into the open.

Chase, filled with adrenaline, his drug of choice, heightened his senses and his reflexes. *I'm back,* he thought as he kicked his horse, which he had named Man of War, the name of the famous racing horse who had the fastest time in the Kentucky Derby, an honor he had held for more than one hundred twenty years. He stole the name but it seemed appropriate, and perhaps it could feed on the skill of its namesake, making Chase a better protector in the process.

The group ran the horses hard to the base of the woods, where the brush and trees made a gallop impossible. They slowed and disappeared into the wood just as the first hint of day began to make itself known to St. Charles, Missouri. Jesse was certain that Buford's men hadn't seen them leave the school, making it very difficult for them to follow the group, not knowing which route or direction they traveled or where they were going for that mater. Jesse smiled at Chase, a smile of victory and relief, as he rode side by side Chase through the woods. Jesse reached over and grabbed his hand, just to make Chase eat his words, allowing both men a smile and an internal laugh.

Chapter 16

Harden entered the camp like a Roman general coming home from a glorious battle with the spoils of war. He tied the ribbon on his horse's harness and let out a rebel war cry when he neared Buford's tent, prompting him to see what the commotion was. He was half-dressed and looked like he had just woken up, nothing odd since it wasn't quite five in the morning. Buford had made about half the distance that he had wanted before he set up camp, not wanting any problems with local travelers or the men he chased doubling back, finding him unprepared for a battle.

"What's all the commotion, Corporal?" As soon as he spoke, he saw Harden on his horse about three feet from him. Josh reached down and gave Buford the note detailing the plans and route of his nemesis.

"Are you sure that they left? She could be setting a trap for us." In the excitement, Harden had not made sure, a detail that he should have attended to before he returned.

"Yes, I saw them leave, heading west." He knew that Buford would waste time making sure and in doing so jeopardizing the operation, so he lied in order to move the plan into action. Harden was more trusting of Elizabeth, playing a large part in his decision to deceive his friend. He dismounted and followed Buford into his tent, closing the flap behind him.

"Josh, this is good news; we're going to make this happen after all." Buford had the look of a mad scientist who was creating a Frankenstein. His eyes bulged from the sockets and his smile seemed to start at one sideburn and end at the other.

"Buford, we need to keep a good distance behind them, but keep pace, so we can ride around their flanks and set the ambush when the time is right. We need to pack up and leave now. Elizabeth will leave ribbons to mark their path and tell us of any changes, but we best not trust her to do all the work." Harden knew just what to say to Buford, and this was the correct time to grease the wheels.

"Good, inform the men to strike the camp; we move out in one hour."

"Very well, sir. Is there anything else?"

"Yes, good job, Josh."

"Thank you, sir." Harden did a crisp about face and exited Buford's tent, which was the only one in which one could stand up. He called a meeting of his subordinate non-commissioned officers and relayed the orders, each non-com quickly getting the rest of the men up and moving, dismantling the camp that had been set up a few hours before.

It took longer to dismantle the camp than Buford and Harden had wanted, but they were in no pressing hurry and could afford a few extra moments. At 6:25 a.m., the ex-Confederate raiders were on the trail to St. Charles and then west to their date with death. That was nothing new to these war-hardened men, who had given as much death as they had taken. Each man's spirit was high and one could see the intense camaraderie that had formed over the years of death that preceded this one.

Julia woke up at the usual time for her classes; what was odd was that Chase was not lying next to her. She had become accustomed to feeling his warm body next to hers in the morning. She didn't think much of it, but was upset that he hadn't said goodbye when he had left to go back to his room. She went about her planned schedule of classes and riding, counting the seconds until she could see Chase, hardly containing her enthusiasm. She had some good news for him that she had been holding onto for the past few days.

After she was free for the night, she rushed up to his room and knocked. She waited for a while and then opened the door, finding nothing but a note on the bed. She was confused to say the least, but managed to pick the note up and read it.

> Dear Julia,
> I have had a wonderful time with you and have the greatest respect for you, but I have to move on. When I came to this place, I was lost, both figuratively and literally, and you were able to help put my mind straight. I will never forget the time that we had

together and wish you the best of luck in everything that you do—because you deserve the very best. Please do not hate me for this. We talked about this possibility, and you had to know that I needed to leave. I will come back for you if I can, but I may be traveling a great distance.

    Love,
    Chase

Julia sat on the bed in disbelief; she had just met him, and he was the man she was going to spend the rest of her life. *I thought that I had him for good, but I must have underestimated his friendship with Jesse.* Tears started to run down her face when she remembered the news that she had for Chase. She put her hands over her face. She had dropped out of school to live with and marry Chase, and now she was without a man to marry.

Cormier had been sleeping somewhat better the last two weeks, with the help of his doctor, but his sleep cycle was turned upside down. He found himself up all night and in most cases during the day, taking a series of short catnaps to compensate for the long days at work, desperately trying to find Chase and his team. He was in the middle of a catnap what he was interrupted by Admiral Townsend, knocking on his office door.

"I'm sorry, Doctor. I can come back later."

"No, I was just thinking. Please come in. What can I do for you this morning?" Cormier was preparing himself for more of the insult trading that had become commonplace over the last month and a half.

"Thank you. I, aah…I would like to speak to you about any progress we've had over the last couple weeks." Admiral Townsend entered Cormier's office and sat in the chair across from his desk.

"There hasn't been any progress over the last few weeks. I'm sorry, I've tried everything I could think of doing, but I can't figure out what happened to them. I'm not really used to being wrong, but I will keep experimenting, and I will figure this mess out. I'll get your people back."

"Doctor, I think that I owe you an…" Townsend closed his eyes and lowered his head, having a problem swallowing his pride.

"Apology?"

"Yes. It's harder than I thought it would be, apologizing. We got off on the wrong foot. I want to explain why I've been so difficult to work with on this project. Chase was more than just one of my men. I thought of him as my own.

When he came to me, he was talented, but green. Everything he did came so easily; nothing was impossible, nothing unimaginable for him. Soon, I realized that he saw things that other people didn't see and had the audacity needed to realize his visions. I took him under my wing, grooming him to take over my command. I made sure he knew exactly what to say, and do, in order to make the appropriate friends. He commanded the respect and adoration of his men and of senior brass."

"Admiral, I figured as much. I saw you and your family with him in a picture that day in you office. I saw the pain on your face."

"Doctor, to be frank, if you, I mean we, can't come up with something new by my next White House briefing, they're going to shut us down. I know I asked you not to send the instructions and auxiliary equipment through the transport, but our time is running short and I thought we could try and mix things up a bit before they shut us down."

"Admiral."

"Please, call me Chris."

"Okay, Chris, I don't want to ruin our new friendship, but I sent that equipment two weeks ago, and we haven't heard anything. I'm sorry."

Townsend just stared in at Cormier. It wasn't an angry stare, but a stare a person might give after hearing they only had a month to live. "Are you sure?"

"Yes, I'm sure. I don't think it's over; we still have time."

"Like I said, they're going to shut the operation down. We have two weeks."

"Two weeks! We need more time to do tests, and experiment with the machine. That's not enough time, you need to get us more time."

"Al, the CIA is going to take over the testing. I visited the CIA building when I was in Washington. I tried to get them to continue the experiment here, but they want to move the equipment to a more secure, top-secret location."

"If the equipment's turned off, I don't think we'll ever find the same frequencies needed to open the portal. If we give up control, we're going to lose Chase forever. There has to be something that we can do to stave off the termination."

"I don't think so. Doctor, I've tried everything I can think of doing."

"Admiral, I don't think you understand, if we can't get them back it means I'm a murderer. It was my equipment, my idea, and my responsibility. We have to do something. What would Chase do in this situation?"

"He would find a way to keep the operation open. He would find a way to win."

"I know we haven't been the best of friends, but we have the same goal. I'm going to make you a promise. If you can keep the project open, I'll find a way to get them back; you have my word."

"Okay, I'll find a way. We'll find a way to do it together, Doctor." Townsend patted Doctor Cormier on the back and hurried to his office. He had work to do before his meeting with the president.

He entered his outer office, where his yeomen stood at attention and opened the door to his personal office. He hadn't thought of it before, but there was one last card he could play.

"Petty Officer!"

"Sir." The young man entered his office and again snapped to attention.

"As you were. Please get me the number of Dick Charles. He's the CIA station chief in Pakistan. That's all, you're dismissed"

"Aye, aye, Sir." The petty officer made an about face and marched out of the office, determined to complete his task. He phoned the CIA, who informed him that Mr. Charles was now the Deputy Director of Intelligence. The operator transferred him to Mr. Charles' line. He in turn transferred the call to his admiral's phone.

Townsend patiently waited for the call to go through, trying to formulate what he was going to say to the new Deputy Director of Intelligence for the CIA, a man whom he had known for almost ten years. His job was to convince him to continue the project at the base, under the CIA control, but in the supervision of Admiral Townsend. If necessary, he had an ace in the hole, one he was reluctant to play, but one he was confident would have the desired effect.

"Hello, you have reached the Deputy Director of intelligence, Richard Charles. Please leave your name, number, and a message. I will get back to you as quickly as possible."

Townsend would have to settle for leaving a message. "Hello, Dick, it's Chris Townsend. Congratulations on your new position. I need to speak with you on an important matter. Please call me at 256-568-2358."

Chapter 17

The only person who really knew the way was a boy. Chase was used to giving the orders, but Tom Truman was a leader in every sense of the word. Chase saw where Harry Truman got his values and work ethic. He led them down a path that seemed to be the less-traveled path because branches were scraping the riders' faces, ruining Elizabeth's day, which had been good until this point. She had informed Harden and had gotten away with it. Now she had to figure out a plan to leave other clues to where they were and going to go. Elizabeth had not really figured that one out, but she would in time, being determined to bring down her companions.

Tom Tidwell was in high spirits and enjoying the adventure that his father had started by stealing the land of very determined ex-soldiers. Chase and Jesse didn't blame Tom for what had happened; some people only know one way, handed down by their parents, and Tom's father had been a carpetbagger. He had no idea that Elizabeth was plotting against his new friends and against him. All he knew was Buford was never going to let him live.

A few hours into the journey, the poor planning and improvisation of the operation became apparent when the team stopped to take a compass reading and eat.

"Chase," Jesse called from the woods where he was going to the bathroom.

Chase knew that Jesse didn't want him to watch him pee, so he went over to him and tried to empty his bladder as well. He waited to get over to him before he answered his call.

"Chase, I made a few mistakes in the planning of this one. I never thought about food or water. I never had to, we had MREs."

"We have the water purifiers, right? We can use them to make water out of the snow and we will just have to kill our food."

"I'm concerned that the gunshots might bring Buford around and give us away. How long can we go without food?"

"A while, I think, but we need the water, so set up the purifier and fill the battle canteens for now; we can all drink from them. When we get far enough away we can think about food."

"I'm sorry, Chase, I should've thought of those things."

"You're sorry, if I didn't have my head up my ass we would have been good to go." Chase slapped Jesse's ass and went back to the group. He went over to his horse and got the purifier from his saddlebag. It wasn't very large, being the battle model and ran on solar power. He set it up, fanning the solar panels out over the top of the machine like a satellite dish. The rest of the purifier was nothing more than a rectangular box with two hoses, one on each side. In a river or a lake, one could put one hose in the water and the other in the container that you wanted to hold the purified water. The navy and army used these to cut back on dysentery and malaria, along with other microorganisms that might be in the water.

The hoses would not work in the snow but it had a way to melt the snow. You put the snow on top of the solar cells; the sun melted the snow and the water passed into the filtration system through a tube that came up through the base of the cupped solar cells. The process took about a half an hour and made the cleanest water ever known to anyone in time.

Chase looked over in the direction of the rest of the group. Margaret, Dave and the two Toms were talking among themselves while Elizabeth was by herself. Chase hadn't noticed it when he had been with Julia, but Elizabeth had been very solitary and defensive about little things. In his experience, people like that were a risk to break down. The navy had trained him to look for people that might break under pressure and she was acting the part.

After about an hour the water was ready and the horses rested enough to push on further west. Jesse had taken a compass reading, finding that Truman was on the correct path; he would just let him lead from now on, giving him and Chase a chance to patrol and double back, making sure that Buford and Harden were not following them.

Buford was following them but with the help of Elizabeth didn't have to actively track them, giving him the much-needed element of surprise when it came time for the ambush. Harden led the way to St. Charles; he had traveled the stretch over fifteen times and could do it in his sleep. The group had everything that they needed: food, water and ammunition, which was the most important one of the three. They would follow silently until the time was right, striking and killing all the evidence of the feud.

As any long journey, the trail was lonely and cold, but the situation kept everyone on their toes, not wanting to be the one to screw up and cost the group a life or more probably, time. Elizabeth tried to hold a conversation with Margaret and Dave, but she had alienated them enough that they ignored her. No one much spoke on the trail, rather preferring to concentrate on making their destination. Tom Truman calculated that they had to travel thirty miles a day in order to make it in time to go west with his dad. He had not asked Chase and Jesse if they would go with him and his father, but he had come to believe that they would have no choice when they saw the women and children in the convoy westward.

The weather turned unusually warm and would make a mess of the trail in a few days; they would have a more difficult time making their thirty miles a day, throwing Tom's timetable off. He was convinced that they would make their destination in time because he knew that Chase and Jesse could do anything that they set out to do regardless of the difficulties.

The next few days passed without incident, and the two SEALs lessened their backtracking to once a day, when the group stopped for the night. The members of the group grew weary without food and almost demanded that they be able to eat. The problem was that they hadn't seen any food to eat in days. It was decided that Jesse would go looking for food. Of all the things that Jesse had killed before, he had never killed an animal for food. He had always had markets and the navy for that. He perched himself on the first large branch of a mature oak tree, which was just newly budding. His M 29 with its electrical firing system was more quiet than his handgun, which he would have liked to use because of its light weight, but he still worried about Harden and Buford. He would have to kill whatever he shot with one shot because it was hard to triangulate a location hearing only one shot. He knew it was unlikely that anyone would hear much of anything with the rifle suppressed, but better safe than sorry in this situation.

The night passed slowly with little luck, and Jesse was about to return with nothing to show for his labors when he saw a small doe in the distance. He pointed his weapon, but had no line of sight. The deer moved away from him and would be gone if he did not act. He climbed from the tree and moved against the wind, towards the animal. Jesse was light of foot and barely made a noise when he moved. It was more a product of training than anything else, but it served its purpose. He was gaining on the deer and would have his shot soon. He stopped thirty yards from the beast and took a sight. The laser was very helpful in the night sky, aiming at its head, squeezing the trigger gently. The shot startled the doe, being a subsonic shot, and the bullet missed its head and hit right in front of the hind legs.

The deer took off into the brush, disappearing into the night. Jesse ran after it, coming to where his shot had hit the animal, finding blood on the ground. He followed it into the thickets, finding her lying on the ground, still breathing. Jesse knelt over it, took out his knife, and slit its throat in one motion. With his knife still in hand, he carefully slit open the doe's abdomen, exposing its insides. With ease Jesse gutted the deer. He tied a rope around its legs and began to drag it back to base camp, where everyone was awaiting the much-needed sustenance.

Everyone was sleeping except Chase, who was on watch in Jesse's absence, when the food arrived. Neither man was skilled at cutting meat for food, but did the best they could under the conditions, carving the meat from the doe and preparing it for everyone in the group, who would be pleasantly surprised in a few hours when it was time to wake. With no way to preserve the meat they would have to settle for only one or two meals, which seemed a waste, but was unavoidable. The remaining snow would afford them some more time with the animal. Chase didn't want to take the chance of making anyone sick, so unilaterally decided, much to the chagrin of the group, that the meat would be discarded. If Jesse and Chase had thought about it, they would have packed salt to preserve the food, but in their haste, hadn't bothered to do many of the things that they should have.

The team members were up, fed, and ready to leave by seven in the morning, each member on their horse and poised to go except Elizabeth, who was nowhere to be found.

"Tom," Jesse called out to Tom Tidwell in annoyance. "Where's Elizabeth? We're ready to leave."

"She said that nature called; she should be back any second."

"Very well, she can catch up; we need to get going." He wasn't going to wait for her or her nature. She was a black mark on the group and somehow Jesse knew it, but couldn't place what it was that made him feel that way.

Elizabeth didn't have a call with nature; she was on a mission to place a ribbon that Harden could find and follow the group further. She tied it to a young sapling near the side of the trail. The note inside simply read "West on trail. February 5, 1866." She rejoined the others about two miles from where they had camped overnight, convinced that she was doing the right thing and that no one was on to her.

In only a few days, the melting snow made soup of the landscape, mixing everything together into a semi-liquid state. This slowed the group down, but luckily, the horses were not impeded by wagons and thus able to trudge through the soupy trail. They hadn't seen a town in over a week, and the one meal that they had had two days ago wasn't enough to keep their spirits high. The snow gave way to an early spring of sorts, which was weird considering the harsh winter storm that the Midwest had just finished having.

Chase looked at his watch. 6:20 p.m., it was almost time to set up camp for the night, but Tom Truman wanted to go a few more miles, insisting that he was on a time table, making Chase think he just wanted to get home. The trail curved in and out of the trees and came out into a pasture, where Jesse was the first to see the wagon, stuck in the open area. It was apparent that nothing short of a crane was going to get the wagon out; not even the team of six horses was able to pull it from the mud that was acting like quicksand.

Chase and Jesse were cautious after what had happened at the white house and decided to pull up, well out of range to the weapons of the day. Chase handed Jesse the digital enhancing binoculars while he informed the rest of the crew, who were following about a quarter mile back, that they were stopping.

Jesse pressed the auto focus on the top right corner of the binoculars and he saw her clearly. She seemed a simple, hardworking woman, wearing a flower-patterned blue dress, and a bonnet of the same color. She futilely worked on pushing the wagon from the mud with a young man by her side.

"That can't be her husband, he's way too young," he said to himself, hoping that Chase was nowhere near. He put the binoculars in his front pouch and approached the wagon. He saw no need to be cautious, waving as he went.

"I don't think that you're going to be able to get it out," Jesse yelled from across the field. He was met with an unsuspected response.

"Says you, mister. I'll get her out eventually, and we don't need your help either."

"That's fine, but you're never going to do it; your best bet would be to go into the closest town and buy a new wheel for it and replace the buried one. If six horses can't do it you're certainly not." Jesse got close enough to see her clearly with his own eyes. She was in the early thirties and attractive in a rugged sort of way. She had definitely lived a hard life, and it had begun to show on her face. She had brown eyes to match her brown hair, which hung below the middle of he back.

The boy she was with looked to be around sixteen or so and was a strong-looking young man, having the same features as his mother. He was almost six feet tall, quite tall for that time, and wore a six-shooter on his side. He intently watched Jesse, making sure that he was on the up and up, and seemed to think so until Chase started towards them.

"That's far enough, mister. We don't want any problems." He pulled the six-shooter, model 1860 Colt .44, percussion pistol and pointed it at Jesse.

"Then put the pistol down, boy, I came to help not cause problems." Jesse saw a red dot appear on the jacket of the sixteen-year-old boy. Without looking, he yelled back to Chase, who was ready to put this boy down if needed. "No, it's okay, Chase, don't shoot him."

The boy was startled by Chase, lifted his pistol, and fired at him. The bullet fell well short of Chase, but he was on automatic pilot, flicking the safety off and taking aim.

There was no way that Jesse was going to let a sixteen-year-old boy die; he plucked a grenade from his shirt and without pulling the pin threw it at the boys head, hitting him between the eyes and knocking him to the ground, just as Chase's single bullet hit the wagon behind where the boy had just been standing. He rushed to the boy, picking up the grenade before his frantic mother arrived, hitting and punching Jesse. He grabbed her and subdued her until she saw that her son wasn't hit.

Jesse propped him up against the wagon just as Chase got there, with Dr. Persons in tow. Chase ran up to him and examined him for a gunshot wound.

"I missed?" Chase was half asking a question and half letting off a sigh of relief. "What the hell happened? All I saw was that kid holding a gun in your face."

"Just a misunderstanding, mister. Thank you for not killing my boy, he's all that I have left. My husband died in the war, and the bank just took my house. We're going west to try to start over. He's only sixteen and has his father's temper on him."

"Thank Jesse, he saved his life. I had nothing to do with it." He pointed in Jesse's direction, shifting the praise to him.

Jesse was using some smelling salts to wake the boy up when he saw his mother out of the corner of his eye. "What's your name?" Jesse liked her spirit and apparent hard work ethic.

"Sara Miller. That's my boy, Scott." She extended her hand to him and cocked her head just enough for Jesse to notice her smile, directed at him.

Dr. Persons was examining the now conscious Scott Miller. "My name is Dr. David Persons." They shook hands less warmly than her and Jesse just had. "Your boy will be fine, he just got knocked on the head."

"Thank you, but now I'll never be able to get this wagon free."

"Why are you moving now? It's not the best conditions for moving; the summer would have been better." Chase was prying where he shouldn't have, but it seemed like a good question to ask.

"Like I said, the bank took my house and land." In the middle of the sentence, she broke up and started to cry, running behind her wagon to conceal her shame.

Jesse shot Chase a dirty look and followed her, finding her looking through her things. "This is everything that I own; they took everything from me except my dignity and they tried real hard to take that from me."

Jesse grabbed her shoulders and pulled her close; it was weird, for he had never felt like this in his life. Before he had landed in post civil war society, he could have cared less about this woman, or any woman for that matter, but now he was holding her close to him and consoling her. They made an instant connection, perhaps because they had the same no-bullshit attitude, or maybe it was just a physical attraction. Most likely, it was a combination of both and Jesse liked the feeling. "I want you and your son to come with us to the closest town and I'll help you get a new wheel for your wagon. I don't want anything for it, I just want to help you out of a jam." He launched a preemptive strike before she could object to his offer.

"I don't know what to say. I would be appreciative."

"Good, we're going to camp the night and move out in the morning. One more thing. Where is the closest town?"

She started to laugh at Jesse who seemed lost to her. "Liberty, about a three-and-a-half-days' ride from here. The least I can do is cook a dinner for you and your friends; it's one of the only things that I'm good at."

"I doubt that, but it would be great to have a good meal; we haven't eaten in a few days." *It couldn't have worked out better if I had planned to meet her in the muddy field,* he thought. He would set up camp for the night, get a meal, and in the morning go to town, help this woman, at the same time correcting his mistake of not having any food when they had left St. Charles.

Finding a suitable location for camp was more than a routine task. The dense overgrowth in the forest surrounding the open space of the field was unforgiving terrain, making camping inside of it impractical. Moreover, the flat ground of the field provided little natural cover or obstructions for a defensible camp. Furthermore, Chase and Jesse were hard pressed to find ground that didn't resemble an African watering hole. The melting snow made a muddy soup of the field, and camping at Sara Miller's wagon, situated in the middle of the field, was unthinkable.

The light was waning and camp would need to be finished before nightfall, making the situation even more precarious. Jesse was on his horse, scouting suitable locations for camp when he found the first real possibility after an hour of searching. One fourth of a mile off the path to the right of the trail, the ground slopped upward enough to form a pool of water at its base, making the high ground relatively dry. With a small amount of preparation the site might just suffice for the night. *At least, it is relatively dry and could shelter the team in case of an emergency,* he thought. Besides, Buford was long lost and the team was getting close to the Truman's place.

Jesse activated the COM set and called Chase, who had been scouting the left side of the field. "Chase, do you copy?"

"I copy, Jess. What do you have?" Chase was happy to hear from his chief, who obviously was having more luck than he was in finding a location to bed down.

"About one fourth of a mile to the right on the back end of the field there's high ground that can be made into a campsite. Have Dave get the rest of the group ready to go and I'll start on the needed improvements."

"10-4. Jesse, I'll inform Dave and then make one last loop of the area before coming to camp, over."

"I copy; we'll have dinner for you when you get back, courtesy of Sara Miller. Jesse out."

Jesse removed his pack and started the process of improving the site. With a little tender, loving care, the hill would make a good camp. He removed his entrenching tool, or shovel, from his pack and began by chipping away the small lump at the crest of the hill, which allowed for quicker draining at the top of the campsite. The hill was dryer than the field, but still had standing water, which he would need to remove. The next step in the drying process was to remove a top layer of soil, a most unwanted and extremely messy endeavor. This was much more labor intensive and tedious than his first task, but just as necessary. Jesse dove right into his task, as he did everything else in his life, excepting woman, who in his mind only complicated matters.

He pitched the mud from the top of the site into the standing water at the bottom, hoping to solidify the mess, if only slightly. The mud slopped as he worked, making a mess of the only shirt that he had, prompting him to remove it and bare the cool night air. His work would keep him warm and the thought of a hot meal hastened his pace.

Three fourths of an hour later, Dave and the rest of the group appeared; in reality they were visible the whole time, but Jesse was on automatic pilot and didn't bother to check their progress. He was so entranced in his work that Dave's voice startled him.

"Goddamn, you scared the shit out of me!"

"We made enough noise to wake the dead; I'm surprised you didn't hear us coming." Dave rolled his eyes jokingly and dismounted in order to help the rest of the group. To his horror, he jumped into the mud that Jesse had removed from the top of the hill. Just as Jesse predicted, it solidified the water, but in the process made a quicksand of sorts. Dave sunk shin deep with both legs, prompting Jesse to start laughing uncontrollably.

"That is the fuunniest shit that I have ever seeen. Ha-ahhhhhhh. Haaa-eeeeeee. Oh my God." With his stomach shaking in laughter and a smile on his face, Jesse stepped down the hill sideways, careful not to slip into the mud and give Dave the same laugh. With great dexterity, Jesse reached for Dave and started to pull him up. Unfortunately, the mud was reluctant to give up its victim without a fight. With one forceful tug, Dave separated from shoe and the mud at the same time, falling face first on Jesse's crotch, giving the rest of the oncoming group a laugh as well.

Dave had no choice but to laugh at his situation, since it was funny as hell and he hadn't had the opportunity to laugh about much since they had arrived in this time. He scrambled from between Jesse's crotch and to his feet, hopping on one leg where he had to decide how to retrieve his shoe from the damn mud pie at the base of the hill.

Having boots on, Jesse waded into the mud and retrieved his shoe, held hostage by the mud. With a popping sound, the shoe was free, baring the scars of battle and needing a good cleaning.

Jesse handed the shoe to Dave, who was thankful for the charity. It was at that point that Sara Miller first got a good look at Jesse without a shirt. His every muscle striated with each movement, only overshadowed by the smile on his face and good-hearted laughter coming from his belly. She found herself attracted to him and his rugged, no-bullshit charm. He had saved Scott's life and she would never forget his kindness.

With the campsite prepared, they set up camp and settled down for the evening, waiting for the food that Sara was cooking as quickly as possible, using her own supplies to repay the group's kindness. With Jesse watching out for Chase, the rest of the group relaxed and spoke of better times.

The camp seemed to splinter into groups of two: Margaret and Dave, Tom Tidwell and Elizabeth, Sara and Scott, and Tom Truman, who stood silently next to Jesse. The conversations were whispered and sullen in tone, giving each group a feeling of tranquility, the whispers foreboding things to come.

Dave wasn't very comfortable sitting on the log that he and Margaret had dragged from the forest and would need to find a more comfortable location to relax; besides he wanted to appear clever to Margaret. He rose from the log without saying a word and walked the twenty feet to the saddles, neatly arranged near the horses for a quick exit. He scooped up Margaret's saddle and returned to the log.

"Dave, that's a great idea. I don't think that I could've sat on this log much longer." She stood and watched Dave place the saddle across the log and returned for his without speaking.

Dave smiled as he walked the twenty feet to his saddle, knowing that his plan was working. He wiped his face clean as he returned to the log, situating himself on the log, facing her. " Now that's much better on my arse as our Irish friends would say." He finally let Margaret see his feeling of accomplishment manifest itself as a smile. He was just where he wanted to be, sitting across from Margaret, wanting desperately to reach over and show her the affection that he was starting to feel for her. He moved his hand towards her, but faltered and adjusted his seat unnecessarily. Words would have to do for now as his fears got the better of him.

"How are you doing, Margaret?" His voice was tender and caring.

"I'm alright, though I need a bath. I never thought I would be in a situation like this one. I mean, I demanded respect in 2099. Here I'm just in the way."

"That's not true, we all respect you. This is just out of our control. You know this is all for you. Do you think the government would have sent Chase and Jesse to save a few inspectors? Most likely not."

"Dave, the only reason they sent them to rescue me was because I know government secrets. That's all it was, nothing more, nothing less."

"Your wrong, Margaret. Besides, even if it is true, which it isn't, the fact is that they were sent. Now if it was just me, I would still be rotting in that camp."

"I don't know, I just feel helpless, like I'm just an afterthought in 1866. At home, I mattered; here I'm just a pain-in-the-ass, middle-aged woman who can't even vote."

"You matter to the group, you matter to me, Margaret. At least you did something with you life."

"What are you talking about? You're a doctor, and there's nothing more noble than that."

"Thanks, I guess we all have our doubts and worries. We're going to get home, I just know it; the scientists that invented the transport system will get us home, and Chase and Jesse will keep us safe in the meantime."

Margaret reached over, took Dave's hand, and nodded her head in agreement. She didn't know just what to say; luckily, Sara, who called the group to dinner, interrupted her before she made a fool of herself.

Dinner consisted of a beef and vegetable stew with a small piece of stale bread, which, when dipped in the stew, became eatable. There wasn't any conversation over dinner, just the occasional grunt from the hungry group. Jesse made sure that he scooped a large portion from the pot for Chase, who he expected back at any time.

With a full stomach most everyone bedded down for the night; a full stomach always made it easier to sleep, with the exception of Sara, who was cleaning up from dinner. Jesse watched as she diligently worked to clean up the mess made by a mob of hungry travelers. She was near completion, and Jesse wanted to take this time to get to know her better. He grabbed another log for the fire and restarted the almost extinguished blaze.

"Sara, sit down and relax; you've worked hard enough tonight."

"Thank you, I believe I will." There was an awkward pause, both Jesse and Margaret looking into each other's eyes. "I wanted to thank you again for this afternoon. I don't know what I would have done if I had lost Scott."

"That was totally my fault; I should have known better than to sneak up on you as I did. I'm just glad that I didn't hurt him seriously."

"He'll be fine. Jesse, that's a good name."

"Actually, my name's Robert, but everyone calls me Jesse. Chase started to call me that over 10 years ago. My last name is James, Robert James."

"I know it's none of my business, but I couldn't help noticing your scars when you had your shirt off. Are you and Chase in the army?"

"No, the navy. We were in the U.S. Navy, but we are just trying to go out West."

"My husband died in the war back in sixty-one. He fought for the Union as well. I think that is one of the reasons the bank foreclosed on the house and land. This part of Missouri is, or was, sympathetic to the Confederate States."

"I'm surprised that no one came courting; you really are very nice to look at…I'm sorry, that was uncalled for."

"No, I'm happy that someone still thinks so, but there isn't much use for a middle-aged woman whose late husband fought for the Union."

"Middle aged, how old are you, thirty-one, thirty-two? I would hardly call that middle aged."

"Actually, I'm thirty-four, but thanks for being so nice; no one's been nice to me for some time now. I guess that's why Scott was so quick to think the worst of you."

"We have to drop the boy off at his home in Greenville, do you know where that is?"

"Yes, it's not far from Liberty."

"Well, I was thinking that if you can wait for us to do that, perhaps you could ride with us for a while."

"Robert, I would like that very much." Sara got up from the fire and walked past Jesse, placing her hand on his shoulder. "I'm going to check on Scott and get some sleep; it's been a long day, but we can talk some more tomorrow if you would like."

"I would. Sleep well, Sara Miller."

Jesse sat by the fire until Chase returned from scouting the area; he seemed tired and would want to eat. He sat next to his friend, who handed the weary traveler his dinner. Jesse may have overstepped his bounds with Sara, inviting her to travel with them, but he liked her and if they were going to be stuck in 1866, he would need to try to make a life for himself.

Chase ate his food in silence; when he finished Jesse sat down next to him, wanting to know the plan.

"So?"

"Jess, I don't think that they followed us; we escaped clean from St. Charles and there has been no sign of anyone at all since we left. What do you think?"

"I think you're right. All we have to do is get Truman home and then decide what we're going to do. I was thinking that we could go west and start a life. I don't think we are going to get out of here."

"You might be right, but I'm not going to give up hope just yet. We go to Liberty, get the wheel for the wagon, return to fix the wagon for Sara, and then take Truman home."

"Chase, I was talking to Sara and she said Greenville was very close to Liberty; perhaps it might be better to finish the mission and then return to help Sara."

"Okay, we finish the mission and then come back, that would be the prudent thing to do. I'm beat. I think it's lights out for me, Jess. I'll see you in the morning." Chase stumbled to his tent in exhaustion; he would sleep very soundly tonight.

"Hey, do you want me to stand watch tonight?"

" I don't think that you need to, do you?"

"No, I think it's safe."

"Okay, goodnight." Chase opened the flap to his tent and literally fell inside. Jesse wasn't far behind.

It was the first night that no one had stood watch. Elizabeth's plan was starting to work; she would have a busy day tomorrow. She had to leave another message for Harden and Buford, giving the location of their destination. "Liberty, Missouri, three days' ride. February 10, 1866."

Harden and Buford were only about five hours from the group and like their counterparts bedded down for the night. Harden and Buford had renewed their relationship over the past few weeks and were close once more.

Buford sat inside his tent, the light of a lantern illuminating a letter that he was re-reading for at least the hundredth time from his mother. He never read the whole letter, just the third paragraph.

> "Son, Melissa has decided to leave with a doctor she met in '62. I was unable to dissuade her from taking Jennifer. I have known about this for some time, but was unable to contact you until you wrote, telling me of your plans to pursue remedies for our land problem. Apparently, Melissa was unable to wait for you to finish doing your duty as she could not stand having no means. I am sorry, and look forward to better days."

Harden stood in the entrance to the tent, having just completed overseeing the camp's defenses and making sure his men had everything they needed to make it through the night. "Buford, when did you get a letter?"

"A long time ago. I was just remembering better days."

Harden could tell that his friend had something weighing on his mind and decided to pry further into his personal life. The company would need Buford at his best. "What does it say?"

Buford looked up, finding the shoulder of a friend; holding the pain in longer was impractical. Knowing he could trust his closest friend, Buford handed the letter to Harden, who read it quickly.

"What, she ran off with someone else? I can't believe she would do that to you. I'm so very sorry, Buford. Why didn't you tell me before? This letter is dated almost a year ago."

"The embarrassment, I guess. The damn war took my country, most of my friends and my family. I had hoped she would reconsider after I got my family land back, but it's been so long in coming, I fear it's too late."

"Perhaps it's too late to get her back, but we can get the land back and start over. We are young, if only in our years on earth. Buford, to tell you the truth, I don't have anything to go back to in South Carolina. Sherman's men burned my plantation and my family was killed in the war. I just want this to be over."

"It will be and we will be victorious. Enough of this dribble. Josh, can you please get that black box we got from Elizabeth? Let's have a closer look at the contents."

Harden opened the box and removed the contents, being very careful not to drop anything. He sat next to Buford and opened the first book.

The book was a completion of smaller manuals, all with the words "top secret" on them in white letters, contrasting sharply with the black covers. The manuals seemed to contain schematics, diagrams, and specifications for army equipment. Rifles, explosives, and optical enhancement equipment were the subheadings.

"Buford, look at this. It's a conversion kit. The manual says it will convert the electric firing mechanism on the M 29/ME assault rifle to the standard mechanical, cased, .223 caliber, 5.56 by 45-millimeter standard NATO round. Have you ever heard of anything like that before?" Harden held up two firing mechanisms used to retro fit the M-29 rifle.

"No, but that must be what they have been using on us. Look at this one, night vision." He handed it to Harden, who read the manual carefully.

"This is what they were using at the white house. Remember I said that we attacked in cover of night, but they seemed to know exactly were we were. This is why. Buford, what are we dealing with?"

"I don't know, but I do know they can die just like we can."

"Buford, what else is there?"

"Not much, just a history book. *World History 1860 to Present*. It's stupid, a history book for 5 years." Buford couldn't imagine the concept of time travel and dismissed the book quickly, a book that would explain many unanswered questions. "Josh, put this stuff back. I'm tired; we can look at it later."

"You're right, we're going to need to focus on killing these men, and not what kind of experimental weapons they have." He placed the books and conversion kit back in the black box and went to check on his men one last time before he turned in for the night.

Chapter 18

Harden and Buford came to the wagon early that next afternoon, finding the ribbon tied to one of the wheel's spokes, giving the destination of her group. It was time to lay the ambush, catching Chase and Jesse, like a mouse that wants the cheese attached to the deadly trap. He would watch as they walked right into there own deaths, unknowingly and with contentment in their actions.

"Joshua, we have them. We'll rest the horses for a few hours; we're going to have to ride hard to beat them to Liberty."

"Column dismount. We rest and then ride hard to Liberty, Missouri, where we'll trap them and end this once and for all." Harden could taste the blood and the glory, knowing now he would have his revenge.

The rest seemed short, but they needed to make sure they beat them into town. They would ride hard ten miles north, so Chase and Jesse couldn't detect them, and then non-stop to Liberty, cutting a full day and a half from the journey if they were lucky, beating the others by at most a day and at least three quarters of a day. It was a hard ride but would be lucrative. Buford could taste victory the same as his friend, Harden; it would be hard not to see it clearly, there was no choice, and he had to have his land, his dignity, and his revenge.

Tom Truman lived twenty miles south of Liberty, and pressed on, without the rest of the group and the problems they brought with them. Chase thought it a poor idea, but he knew that he probably would be home quicker than if they escorted him, especially since Jesse had volunteered them to help Sara and her son, Scott. Chase and Jesse agreed to meet Truman at his home in a few days and discuss helping with his father's wagon train west, which made Truman very happy. He turned south a half-day's ride from Liberty, giving Chase a bit of relief, having such an important task completed, the whole reason that they had traveled across the state in the first place.

Later that same day they arrived in Liberty. It was a larger town, home to William Jewell College, and the Clay County Savings Association, the largest bank in the area. It was nothing like St. Louis, but it did have a quaint look to it, a homey feeling that Chase would soon discover was not lasting. It was February 13, 1866, the day before Valentines Day, and the weather had turned cold just in time. The mud of a few days ago turned into ice, and the budding trees iced over, killing any chance of an early spring. The town was a prototypical town of that era. The main street housed the stores, saloons, and the bank, along with the mom-and-pop stores, all neatly confined to Main Street. The rest of the streets, which all led to the main drag, had people's homes, and on the left side of town the college took up most everything from the far edge to just before the main drag.

The group agreed to stay the night outside the town because all of the stores were closed and they didn't have the money to stay in a hotel. They camped unaware that Harden and Buford were waiting for them less than a mile away. Chase and Jesse felt confident that they had lost the two men and were careless with the watch and security. They didn't even scout the town before bedding down, a fact that would haunt Chase in the morning.

Surprisingly they slept well and were refreshed in the morning. It was early when they went into town, proudly riding into the town with a name that summed up everything that they had ever done in their lives, fighting and killing for liberty. Chase finally realized who he was; it was a weird time to realize it, but he welcomed the epiphany regardless. He patted his friend on the back and smiled at him. Jesse had helped him work through the problems; he would have to thank him properly with a bottle later. They made their way to the hardware store, looking for a wagon wheel. After talking to the owner, who had to prepare one, taking a few hours, they decided to go to the saloon. The saloon was open twenty-four hours a day, seven days a week, catering to the cowhands who made their way up from Texas and Oklahoma.

They entered the establishment through two shutter doors that went the length of the doorway that opened both inwardly and outwardly. The two friends found two open seats at the bar and ordered a bottle of whiskey. Chase had his opportunity to thank Jesse properly quicker than he had thought he would, but it would do.

Chase poured two shot glasses full and raised his glass. Jesse followed suit, but waited for Chase to make the toast; the person who raised their glass first makes the toast.

"Jess, to the United States of America, the navy and all the best things they stand for, and to you for helping me overcome my demons. You're a true friend, a brother and I love you."

Jesse nodded his head to the toast, but welled up inside at Chase's sentiment; he loved him too and thought of him as his little brother. "I feel the same way and I am glad that you came to your senses before someone killed you."

They passed the time drinking to all of their friends who had been killed over the years, finishing the bottle quickly. Both men were avid drinkers and could have finished another bottle if it weren't for their business. They walked towards the door just as it opened, where one of Buford's men stood face to face with them.

He was a small man in stature, with blond hair and one lazy brown eye, the other being blue. He pulled his gun just as Chase came to him. Chase didn't hesitate, grabbing the Remington .44 caliber in the man's hand, twisting it up, loosing the grip on the gun. He didn't stop there. Chase brought his full weight down on the man's arm, snapping it in two, turning square with the man, who's arm had a compound fracture and was bleeding profusely on the floor, and with an open hand, thrust his nose up into his brain, killing him instantly.

The dead man fell to the floor, startling the other patrons in the bar, who had missed the action as it had happened so quickly. Jesse went to the door of the saloon, securing the exit. The street seemed clear, but Buford and Harden were bound to be near, and the two men only had their 10mm navy-issue handguns and five clips each. They ignored the other people in the bar, drew the futuristic handguns from the holsters, and watched for any sign of their enemy.

"What are we going to do? Chase, do we make a run for it or do we wait it out here?" Jesse was not really asking Chase, but going over their options aloud.

"This seems to be a good defensible location, but Dave and Margaret are not protected and could be vulnerable."

"Shit, Chase, Dave has both machine guns and the grenades; I think he'll be okay. We have to find a way out of this; I have a feeling that they are waiting for us to exit."

"Holy fuck, I can't believe that I forgot. What's today's date?" Chase's face lit up like a Christmas tree.

"What?" Jesse was confused but only showed discomfort in Chase's comment.

"What's the date?"

Jesse looked at his watch, the same one that Chase had left with Dave in order to keep coordinated. "February 14, 1866. 1:47 p.m. Why?"

"1:47. I know what we need to do. In thirteen minutes the real Jesse James is going to rob the Clay County Savings bank."

"You're shitting me."

"No. I feel stupid, he was my favorite subject in grad school. I studied everything about him. Why do you think you got the nickname?" Jesse shrugged his shoulders; he had never taken the time to learn about his namesake, or at least where he got his nickname.

"Fill me in; we only have a short time."

"It is the first daylight bank robbery in U.S. history, with the exception of a group of Confederate raiders, who robbed one in Vermont, but that was war and doesn't count. If I remember correctly, they had to shoot their way out of town and avoid a posse that was sent after them. The funny part of it is that Jesse and Frank James just live one railroad stop north of here. Did you notice where the bank is, Jess?"

"I think I remember seeing it right next to this building; yes, it's next to us on the left." Both men were looking out the window for the bank robbers when they came riding down the street. Twelve men came down the street, wearing long soldiers' overcoats, with six-shooters strapped over the coats. The first three riders dismounted in the square and covered the others who rode up to the bank. Two men dismounted and entered the bank: Frank and Jesse James.

"Chase, what happens inside?" The story hooked Master Chief Robert James; he was witnessing history, and he loved every second of it.

"Frank and Jesse go inside and warm themselves on the stove. The cashier—his name was Greenup Bird—labored over accounts at a desk behind a wooden counter while his son worked the teller window. After a moment Jesse walked up to the counter and…

Jesse slid a ten-dollar bill over to William Bird on the polished wood teller window. "I'd like a bill changed, please." As William reached for the bill, Jesse's six-shooter greeted him, pointed at his face. Almost as an afterthought, he broadened his request. "I'd like all the money in the bank."

William jumped back as the two brothers jumped the counter, Frank brandishing his revolver on Greenup, Jesse pistol-whipping his son. "Make any noise and I'll burn you down," Frank said as he covered Jesse, who pushed William to the open bank vault.

"Damn you, be quick!" Jesse shouted as he shoved William over to the money, where he gathered gold and silver coins from the shelf and stuffed them into a grain sack Jesse had taken from his coat.

Frank James, standing at Greenup's desk, pointed his gun at his head. "Where is the paper money?" He pressed the revolver into the scared man's temple.

"In the box," he replied, pointing to a large tin container on the table. Frank didn't miss a beat; still holding the gun on his attentive bank clerk, he stacked the contents, currency, bonds, bank notes, and sheets of revenue stamps in anticipation for Jesse's exit from the vault.

When Jesse emerged with a bulging bag, Frank added the legal tender and motioned Greenup to join his son in the vault. Jesse slammed the door shut so hard that it didn't latch tightly, but he was in too big a hurry to notice.

"Stay in there. You know all birds should be caged." Jesse and Frank James had just started the longest and most famous bank robbery gang in history, but the fun was just starting for Chase and Chief James, who waited patiently in the saloon next door, and Buford and Harden, who were across the street.

Neither man had any idea that the bank was being robbed across the street. The whole town was in the dark, but would soon be awakened to the sweet sound of gunfire. Harden was perched inside a candy store and Buford was two buildings down in a dress shop. Their whole crew was ready to strike, hungry and lean. They watched as Jesse and Frank James came out of the bank, followed by Chase and Chief James from the saloon next to it.

Chase and Chief James were making their move, thinking that the real Jesse James would cover their escape. The horses were at the hardware store down the street. They busted from the saloon in a standard covering posture, one man covering six to twelve and the other twelve to six. As soon as they entered the street, Buford and Harden's men all came out to play. It was an unique situation, three groups coming together, which should have never met. Chase hoped that it would turn out fine historically, but was more concerned with the life of his friends and himself.

The lock on the vault never locked; after a few moments the two birds opened the door and went to the window, calling for help. What they saw was chilling. The bank robbers defended themselves from a group of lawmen stationed across the street. Greenup saw that they wore badges and rejoiced in the fact that the money was sure to be retuned. In fact, he would never see that money ever again.

Harden watched as his men were attacking Jesse and Frank James; ironically both sides of this battle were Confederate raiders during the war, but the marshal badges were an invitation for Jesse James to kill. Harden focused on Chase and the chief, who were almost to their horses. He aimed his gun at the two horses tied up at the hardware store. The Henry rifle he chose for the battle had the distance and accuracy to hit his target. He fired three shots, killing the horses, and stopping Chase and Chief James from making an exodus.

The mounts dropped right in front of Chase, who was lucky that he wasn't hit by one of the rounds. They took cover behind the dead horses as the battle approached their position. They had not fired a shot, but that would soon change. Harden's men pushed Jesse and Frank James back to where Chase and the chief were, bullets flying everywhere, which prompted Jesse and Frank to dismount and take cover. Chase could see both brothers standing in the middle of the street, helpless. Over half of their gang had been killed and the others were pinned down by the bank.

Chase had to save the James brothers; they were an important part of history and couldn't be killed prematurely because of his actions. He stood, took aim with his laser sight, and fired one shot after another, killing Buford's men with ease. He covered Jesse and Frank as they made it to Chief James' position.

"Thanks, man. I'm Jesse and this is my brother, Frank." All four men were flat on their backs behind the horses. "All we have to do is make it to the end of the street; we have some back-up mounts their, enough for you as well." Jesse had everything planned well, except for forty armed men in position to kill them before they even robbed the bank.

"Good, my name is Chase and this is Bob, nice to meet you both. Jesse, two and two, we cover you and you cover us."

"Sounds good. I'll take the honors, on three." Jesse and Frank James were fighting alongside him, Chase felt a chill up his spine as he heard three and took off running, his chief at his side.

He turned just in time as Frank and Jesse followed down the street. Chief James dispensed his usual nasty taste of death, killing three of the now rushing bandits. Chase was just as accurate. He looked behind him where the James brothers had set up under cover and began to fire, allowing them to retreat to the horses.

The two groups repeated the process until they were at the end of the street with a wake of dead bodies behind them. Frank James came out from around the corner with four horses, one for each of the men. Unfortunately, the two of Jesse's found themselves pinned down behind a building near the end of the street. Chase was already on his horse when the real Jesse James made his break for his mount.

Chief James had not expected Jesse to run for it; Buford's men had consolidated their fire into a heavy volume right where the famous James brother had taken off, creating crossfire sure to hit anything running through the street. Chief James, without thinking, ran after him, firing through his armpit at Harden and Buford's men as he went, tackling Jesse as three bullets entered his back, expanding and ripping large holes. Jesse James jumped up, mounted his horse, and grabbed Chief James, who was flat on the ground, from the cover behind his own mount. He placed his new friend over his horse in front of him, riding out of town behind the others.

Frank James led the way, following their prearranged plan, heading south to the county church, where they planned to divide the money and split up. Harden and Buford had changed that plan slightly, neither James brother knew if any of their gang had escaped the wall of lead in town, and they knew if it weren't for their new friends they would have joined them in hell. The men arrived at the church and scrambled inside with Chief James. The church was simple and quaint, lending to the mystique of the town and countryside. It was empty and cold inside; Chase carried his friend into the church and laid him onto a bench.

"You're going to be okay, Chief. I'm going to get the doctor and he's going to fix you up." Chase opened his coat and shirt, finding his Kevlar jacket. "You wore your jacket, thank God."

"I always do, Chase, but it must have been a rifle because it went right through it." Chief James struggled to speak as three of his ribs were broken

"Okay, save your strength." Chase was concerned, but the fact that Chief James had his Kevlar jacket on gave him a hope that he would make it out alive.

"How is he? He took three in the back; it looked bad." Jesse didn't look at Chase; he just continued to divide the money. "Look, you didn't help us rob the place, but you did help us escape. Frank and I want you to have some of the money." He dropped a sack of money by Chase and headed to the door where Frank was watching for any sign of a posse. "Thanks, you saved our lives. I hope that your friend's alright. You better get moving; they're bound to come looking for us."

Chief James held out his hand, stopping Jesse James on his way to the door. "It's been my pleasure, Jesse. Good luck and don't give up robbing banks because of what happened today."

"I won't. You take care of yourself, and maybe we can get together on another job." Jesse didn't really mean it—he thought that the chief was too far gone—but he had never met Dr. Persons. Jesse and Frank James smiled at Chase and Chief James and walked out of the church and into history.

The town of Liberty, Missouri, was in shock; no one had ever had the audacity to rob a bank during business hours, and the town's leaders right down to the common farmer wanted revenge and their money. There was no FDIC to insure the money people put into the banks; it was just lost, taken by the most accomplished bank robber in all of U.S. history.

The town marshal, county sheriff, and Buford, who represented the U.S. government but had his own agenda, gathered at the bank to investigate and eventually form a posse. It was decided that Buford would lead the posse, which had many war veterans who gathered what weapons they could and stood ready to defend their town from thieves and murderers.

"Josh, I know that we got one of them. I saw him fall; they couldn't have gotten very far with an injured man."

"Buford, did you ever think that he is dead and they just left him?"

"No, not these men; they're too close to just leave the other to die. Remember what they did with our men at the white house? They killed those men and they still took care of them. No way they left each other."

"You're right. How do you want to proceed?"

"One of the townsmen picked up the trail. They headed south; we need to get on the move. The temperature is dropping and a front seems to be moving in, so we need to start now."

Harden addressed the posse and his own men, briefing them on the plan. With the infusion of new blood from the town, who had the same desire to kill, for obviously different reasons, Buford and Harden bolstered their numbers well over one hundred once again, giving them the numbers needed to overrun Chase and an injured Chief James.

Dave and Margaret waited with Tom Tidwell, Elizabeth, and their newest travelers, Sara and Scott Miller, who had all been instructed to wait five miles out of town on the road heading to Tom Truman's place, for Chase and Chief James to return with the wheel. They waited under the shelter of a group of large evergreen trees just off the road in silence. They heard the gunfire coming from the direction of town and were concerned that it was Jesse and Chase who had sparked the gunplay. Only Elizabeth knew what had happened, but Chase and Chief James were too skilled and too smart to have been caught by Harden, but they had paid the price and Chief James would need attention.

Margaret was the first to spot Chase and Jesse riding side by side, Jesse slumping forward on his horse, trying to hold on with the all the strength that he could muster.

"Dave, look." Margaret hit Dave on the shoulder, prompting him to look up at the two SEALs.

"Holly shit." Dave didn't waste any time; he rode to Chase's position, finding Chief James half delirious and still bleeding from his back. Chase did his best field dressing of the wounds, but couldn't stop the bleeding. He dismounted and helped Jesse from the horse, catching him as he slid off. It didn't take long for Dave to come to his conclusion.

"We need to get him inside so that I can work on him; he's lost a lot of blood and isn't going make it if I can't get the bullets out and close the holes quickly."

By this time, the rest of the group, excepting Elizabeth, who remained by the evergreens, were huddled around Chief James, trying to get a look at the fallen hero. Scott had never seen a gunshot wound and was intrigued by the man's story and history; he had appeared so collected earlier when they had met, he regretted holding the gun to him, but had thought that he was going to hurt his mother. He had saved his life because he was so calm under fire. "There is a house up the road a bit. I used to have a friend who lived up this way, and we would camp out at this place; no one has lived there in years, so we could use it."

Chase didn't answer the boy, he just motioned him to mount his horse. Scott got Chase's meaning and led the way to the hideout that he hoped was still standing; it had been two years since he had been there.

Chase passed by Elizabeth, seeing a red ribbon tied to a branch next to her, but he was too preoccupied to derive a conclusion and just passed her by, waving his hand, motioning her to follow behind them. They followed Scott Miller into the forest, Elizabeth still lagging at the foot of the forest. She shoved the note into the tie of the ribbon, simply saying "forest." She didn't know anything else.

The cabin was made of tree logs and was in poor shape, but they weren't going for comfort. Dr. Persons had to operate on Jesse, who had been hurt worse than this in the war. *He'll make it.* That was what Chase kept telling himself as the good doctor was working inside. Chase roamed the woods, trying to figure out how Buford had found them and beaten them to a town, one that they had just decided to go to a few days before. That fact prompted him to think that it was just a coincidence, but if it was a coincidence it was such a long shot. *Harden and Buford have to be the luckiest people in the world.*

After a few hours, Chase went inside to check on Dr. Persons' progress. Upon entering, he saw that the operation was complete and Jesse was resting comfortably in the bed.

"Chase, the operation went smoothly, but he has lost so much blood that I can't keep his blood pressure high enough to sustain his bodily needs. I give him a thirty-percent chance.

Chase grabbed Dave by the coat, lifting the two-hundred pound man off the ground. "If he dies, I'll bury you with him, you understand me?"

"Now wait a second, how dare you say that to me? I'm not the one who always gets into these messes."

Chase let him down and went over to Jesse, ripping his dog tags from his neck.

"AB negative, does anyone have AB negative blood?"

Margaret stood, cautiously raising her hand. Chase had scared her, knowing that he could and would back his words up with actions. "I have AB negative."

Chase rooted through the med kits, finding two syringe tips and a rubber hose used to tie off an arm before an injection and for person-to-person blood infusions in this case. Everything in a combat med kit had at least two uses;

they were packed for efficiency, and one just had to know what to look for. He handed the equipment to Dr. Persons, who felt a bit stupid that he hadn't thought of this earlier.

"I'm first. I have O positive, and everyone can use it. You take two pints from me, and one from Margaret. Do you think that three pints will be enough?"

"Enough to get him out of danger, but it's not safe for you, loosing two pints." Chase glared at Dave. Dave then understood that Chase wasn't kidding; he would do anything to keep Master Chief Robert James from dying, and probably go through with his threat, though Dr. Persons didn't think so. He was just under an enormous amount of stress. The transfusion was an easy enough thing, but he would have to watch Chase closely; he wouldn't quite be himself, low two pints of blood.

The snow started to fall as Buford and Harden arrived at the county church. Buford was weary of the snow, which had stopped him once, determined to end this before the impending storm halted his search once more. Inside the church, his men found some paper money and a lot of dried blood on one of the benches.

"So we did get one of them, good; they should be close, hiding out." The size of his posse again slowed his pursuit, but he found out the hard way that a few men couldn't handle these trained killers, who even fought their way out of an ambush. Harden even learned a bigger lesson, losing over sixty men to them at the white house. *It isn't going to be the case this time; one is shot up and probably too injured to fight, and one man can't take on one hundred thirty men, not even a man as skilled as these two,* Buford thought.

"Sir." Harden had some good and bad news to tell his commander. "We found the trail, but there are two of them; one heads south and the other west towards a river crossing. Both are two horses and both are heavy."

"They split up; take fifty men and head to the river crossing. I'll head south, following the other trail. Just find them and report to me; do not, I repeat, do not engage them without me."

Harden didn't appreciate being spoken to like a child, but he had made the mistake of attacking them at the white house where they had massacred his men. "Yes, sir." He was off, hoping to find Chase and Chief James, but he would only find a few more pieces of the banks money and a blizzard, which was moving into the area.

Buford would spend more time at the church than he wanted to, trying to organize his new men; they didn't use their heads to make decisions and could be a liability if Buford couldn't whip them into shape. It had been three hours since Jesse James and Chase had split up, and it would be two more before Buford would move out.

The transfusions had been a success and Jesse was awake and talking, but couldn't be moved for a few days. After the transfusion, Chase had to take a nap, trying to regain his strength. It worked to a point and he was up, planning the group's next move.

"How are you? Jess, I was worried for a while, but Dave said that you are going to be fine." His friend was lying on his stomach, tied down, so as not to move around, opening the wounds.

"Who would have thought that Dave Persons would save my life? He told me what you did. I'm grateful, as I said; you're always there when you're needed."

"Buford's bound to be looking for us. I'm thinking that we could lead them away from you; besides, I'm worried about Truman. If they get him, history will pay the price."

"That could work. I'm sure not going to be able to ride. You can backtrack to the forest and head out from there to Truman's place; it would look like we had stopped, but then pressed on.

"Are you sure? I don't want to leave you alone."

Chase heard a voice from the corner. Sara Miller had been eavesdropping and wanted to help. "Scott and I will stay with him; he and I would only slow you down and he saved Scott's life. I figure we owe him."

Chase looked at Jesse, who nodded his head in agreement. "Go, everything will be alright. You had better leave now." Chase grabbed his best friend's hand, who just winked at him, prompting Chase to turn his attention to Dave and Margaret.

"Let's go, gather your things; we're moving out. That means you too, Dr. Persons." Chase had cut him off before he could protest; he knew that doctors always wanted to stay with their patients. "There's nothing more you can do for him, you said so yourself, and I need your gun."

Chase turned, bumping into Elizabeth and Tom Tidwell. "Chase, Elizabeth and I were thinking that we should stay here as well." It was really Elizabeth's idea, but Tom was the man and had to act as if he made the decisions.

"No, Buford is after both of you; the whole idea is to misdirect them away from Jesse, giving him the time he needs to get back on his feet."

"But I—"

"But nothing. Get your fucking things together. We go to Tom Truman's place in Greenville in ten, let's move." Chase was giving orders as if these people were in his SEAL team, but someone had to get things accomplished.

Elizabeth acted like she was upset and stormed outside where she put her third to last ribbon on the door of the house, which opened outward, hiding the ribbon as they left. She put the note in the usual place. "Greenville, Truman house."

Chapter 19

Harden followed the trail to the Missouri River crossing into Kansas, where it ended; he had lost the trail in the heavily falling snow and would have to turn back, following his instructions, taking the posse back to town. He figured the snow would stop the men he was chasing, and they would not lose any ground, just lying at the white house. *Buford will either send word or meet them back at Liberty,* he deduced. Harden was disappointed, but knew Buford would find something significant. They still had an ace up their sleeve in Elizabeth; for some reason he was positive that she wouldn't let them down.

They started back to town, battling the snow; they all wanted to the men who had robbed the bank, but good sense told them to continue the search when the snow stopped. Harden followed some of the local men, who knew their way around the countryside. He wondered if Buford had had any luck. He could feel this madness starting to end; the feeling made him warmer inside somehow as the temperature dropped to near zero.

Chase and his group came to the edge of the forest only about twenty minutes before Buford, riding south to Greenville where they would check on Tom Truman and hopefully get his parents to leave with him while Chase dealt with Buford and Harden. This tactic was risky, knowing they could be surrounded by Buford's men if the group all stayed in the cabin. This way their tracks headed south and not into the forest. Chase had made sure that he covered any evidence that they had ever gone into the woods.

The snow was coming down as hard as it had on the trail to Liberty, but they had to press on. Chase had made his two principle concerns, Dave and Margaret, put on the other environmental suits, giving them all the heat that they needed. Tom Tidwell and Elizabeth had to struggle to stay warm, but they were not his primary concern; they would just have to tough it out.

It was only about fifteen miles to Greenville, and they could make it in three or four hours if they made good time. For Chase it was time to put his body into overdrive; he was tired, low on blood, hungry, but he had thrived on adversity his whole life. If it was easy it was never worth having; he lived by that and these had been the hardest few months in his life. He was going to enjoy himself when this was over. He felt the conclusion looming over him, finishing this mess, and celebrating with his friend Jesse.

Buford followed the trail to the base of the woods, but the snow was starting to cover any trace of Chase and Jesse. Buford was visibly upset, throwing and kicking the snow until he saw it. It was the most beautiful thing that he had ever seen in his entire life, the red ribbon tied to a low branch of a tree. She would have to have been standing on her stirrups to reach it, but she had given the break Buford needed. He ordered one of his men to remove the note inside the ribbon. "Sir, it says 'forest.'"

"Nothing else, just forest?"

"Yes, sir, just forest. They have to be somewhere close by, a cabin in the woods perhaps."

We will find out soon enough, Buford thought as he led the way into the woods, ordering his men to spread out and look lively. This was the moment for which he had waited for nearly three months.

They came to a clearing, a dilapidated cabin in the middle of a treeless area about an acre on each side of the cabin. The only way one could tell the cabin was occupied was the smoke billowing from the chimney. Buford approached with caution, knowing what they had done to his men in Virginia and at the white house.

"Hey, there are a whole bunch of men outside coming this way, about fifty or so." Scott's voice was shaky, filled with fear and excitement at the same time. Jesse forced himself to get out of bed, using every bit of his reserves. He put his pants and boots on and went to the window, looking out at Buford's men.

"We're fucked," he mumbled. He thought he'd said it soft enough so Scott couldn't hear him, but he had sixteen-year-old ears. Scott looked up at him and started to cry.

"Get it together; if we're going to die today it's going to be in a fight." His automatic pilot kicked in; it had never failed him. He loaded his 10mm, checking his ammunition supply. *Five cartridges, seventy-five rounds.* "How many bullets do you have, Scott?"

"Twenty-four plus what's in the gun."

"Okay, this is it; you fire at targets that you can hit, don't waste your ammunition. You start shooting when I do; you might want to save one for yourself and your mother." *God knows what they will do to her,* he finished to himself. Jesse turned to Sara; he had come to like this woman and hoped to start a new life with her after this was over. *There is a chance I will make it out of this. I have done it before, how ever unlikely. I'm king of making it out of situations that I shouldn't.* "Sara, I'm sorry." He grabbed her and kissed her firmly and passionately. Without another word, he went to the window, his bullet wounds already bleeding from moving around too much. Adrenaline was a funny drug; a person could do extraordinary things on adrenaline. *It was time to meet destiny head on. Live or die, he had made his mark on the world, in 2099 and 1866.*

Buford wanted this battle to go smoothly; he sent two groups around the flanks and concentrated the rest of his men in the center, numbering around fifty. He was using the same strategy that had won the battle against Tidwell in Virginia. This time he would hold his flankers in reserve, so they could overwhelm the men when the time was right. The weapons that he had were not as accurate as his two adversaries' he now knew from the manuals in the black box; he would take some casualties getting into range, but that was the nature of war. *I just have to go seventy more yards.* When the shooting started he would order a charge, minimizing the amount of people killed.

"Scott, my gun has a much further range than yours does. I didn't think of it before; you're going to have to wait until they get to about the shed until you start. Remember, pick your targets wisely."

Scott nodded as he trained his eyes on the approaching men. Jesse's first shot startled him, and he jumped about an inch off the ground.

Buford would close the gap as fast as he could, Jesse knew so he had to work fast. His laser sight would have been an advantage, but the falling snow reflected the beam and he couldn't get an accurate aim. He would have to do it the old fashioned way. He picked up the first man, who was leading the group. He could tell that he was a soldier because of the coat he had. That made Jesse feel better about killing him; he would've known the risks when he had started this insanity. His first shot rang out into the dusk air. One shot, one kill. He had a chance if he could keep this up.

Buford ordered the charge, and his men raced to Jesse's position; for some it was the worst decision in their lives. Jesse acquired and dispensed targets as quickly as he could, loading, firing, and reloading with the hypnotic humming of a well-oiled machine.

The charging men made it to the shed and Scott Miller opened fire. He was the antithesis of Jesse—he couldn't hit a thing—but they were still a ways off and he would have more opportunities. He stopped to reload and looked over at Jesse, who had a look of determination on his face and the look of the devil in his eyes.

Buford's men hit their maximum effective range; he had expected to lose more men, but the two men weren't using their futuristic guns. *They must have been to large and heavy to carry all this way or perhaps only one of the my two enemies is inside the cabin,* he thought as he advanced. Half of his men dropped to the snow-covered ground and opened fire, covering the advance of the other half. Buford would simply continue to move up in this fashion until he took the cabin.

Buford's first volley hit the cabin, but the thickness of the logs stopped ninety-five percent of the bullets. He watched as his advancing team fell, one at a time, dead or dying in the white snow. *It's as if the snow cleanses them of all their sins as it hits their bodies,* Buford thought.

"Aim for the windows." If he could make them take cover, they could advance without taking casualties. The next volley of covering fire slammed into the cabin around the windows. It was time to advance; the first group took a prone position and laid down covering fire as the rear group advanced.

Jesse took cover for the second volley, but Scott, being inexperienced, didn't; he was killed insistently. Sara ran to him, finding his head with a fifty-caliber hole in it. She curled up with him in her arms and cried, she felt death hanging over her, and she would join him soon enough.

Jesse used clip after clip, killing about eighty-five percent of the people at whom he aimed, thinning Buford's group out enough where he could envision surviving. He loaded his second to last clip, and gathered Scott's revolver and ammunition belt. He would make his last stand, taking aim and firing just as the flanking men appeared from out of Jesse's sight line. He used his last two clips quickly, saving the last two bullets. He looked over at Sara, who was still holding Scott.

"It's okay, Jesse, there really is no reason to live." Jesse pointed the gun and pulled the trigger, devoid of any emotion. He made sure the bullet killed her instantly, shooting her in her temple on a downward angle, so the bullet ripped through her medulla oblongata.

He didn't watch her body slump onto the floor; he had other things he needed to attend to. *There is no way I'm going to end my own life; I'll fight like a man until the very end.* The door to the cabin flung open and the man fired blindly into the opening. Jesse was behind the door. He slammed the door back into the man's face, startling him. He reached over the man's shoulder, using his last bullet on the man behind him. After using his last round, Jesse grabbed the first man's head and rotated with him through the doorway. His friends took care of that problem. Before the man fell, Jesse grabbed his revolver from his holster and fired all six rounds. Six separate men fell dead to the ground. The seventh man's bullet entered Jesse right under his ribcage on the right side. With one last show of strength and skill, he snapped the man's neck before falling in a platoon of fifty-caliber musket bullets.

Buford arrived at the cabin, seeing two men and a woman dead on the floor; he inspected the bodies, trying to identify both of the men. He was happy to get out of the snow that had begun to blow. He knelt over Scott's body.

"This is just a boy; the man I am looking for looks like that one." He pointed to Jesse's corpse.

"Sir, this was pinned to the door." The man handed Buford a red ribbon with a note in it. He read the note, turning and walking out of the cabin. He stopped in the doorway and surveyed his dead. "Get a detail together and take care of the bodies; we head back to town in thirty minutes." He would need Harden and the rest of the posse to take on the other two men. He decided that the snow and wind would stop Chase, and he could still surprise him when the storm cleared.

In the month since the last briefing, there had been no new information to report, the team was still missing and Cormier wasn't any closer to solving the mystery than he had been the day it happened. As Townsend approached the briefing room, he knew that the program had run its course, and prematurely doomed to be terminated if he couldn't come up with something quickly. The thought of lying crossed his mind, but just like his missing friend, he had to do his duty the best he could. That didn't include lying to his commander in chief, no matter what was at stake.

He had just come from his secret weapon, Dick Charles, who had given him some ammunition to bring to the meeting. General Mathews was reportedly bragging to his collogues how he would soon be in command of the military aspect of the new technology. Townsend deemed the possibility of Mathews running the program unconscionable and vowed put an end to Mathews' plans if it cost him his career.

He entered the same briefing room used in his last meeting; this time he was the first one inside. He used the free time to call Cormier; he might have something new to report before the president arrived.

"Hello. Dr. Cormier."

"Hi, Al, it's Chris. I just wanted to call and see if there was anything new since I've been in transit."

"No, nothing, Chris. I'm sorry."

"Thanks, I'll let you know as soon as I do what the verdict is."

"Okay, good luck."

Townsend hung up the phone as General Mathews entered the briefing room. Townsend walked over to Mathews, who seemed to be gloating over the fact that he would soon have his revenge on Chase.

"General, I've heard you're going to be heading up the military arm of this new technology." Townsend stopped toe to toe with Mathews, who didn't bother to take a step back before answering.

"You heard correctly, Chris. I'm going to be working for with the CIA in a joint DOD/CIA effort to utilize this technology. It was my idea to use this transport in the first place and now that it has yielded some unexpected results, I'm going to try and find a way to use it as a weapon system."

"Not if I have anything to do with it, General. We both know why you're pushing for the current project to be canned."

"What's that, Admiral Townsend?"

"The whole reason you're pushing for the termination of this project is because Chase was in command. You want to kill him and then discredit his name, just like he did to your son."

"How dare you speak to me like that? I am a superior officer and you will show me the proper respect."

"There's no one else here, you piece of shit. I promise you that you will not get that command. If it costs me my carrier, you will not be given the satisfaction of smearing Chase's name."

"You don't have the power to take me on, Townsend. You're going to start a war you can't finish."

"I'm a SEAL. Mathews, if you want a war, it will come fast and hard. You will never know what hit you until it's too late. Remember, SEALs never leave a man behind, and I'm not going to let you leave Commander O' Sullivan behind."

Townsend took another step closer to Mathews, who was not about to back down. A fistfight seemed to be imminent, but the altercation was broken up by the arrival of the president and his staff, who were ready to begin the mission.

Unlike the last briefing, Townsend was required to present his information first, due to other briefing needs required by the president. He was ready to scuttle his career to save Chase, but hoped it wouldn't be necessary.

"Mr. President, I regret to inform you that there are no new developments to report."

Mathews smiled and decided to slam the door shut. "Thank you, Admiral, that will be all."

"No, sir, that is not all. I think the rest of the group needs to know the truth—"

"Admiral, you are close to insubordination. Stand down, sir." General Mathews had to stop Townsend before he made a fool of him.

"I really don't give a shit. With all due respect, Mr. President, I think you need to know the whole story. Two years ago, General Mathew's son was held hostage along with army and marine personal in a captured base in Pakistan. Commander O'Sullivan and his SEAL team were ordered to rescue the hostages and extract them to Afghanistan. After the rescue was complete and the team was ready for extraction, they came under heavy fire and were forced to fight their way to safety. General Mathews' son demanded command of the team. Chase refused and led the team to safety. The General's son was wounded after he disobeyed an order and was subsequently forced out of the army. The general has been plotting his revenge ever since. This is all a plan to discredit Commander O'Sullivan."

"Admiral, that's totally false; you have no proof substantiating those charges."

"Only your actions and this file." Townsend slid a manila folder across the table to the president. "Mr. President, this file shows that General Mathews knew that the transport system malfunctioned when used in conjunction with new electromagnetic pulse rifle. As the military liaison to the original transport system program, he was privy to the top-secret test the DOD and the CIA conducted using the new rifle. This test yielded the same results as at the Arab compound. They classified the test, for their eyes only, but it shows General Mathews as the convening authority. NASA and the White House were kept in the dark, the test results were sealed, and the aftermath of the test covered up. This all leads to one conclusion: The general knew about the flaw and ordered the transport system used, knowing I would use my best team, led by Commander O'Sullivan. General Mathews is guilty of attempted murder, and contact unbecoming a commissioned office."

The president read the file, flipping through every page, knowing he had made a horrible mistake approving the use of the transport system. He had been duped by his advisors and unwillingly sent those brave people to there deaths. "General Mathews, you're relieved of your duties pending an investigation. Admiral Townsend, I don't know how you received this file; frankly I don't want to know. The project will remain under you command until further notice. Gentlemen, I believe this meeting is over; please have General Mathews taken into custody."

Townsend stood, never taking his eyes off General Mathews, who was in shock and unable to speak. He exited the room and fished his cell phone from his pocket in order to call his new friend, Al Cormier.

Chapter 20

Chase arrived at the Truman residence just as the snowfall reached its heaviest; opting not to say hello, he just dropped the others off and started back to the cabin. He had to keep Margaret and David safe, that was his original mission. With that accomplished, he could turn back for Jesse.

"Dave, I'm sorry about what I said earlier; he's the only true friend that I have ever had. Thank you for taking care of him."

"That's what doctors are for." He borrowed Jesse's line in order to prove a point. "I'm your friend, too."

"Thank you. I have another favor to ask you." He handed Dave an M29 and ten clips of ammunition in a bag. The bag also contained night vision goggles and three grenades. "The grenades with the white stripes are concussion grenades and the other one is a stun. I'm counting on you to keep Truman and Margaret safe while I go back for Jesse."

"I'm up for it, Chase."

"I know you are. Tom Truman has to stay alive at all costs. You realize what's at stake: His son changes the world, and he's a very important part of history. At all costs, Dave."

The doctor turned and started to the house. "Good luck, Chase."

"Don't you know by now that it's never luck?" Chase was on his way back to Jesse in the snow and wind, but he had his ace in the hole: technology. He put on all the accessories of his environmental suit, which shielded him from even the harshest weather.

He made the journey twice as quickly as he had with the others in tow; they just slowed him down, and he was determined to get back to his friend. Jesse understood the mission and had made it easy for Chase to leave him, but a SEAL never left a man behind. It was necessary to get Dave and Margaret to safety and at the same time keep Tom Truman alive, but Jesse knew Chase would come back for him; it wasn't the first time Chase had come back for Jesse.

He passed the red ribbon and entered the forest. *What an odd place for a decoration*, he thought, but it was inconsequential and trivial. The snow had covered Buford's tracks and the blood from the battle, so as Chase approached the cabin, everything seemed fine. He got to the door and opened it.

"I can't believe that you let..." What Chase saw made him sick; he had seen hundreds of dead bodies but never like this. Jesse was hanging by the neck from the rafters, naked, his body pale and bloodless like Rodriguez had been when they had first arrived in 1865. The other two bodies, obviously Sara and Scott Miller, had just been thrown into the corner like pieces of trash one would toss from the window of a moving car.

Chase couldn't take it; he had to step outside where he threw up by the door. His best friend had been murdered, tortured and humiliated. "Those motherfuckers will pay for what they've done. Pay!" He gathered himself and went inside, where he cut Jesse down and covered his body. There was no way that he could bury the bodies in the snow and frozen ground, so he lined them up and placed any type of burnable items on and around the dead bodies. He took his Zippo lighter from his shirt pocket and set the cabin on fire.

Chase stood outside and watched as the cabin slowly went up in flames. He had made sure that the bodies would burn completely.

"Jesse, I will avenge your death. I'll be there for you one last time; those fuckers will pay for this." He didn't have any of his own words, so he decided to use someone else's. "Jesse, when I was a boy my grandfather used to sing Irish folk songs to me when I couldn't sleep. One song in particular I liked. I want it played at my funeral, but I don't think you will mind if I sing it for you today."

Chase took out his flask that he had filled in the bar in town. "I hope I can remember the words, and I don't sing all that well, but here it goes."

"Oh all the money that I spent, I spent it in good company.
And all the harm that I've done, at least it was to none but me.

And all I've done for want of whit, to memory now I can't recall.
So fill to me the parting glass, good night and joy be with you.
Oh all the comrades that I've had are sorry for my going away.
And all the sweethearts that I've had would wish me one more day to stay.
But since it falls onto my lot, that I should rise and you should not,
I'll gently rise and I'll softly call, good night and joy by with you.
God Bless, Robert James, Master Chief, United States Navy, rest in peace."

Chase lifted his flask and took a gulp, spreading the rest on the fire in an offering to Jesse.

He looked down, his feet having unearthed something red. At first Chase thought that it was blood, but when he bent down he saw that it was a red ribbon, similar to the one on the tree in the forest. Then it clicked. "Elizabeth. Elizabeth gave Jesse up, that's how Buford followed us to Liberty and got in front of us to set an ambush. That's why he never attacked us in St. Charles; he was waiting for Elizabeth to give him the signal. That stupid, back-stabbing bitch."

Chase hopped on his horse and started back to Tom Truman's where Elizabeth was going to pay the piper and Buford was next.

Buford arrived in Liberty with the news that one of the bank robbers had been killed; he knew that it was a lie, but he had to keep his new men happy. They would start to Greenville when the weather cleared, going after Chase and the rest of his group. They all had to die and Buford was the one man willing to do the dirty deed. Most of his men were put up for the night in town, many of the new men stayed at home with their families, but twenty of them were assigned to stand guard in town. Buford did not want Chase coming into town in the middle of the night and felt that twenty men would be sufficient to stave off any surprise attack. He personally stationed the men with the help of Harden and retired for the evening. It was early when he went to bed, 9:45. It had been a long day, a prosperous one, and he wanted to be fresh for the killing tomorrow. Tomorrow it would be over and he would start home with his friend Harden and what was left of his men.

Chase hesitated before he approached the house; he decided that it would be best if he warned Dave before approaching. The problem with that was Buford could have taken Dave, Margaret, and God forbid, Tom Truman, putting him right in the teeth of a trap. He contemplated his decision for a few seconds and figured that if everyone was dead, what did he have to live for, except perhaps Julia.

"Dave, it's Chase. I'm alone and coming out."

"I hear you, come out." Chase was happy that Dave was still standing watch, but knew that he wouldn't like what Chase had to do next. He walked into the open with his horse lagging a bit behind him and started towards the house.

"Where's Jesse? I thought that you were going to get him?"

With no emotion in his voice, Chase answered Dave; he had no more emotions to show anybody. "Dead. I want you to go inside and search Tom Tidwell's and Elizabeth's things. I'm looking for red ribbons or anything that doesn't belong. Don't say a word, just go do it."

Dave went inside with a crushed look on his face; he had put so much time and effort into fixing Jesse, he had no idea that he had been ambushed, thinking that he had forgotten to do some little thing, and it had killed him.

Chase collected himself before he confronted Elizabeth; he was certain she was involved but had no idea about Tom. He would have to play them and see who started singing. *Don't go too far over the edge; you might not come back.* He had to keep a clear mind, but he knew that it would be futile.

He turned the doorknob and opened the door. Tom Truman was there to meet him with his father. Chase didn't pay any attention to either of them; he had tunnel vision. Tom Tidwell was sitting on a handmade rocking chair, sipping wine and talking with Tom's mother. Chase walked right up to him, and with as much force as he could use without killing Tom, Chase rammed the butt end of his rifle into his forehead; he purposely missed the nose. *He might not know anything about it.* The first thing that Chase had learned about fighting was to always take the toughest target out first, striking quickly and hard with the element of surprise.

Tidwell flew from his seat and over to the fire pit, where his shirt temporarily caught fire. Chase stomped out the fire with his foot, using more force than was needed, and grabbed the half-dazed man's burned shirt and dragged him into the kitchen, where Elizabeth and Margaret were cleaning up after dinner, showing their host the proper respect for feeding them.

Chase let Tom go on the floor and took hold of Elizabeth's hair, pulling her to her knees and striking her, closed fist, in the head. She flopped to the ground, crawling to all fours. Chase brought back his leg to kick her, but Margaret intervened and took the blow.

"Chase, she's pregnant. What are you doing?" Margaret was in pain, but she couldn't let Chase beat a pregnant woman.

He took her by her hair again and sat her in a chair that he then moved to the corner of the room. Chase looked at his target; she was bleeding badly from her nose and above her right eye. He moved Tom from behind him into the corner and told him to sit next to Elizabeth. He refused and Chase took offence, pistol-whipping him again, buckling his knees. He hit the ground and pulled himself up on the chair, hanging on next to Elizabeth, who just looked at Chase.

Margaret had moved out of Chase's way, but again intervened. "Chase, what is going on? You need to calm down."

"I am calm; you should see me when I'm not." That wasn't true, but Chase had to have total control of the situation. "She gave us up to Buford, and she killed Jesse. She probably gave us up, too."

"Jesse's dead?" Margaret's voice trailed off as she stepped out of the way.

"They hanged him from the rafters, naked, after he was already dead. Buford will get his, but first I need to find out what they know."

Chase took the two red ribbons from his pocket and tossed them at Elizabeth, who was scared at the fact that she had been found out. "I found those, one on a tree branch where we went into the woods and the other on the ground where Jesse was killed. The only way that Buford could have followed us was if she tipped him off. We left St. Charles in secret, no one saw us leave the stables, there was no one on the trail to Liberty, but somehow they beat us to the same place we decided to go only three days before. They were waiting for us. If it wasn't for Jesse and Frank James robbing the bank, we would have never gotten out of town. My chief paid the price for that. You want me to believe that the ribbons, Jesse's death, and Buford setting a trap are all coincidences? No, you set it up and now you have to pay the piper."

Dave appeared from checking their stuff holding a red ribbon and a cylindrical rock. He handed them to Chase and went over to Margaret, standing side by side with her, their full attention on Chase.

"Identical, the ribbons are identical." He paused, waiting for a response. "Talk, goddamn it, fucking tell me what I want to know or I swear to God you'll wish you were fucking dead, do you hear me!" Chase was yelling so loud that his voice was cracking.

"Tom had nothing to do with it. I set everything up myself. The ribbons were a sign. I made a deal with Buford and Harden, you and Jesse for Tom and me. You aren't from here, you don't fit, and you deserve to die. I was just trying to save our lives." She was crying and had little hope of living, but she wouldn't kill Tom as well. Her only chance was to come clean and hope that he could not kill a woman, especially one who was over three months pregnant.

Chase filled with rage and hit Elizabeth with his pistol, knocking her into Tom, who pushed her back upright and faced her.

"Why, these men took us in, they saved our lives. How could you betray them?" Tom spit on her face and turned back around to Chase, who had just finished loading his 10mm.

Chase picked up the cylinder from the floor. "Where did you get this?"

"In the ammunition box back at the white house, I took it out before I told you about the box that just appeared out of nowhere. I was going to keep it for evidence."

Dave and Margaret moved closer to the black stone; Margaret beat Dave to the question by one second. "What is it?"

Chase shook his head and tried to remove the top of the stone. However, it wouldn't come off. He set the stone on the floor, lying on its side, and picked up his rifle, bludgeoning the stone until it broke. He had to hit the cylinder twelve times before it broke, breaking the adjustable stock of the M 29/ME in the process. He reached down and pulled a smaller cylinder from inside the broken pieces.

"It matches the firing mechanism in the EP450, electromagnetic pulse rifle. An electromagnet, they sent this to us; it operates the EP450." Chase got the last rifle, the other two were lost in the river, and disconnected the barrel from the base, finding an identical magnet with electrodes connecting wires from the base to the magnet. He removed one wire at a time and attached them to the new magnet, then replaced the barrel cover and pointed the rifle at Tom Tidwell's head. "I wonder if it works?"

"No, please," Tom begged for his life. Chase pointed the rifle, squeezing the trigger, but he deflected the gun upwards when it discharged, putting a softball-sized hole in the Truman house.

"I guess it works." He set the EP450 in the corner of the room and removed his 10mm from its holster, pointing it at Elizabeth. He stared at her for almost five minutes, ranting, waving his gun in her face, but he could not kill an unarmed woman who was carrying a child, even one who stabbed him in the back. He put the gun down. "Fuck it, I can't do it. Get out of here, take your shit and go. No horse, you walk. The weather will kill you for me." He turned and started to walk out of the room when he heard a single gunshot echo in the small room. He turned to see Elizabeth, with a bullet in her head, slumped over in the chair.

Chase panned over and saw Margaret with Dave's 10mm. "She didn't deserve to live."

Chase just turned and walked out of the room. Dave and Margaret followed slowly. They walked past the Trumans, who were huddled in the corner.

"Dave, you and Margaret stay here. I'm going back into Liberty to find Buford and Harden. I need to strike before they do; no doubt they're going to come here tomorrow and we can't let them get Truman."

Chase laid out his battle gear and prepared for war. He was wearing his full combat outfit, down to the helmet, grenades, repelling harness and his newly repaired EP450. He painted his face black and went to the door, stopping.

"Dave, do you remember how to use the EP450?"

"Yeah, I remember."

"Good, take this." Chase handed him the pulse rifle. "You need to defend the place, it should take care of anything that comes your way."

He opened the door and walked outside. Margaret followed him to the doorway.

"Good luck. Chase, God speed," she said under her breath. She watched Chase until he disappeared into the night.

Chapter 21

Chase tied his horse up about three miles from town and ran in; he was in great shape and the run allowed him to vent his anger. His venting didn't change his mission, but calmed him enough that he was able to make reasonable decisions. He entered the city from the back, where William Jewell College stood, crossing the campus in the shadows and coming out in the righthand west corner of the main street. He had his night vision goggles on, but he didn't really need them because the snow on the ground lit the city up. He saw about twenty men, but the exact number he could not ascertain from his position. He had to get up high, scouting and waiting for the men to become tired and lazy.

He looked around, finally finding a good position: the top of the college's bell tower, which looked out over the town, far higher than anything else he could find. He came to the base of the tower and fixed his repelling harness; like the med kit, many of the combat-issued equipment had duel roles. He fastened the suction cup, which would adhere to any surface and support over seven hundred pounds, to the side of the bell tower facing the campus. The cup was attached to a rope, attached to a winch on his belt. The attribute that made the cup work effectively was the fact that one could slide it up, raising your elevation, but could not slide it down. This allowed you to climb a perfectly flat and vertical surface with little effort.

Chase scaled the tower without detection, sitting inside the tower platform where the bell was with nothing but his night vision goggles showing over the wall. He could clearly see seventeen people, tactfully spread out over the town, evenly distributed on the left and right side. The lucky thing was that many of the positions were out of view from the others, allowing Chase to strike one on one. He looked at his watch, three hours until sun up; he would have to go in and get out in less than an hour and a half.

He spotted his first target, a fat man with long black hair and overalls on under his winter coat. He certainly wasn't one of Buford's men, but the posse killed the wrong Jesse James and would have to die as well. He was on the other side of the street one building over, hidden. *He thinks he's so sly.* Chase shook his head. *He isn't sly, just fat, and dead.* He let out the cord on his harness and tossed it across to the building. *Who would think to look up?* Securing the cup on the lip of the other building, he grabbed the other end of the cord and attached it to the tower, allowing him to cross with the winch, taking in one side and letting out the other. He stepped off the tower and activated the winch, shooting over to the other side of the street, with a low hissing noise. After he was safely across the street, he deactivated the cups and the winch collected its rope.

He looked down on the man as he propped himself on the wall right under Chase. Chase attached the cup to the roof and repelled down, horizontally, stopping five inches from his head.

"Hey, fsst." The man looked up and Chase snapped his neck in one fluid motion. *One down.*

The next man was on the other side of the building in the front by the store window. Chase crawled on his belly to the corner and then around it, finding the coast clear. He made his way to the far side of the back of the building, carefully avoiding making a shadow. He had to get the attention of the man. He removed his lighter from his shirt pocket and started to tap the brick, tempting the man to investigate. Eventually the man wandered over to the back of the building, turning the corner. Chase greeted him with his ten-inch combat knife through his larynx and out the back of his neck. The man had no voice box to yell, falling to the ground; bleeding out, he would die slowly. Chase pulled him behind the building and set his sights on his next prey.

He had to cross the street undetected, a difficult task at best. There were two men who could see him, the first across the street, catty-corner to Chase's position, and the next straight across the street on the same side as Chase, but a large wall protected him. These were three of the men who could see each other; he did not have much time before his third friend got curious and came looking for dead man number two. *If I scale the wall, I'll be detected, so I have to kill both men at the same time.*

He jimmied open the back door to the building that he was hiding behind, finding a gunsmith. *I have guns but cannot use them,* Chase thought, continuing to look around in case there was something of use. He was out of luck, but it was hardly ever luck. He ran for the building and over to the wall, finding his third victim sitting on a stool by the corner. He could also see the fourth man standing across the street. He took his only mace grenade out and put his re-breather on. He checked the wind, pulled the pin, and dropped it over the wall. Unlike a stun or concussion grenade, a mace grenade did not explode, it let off a spray of mace good for thirty feet.

He attached his cup to the top of the wall and waited. The first man started to choke and his eyes violently watered, alarming the man across the street. He had no idea someone had planned this; he was concerned for his neighbor and friend, who stood watch with him. He crossed the street, leaving his rifle on the other side, wanting to help his friend, who was in great pain. As soon as the man hit the mace cloud, Chase activated the winch and vaulted the wall, descending on the two men, who could not see him through the mace. Chase ran his razor-sharp knife over the first man's neck, in a near-to-far motion, slicing his jugular vein. He never stopped the knife's motion, jamming it into the next man's skull, pulling him forward with the knife, which was stuck in his head. Chase stepped on the dead man's skull and pulled out his knife. *Four down.*

The next few minutes were spent waiting for the next move to present itself. He had thirteen more men to kill tonight. *I'm a killer. Jesse was right, you can't change what you are, it picks us, and we're all slaves to our talents.* Chase was stalking and killing any person who crossed the United States of America; he was the best and Buford was going to feel his wrath.

Chase hurried across the street and up one building, trying to get a beat on his next man. This part of town seemed well lit, making it hard to stalk his prey, knowing he needed to kill them quickly. *Three up and three down,* he thought as he affixed the suppressor to the rifle. Chase was about to rear back and throw his hundred-mile fastball. He slid the suppressor into place, making the rifle quiet but not silent. He hoped he could get all three without being detected. He climbed to the top of the building, using his modern rappelling harness, finding a perfect spot to fire. This was a gamble, there was no guarantee that the suppresser would work, and he might find himself in a firefight very quickly.

He acquired his first of four targets, *it was now, or never*, he fired one round, making a popping noise, like a confetti popper that a child would play with on July 4. As the first man fell the other three looked in Chase's direction. He targeted the second man, dropping him out of sight. The other two jetted into the street, looking for Chase. He had no choice but to put them down in the street. Two more pops rang out in the night.

No one else came out of their posts, so Chase rappelled down the other side of the building and ran to the two men in the street, dragging them into an ally. He went back into the street and covered the blood with snow, and moved down the side of the building, scanning for others to kill. He had to move quickly; time was running out. He rounded the next corner and almost ran into his tenth target. Chase's knife was out of reach, so he pulled the repelling wire out and wrapped it around the man's neck, pivoting behind him and crossing the wire. It embedded into the man's throat, cutting his airway. He made sure that the man was dead before he moved on, laying him in a pile of trash behind the saloon.

He dropped the next two with the M 29 but the last round startled the nearby guards. He was close to the end, having only one more mission. Traveling on the left side of the street, he came to his last target, who was standing by the flagpole between the bank and the city municipal building. Chase surprised him and plunged his combat blade into his spine, under the base of his skull, separating his spinal cord from his brain, stopping any nerve impulses from getting to the rest of his body; death was instant. He tied the rope from the flagpole around his neck and pulled the body up so that his chest was eye level with Chase. He took out a piece of paper and a pen, scribbled a message on it, and attached it to the already dead man with his combat knife, jabbing him in the solar plexus, and running the man up the pole, tying the rope off and disappearing into the night. He had to return to Truman's and prepare. Tomorrow would be the end of it; one way or another, it was going to end tomorrow. Either Buford and Harden or him and his group were going to die.

He arrived at the Truman ranch about an hour after dawn, where Dave greeted him fondly; no matter what had happened or what was said, Dave truly liked Chase. He had dragged Elizabeth outside and put her by the woodpile; no one showed her any respect.

"Dave, help me with her." They carried her to the largest tree on the front of the property. Chase tied a hangman knot and put it around Elizabeth. He stood on Dave's shoulders in order to get it around the lowest branch. Next, under protest from Dave, Chase stripped her down and strung her up in the same fashion in which Jesse had been in the cabin. His message complete, he went inside and finished his work. He had to check his ammo, decide the best placement of his assets, and finally get about twenty minutes of sleep. It was time to make good on his promise to Jesse, but first sleep. He set his watch alarm for twenty minutes; any more than that, his body would shut down, and he would be lethargic for the battle.

Chapter 22

Buford woke before dawn in order to prepare for battle, most likely his last; by tomorrow he would be traveling home to reclaim his land. His trusted first soldier, Harden, woke with the sun and quickly went to see his men, who had been standing guard throughout the night. Because of their long night, the lookouts would be in the reserve for the battle today, twenty in all. What Harden didn't yet know was that seventeen of them had been executed with extreme prejudices by Chase's hand. He walked down the street, finding the three surviving men, who because of their proximity to the Confederate camp had been spared a gruesome death, sleeping. He went over to yell at his negligent men when he saw the flagpole, which was shielded from the camp by the hardware store

"Get up. Get the fuck up!" he bellowed at his slipshod men, who at the sound of Harden's voice snapped to their feet, fearing the consequences of sleeping on watch. "Quick, get Captain Buford." The men were off, running to where Buford went over his battle plans, thankful they had not been punished.

"Sir, Sergeant Harden needs you in the town square. It's urgent." The three men just stood outside as Buford departed; they didn't want to remind Harden that they had been found sleeping, so they just stayed in the rear, out of sight, out of mind.

Buford arrived, visibly upset with the disruption until he saw why he had been summoned. Harden was pulling the message holder down from the flagpole. Harden removed the rope from the man's neck and then the knife from his chest, freeing the note. Harden caught it before it hit the ground and without reading it, gave it to Buford. Harden was too concerned with his man to bother to read a note. He ordered two men to take the man to the city mortician and joined Buford at the bank, away from prying eyes.

"Buford, what's it say?" Harden grabbed the message from Buford, who could hardly keep his temper from showing. Harden grabbed his friend behind the arm in order to steady him and looked down at the note.

> Dear Buford Walton & Joshua Harden:
> Your men were weak and easy to kill. If you are a man, which I have no doubt you are not, bring your men to the Truman house and finish this. I promise that I will kill you quickly.
> Chase O'Sullivan
> Commander, United States Navy

Harden handed Buford the note and pulled him behind the bank in order to speak with him in private.

"Buford, he's trying to pick the battlefield; he'll have a tactical advantage over us. We can't afford another battle like at the white house; we need to draw him to us, on our terms."

"Perhaps, but I think that we can overwhelm him; he's only one man, and we have over a hundred men, all wanting to be the one to kill this bastard."

"No, we draw him out, it's the only way. I charged with sixty men on a fortified position, thinking the same thing, and he killed every man. They didn't even break a sweat; they are killing machines. I'm telling you our only chance is to pick the terms of battle and have a trap set."

"All right, but where do you want to have the battle?" Buford was in no mood to argue with Joshua.

"On the other side of the river, the sheriff told us of a spot, completely open. We draw him in and then use our numbers to kill him. We can set up a flanking platoon and use the river as a natural obstruction." Harden walked around the corner to find a stick to draw his plan in the dirt and literally stumbled over the two bodies Chase had put in the trash. "Corporal."

Buford came running at Harden's order, finding two more men dead by Chase's hand.

"Sir."

"Corporal, form a detail and police the area for any more men like these." Harden pointed to the dead townsfolk.

"Yes, sir." He was off in a flash; little did he know that he would be busy for the next few minutes.

Harden picked up a stick and drew a picture in the dirt.

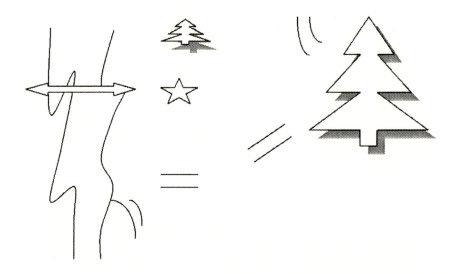

"We make him cross the river at the bridge; it's the only crossing. Then we get him to commit to our troops by offering him decoys, luring him in close where we have three groups, two straight on and the last on the corner, with their backs to the river. When the shooting starts, he'll be in the middle of crossfire. If he is still alive, we can send in the fourth unit that is hiding in the trees. It is a bit of a run to the battlefield, but we send our best shots."

"What if he retreats? We will be stuck on the other side of the river."

"There's too much distance to cover; he will never be able to make the bridge. If you are concerned about it, we can use the flanking unit to slow his retreat. Even if the other man is with him, we will be able to escape."

Buford looked at his friend with a smile on his face and patted Harden on the back. "I like it; now we just need him to bite. Send a rider to the house and see if we can get him to our spot. Then take care of this mess and get the men ready to move; we need to be ready for him."

Harden walked out from behind the building to find ten dead men—some were townspeople—lying in the middle of the street. Harden might be able to use that to his advantage. If the town was upset enough it could bolster his numbers for the battle.

If he could get Chase out in the open, they could kill him. *The question is how many people are going to die by his hand before he is dead?* Harden put such thoughts out of his mind and went about preparing for his men to pull out as the townspeople filed out to see their slain friends. The effect was just what Harden hoped: They all wanted to join the fight. He decided to play hard to get, turning the enraged people down, but that just strengthened their resolve. When Harden thought that they were hungry enough, he agreed to let them come, and die, but he left that part out.

Chase was ready by mid morning, but all his quick preparation just gave him some down time, time to wait for death. His body was being pushed to the limits and would have to shut down for a short time if he were going to be effective. He went about fortifying the house as best he could in the short time he had before the battle, moving the Trumans' winter woodpile to the front of the house at the corners to protect from being overrun from the rear, and by the door so he could move around the house more easily.

Dave was responsible for the rear of the house; he was to stave off any flanking maneuver, allowing Chase to dispatch the lead element. It was not much of a plan, but Chase counted on superior firepower to compensate for the lack of tactical superiority. Dave made sure that his area was secure and went out to see how Chase was. They had much more time than they had expected to have and started to wonder if Buford was even coming or if Chase had scared him off with last night's action.

"Chase, the back's done the way that you wanted. What else do you want me to do?"

"Help with the rest of this wood, there was more than I thought." Dave immediately started moving the wood from the side of the house to the bunkers.

"Chase, do you think that they're coming? I would have thought they would've been here by now."

"Me too. They could just be cautious." The men had stopped working and were scanning the countryside for any sign of Buford and Harden. Chase used his binoculars while Dave struggled with his naked eye.

"Chase, I don't see anything. Do you?"

Chase just nodded his head yes and handed the binoculars to Dave. "Do you see him, with the white flag?" Chase pointed in the direction and Dave followed with the binoculars.

"Yeah, there he is, he's coming in to talk, I think." They waited ten minutes before he was in range of the naked eye. The messenger stopped where Elizabeth's body was hanging.

"Buford sends a message; he wants to meet you at the river crossing, the only one in these parts. He said if you're man enough you'd show up."

Chase smiled at the man. "You tell Buford that I'll always be more of a man than he is. Tell him that I'll be there. You have to do something for me. I want you to cut down her body and carry it to Buford. She was a spy and it's his responsibility to bury her."

The man reluctantly cut Elizabeth down and put her over his horse. He slowly backed out of the yard and disappeared into the trees. Chase watched him disappear, just to make sure it wasn't a ruse to get him to leave Dave, Margaret, and Tom Truman.

"Chase, you're not really going to go after him, it's obviously a trap. He wants to get you to a battlefield where he has the upper hand."

"I know, but I have technology on my side. I can scout his positions and form a plan. Another thing that I have going for me is I can fire from greater distances, sniping his men, where he can't return fire. I'm going to wait a few hours just to make sure Buford is not coming and then I'll leave."

"I'm coming with you, Chase. Two people are better than one."

"No, you stay and look after Margaret. This is something that I have to do alone." He walked inside without letting Dave argue the point.

After a few hours he was satisfied that Buford was not coming, although he spent them sleeping; he had no choice, for his body was at its limit with all that had happened, including giving his friend two pints of blood and then finding him murdered.

The sleep refreshed him, being used to sleeping in small increments and pushing himself and his men to the extreme. Chase's path was set and he would have a hard fight ahead of him; he welcomed the challenge, but also needed to end the situation, either with the death of Buford or with his own. He had made a promise to Jesse and he was going to keep it if it cost him his life, but he couldn't ask Dave and Margaret to do the same; that's why he refused to let Dave come. They had more life to live, and it could be a prosperous one, knowing what was going to happen for the rest of their lives. They could quickly make some money and stay out of history's way. Chase's original mission was to save them; if they lived, he would finish his career without failing to complete a mission.

Chase prepared to leave, packing his weapons: the EP450, M 29/ME, a variety of grenades, and Jesse's knife. He also had his night vision and binoculars. The ammunition situation was a bit precarious, but he would make it work. He decided that he would only use the EP450 if it were absolutely necessary. *Bringing the pulse rifle into battle could seriously undermine history; introducing that type of technology into 1866 might jeopardize Dave and Margaret, after I am gone.*

"Chase, you're leaving?"

"Margaret, how are you doing?"

"All right, considering everything that has happened. Chase, do you think less of me for what I did to Elizabeth?"

"No, you did what you believed correct. God knows that I wanted to do the same, I just, I don't know, I couldn't do it."

"What happens now? I'm scared; this place is so foreign to me if I lose you and Dave, I don't know what I would do."

"Dave's going to stay with you; this is something I have to do by myself. Jesse was the only true friend I have ever had. In my business, friends are somewhat of a liability, but Jesse always seemed to come out alive. We built a friendship over the years; I have to avenge his death."

"I'm sorry; he was a good man, and we'll miss him as well. You be careful and make it back to us." Margaret's words were genuine but hollow in some way; she didn't really believe he would live.

"Thanks. Margaret, tell Dave thank you for being a good doctor and a good friend." Chase mounted his horse and began his journey to finish what Buford had started three months and a lifetime ago.

Harden prepared for battle as well, placing his men in the correct locations according to the plan; it was decided to place all his sections in the surrounding woods, masking his plan and giving Chase a false sense of security. The plan was simple and hadn't changed much since the dirt road in Liberty. Now all he had to do was make sure that his men correctly executed the plan and prepared for action.

He was surprised when he posed the challenge to the townsfolk to defend and avenge the death of their fellow townsmen. Seventy-five more men volunteered in addition to the posse formed earlier, bolstering his numbers to one hundred eighty-two men. He had more than enough for his plan, more than enough to kill one man.

He visited all his men and made sure that they had settled in for the night. On the other hand, Harden and Buford wouldn't get much sleep; they had too much at stake to sleep. They walked from one group of men to the other, making the final arrangements for the festivities that could come at any second.

All four groups were set and ready for battle. The first two lead elements bivouacked just inside the tree line; the group near the river was further back, and they would be the driving group, marching on Chase when the first two groups had him engaged, driving him into the flanking group, who had the task of cutting off his retreat. Chase would be caught in crossfire, hopefully a deadly one. Both Buford and Harden expected casualties; they had seen him in battle, but figured that their numbers would prove too much for him in the end.

Chase traveled by horse until he was three miles out, where he set his mount free. *I won't need her anymore,* he thought as he watched her run through the trees. He loaded his equipment into his pack, needing his full battle pack. He could make the three miles in about twenty minutes, but would have to scout the location before acting.

He came to the river, scanning his enemy's positions with his night vision, trying to catch his breath after running the three miles to the battleground. He saw the first two columns and the flanking unit, but the river unit was not in sight. Chase couldn't cross where Harden and Buford wanted him to, so he headed upstream three quarters of a mile. *Dave was right, they would have a trap laid for me,* he thought, but he would set one of his own in a desperate attempt to survive. Chase's environmental suit had proved itself in the Mississippi River in St. Charles and would get another chance in the Missouri, keeping him warm in the icy river. He completed the suit with the gloves and headpiece, put on his MBA, and started to forge the river.

The river was swift; Chase used ever muscle in his body to keep from flowing, with the river, downstream, losing precious time and having a greater distance to cover to make it back to the prearranged battle sight. Of course, Chase would have to even the odds before the battle.

He crawled from the river and started to the battlefield. He replaced his MBA with night vision and covered the three quarters of a mile, scanning the ground for any sign of Buford and Harden's men. He was swift and silent, coming to where the flanking team was bivouacked for the night, finding them mostly sleeping. Guards kept watch for the others, but they were not expecting Chase. He had a few surprises for them.

He crawled on his stomach behind the first guard, who was sitting on a fallen tree trunk. The man was half asleep, his head slumping in boredom. Chase pulled himself to his knees on the other side of the trunk, reaching up and grabbing the man, one arm around his neck and the other covering his mouth. The surprised guard kicked in vain as Chase squeezed the life out of him. The first guard dead, he set his talents on the next man.

The next target would be harder to kill; he was standing in the open, and his back was turned to the lights of the camp. Chase used the shadows to move closer to him, twisting from one to the other. He was diagonal to him about five feet to his left. If he got this one, the other three would be easy to kill, completing the first phase of the operation. Chase would have to risk it, jumping into the open and closing the five feet quickly, overtaking him before he could shoot or even yell. Without stopping, Chase ran past him with his arm extended, curling his head to his chest. Chase moved into the thickets, dragging the ex-Confederate Civil War hero, snapping his neck in the process. He paused, searching the night for any sign that someone had seen him kill the second of five guards. Secure, Chase made his way to the next set of guards, having to make quick work of the last three; he had a lot of work to do before dawn, which was less than two hours away.

The last three men were all sitting together by a fire, trying to stay warm and talking about old times. It would be the last thing that they ever did. Chase approached from the rear just right of the men, all three huddling together. Slowly and methodically, Chase unscrewed the suppressor on his rifle and fixed his bayonet, switching it to single shot, and waited for the right moment. That moment came two minutes later when the closest guard to his position turned to face his friends. Chase darted from behind cover, sticking the turned guard in the back with his bayonet. Chase thrust the knife into his back with enough force that the rifle also entered the wound, incasing the barrel in his chest cavity. Chase fired three rounds, quickly killing the other two men. The body of the first guard acted as a suppressor, silencing all three shots, trapping the gases in his body.

He dragged the bodies into the brush and scanned the camp for any guards that he might have missed. *The first part of my plan is complet*e, he thought as he started towards the main force. *Now I will have to set the charges.*

He placed the C40 charges in tactically sound locations, making an educated guess on where they would exit the woods and enter the battle. The C40 was spread out, some charges set in the trees, some on the ground, but all the charges were shaped to explode outward, killing anything near their blast pattern, which had a radius of twenty-five feet in all directions. Chase had one more explosive charge to set—the initial priming charge—but the hard part was stringing them together in a parallel circuit so that one charge would set the rest off. He had started close to the camp and ended near the edge of the forest. The furthest charge would act as the detonator. He strung a trip wire attached to the detonator to the last charge near the edge of the trees. When someone tripped the wire, he would set off a chain reaction, killing most of the men charged with flanking Chase and disorientating the rest.

The last charge was complete and he was going to make his way back across the river when he heard something crunching the forest floor. He looked up with his night vision, finding one of Buford's men, half asleep, coming towards him. Chase pulled his knife while lying completely flat on the ground. The man stopped, six inches from Chase's feet. Chase was ready to strike when he felt something wet falling on him. *The fucking guy is pissing on me*, Chase thought as he watched him zip up and walk away, having no clue that the man for whom they were looking was right at his feet, almost helpless.

Chase's work complete, he made his way to the river, crossing in the same spot he had earlier, at the same time cleaning the urine from his uniform. Chase quietly laughed as he slipped into the river. *I just let a man piss on me and didn't kill the bastard. I must be getting soft.* That wasn't the case, of course; he was ready to fight the fight of his life tomorrow. Mean and hungry, he would go into battle, for the first time not caring if he lived or died, just that he fulfilled his promise to Master Chief Robert James.

Chapter 23

The sun was about to rise and Dave wasn't going to leave his friend to die alone. He understood Chase's motivations, but couldn't let him throw his life away for revenge. He readied two horses, one for him and the other for Margaret, who was against the whole idea—as usual.

"Dave, this is asinine; you're going to get killed. Hasn't there been enough killing?" What she wanted to say was, "I love you; I don't want to lose you."

"I've lived my whole life afraid to take chances, afraid to do what was right, but now I live my life the way that one ought to, and I will not stand by while my friend dies. Margaret, I haven't been much of a man in my life. I used to run and hide from things that I was afraid to do. I see why I was sent here: to become a man, a real man, one who is accountable for his actions and doesn't run and hide."

"I can't dissuade you from going, can I, your mind's made up?"

"Yes."

"Then I'm going with you." She mounted her horse and started ahead of Dave, who quickly caught up. They had no idea what they were getting themselves into, but didn't much care. Chase and Jesse had been there for them and now they would return the favor.

As the garish sun began to show itself on the horizon, it painted the few clouds that scattered the winter sky with the color of blood. *A fitting sunrise,*

Chase thought as he made his last preparations for battle. He stopped and watched the sun rise slowly over the horizon. Its powerful rays reflected off the ice particles in the river, making the Missouri look like a river of diamonds. It climbed above the tree line and let itself be seen by the whole world. For some reason, Chase was moved by this sunrise; it stood out from the hundreds of others he had seen, brighter, more magnificent, having a grandeur fit for a king.

The morning was magnificent, but it was time to pay the piper. Chase had always found a way to avoid his toll; today he feared would be the day that the piper collected his past dues. Without the benefit of a horse, he walked towards the bridge, scanning the field for any sign of his fight, which would come in due time.

The bridge was well made from hard wood and was grand in scale, as everything seemed to be this morning. It spanned the expanse of the river with ease and grace. The width was enough to fit two carriages on it at the same time, with railings that were made to keep the travelers on the bridge in an emergency, unlike the one in St. Charles. Chase made his way across the bridge, knowing that he was entering no man's land. He would be hard pressed to retreat if he went any farther, but he knew that Buford wouldn't show himself until he was well clear of the bridge, which afforded Chase the option of retreat.

He walked to the middle of the field width-wise and started down to where Buford had the bulk of his men. Over a hundred men in the front, which was the only part of the battlefield he had to contend with if his charges did their job. The snow made it difficult to advance on Chase quickly, a factor that would play into his hand in the long run. He had greater range with his rifle and would be able to thin Buford's lines before they could bring their guns to bear on him.

When Buford was able to fire, Chase would have to find cover quickly. The field was just that and offered little in the way of cover, but Chase had a plan that he hoped would give him the shelter that he needed to stay the course of the battle. He decided to move to his left of the soon-to-be oncoming men, maximizing his advantage, and stopped just inside the accurate range of his rifle.

Buford and Harden stood side by side watching Chase come closer to their position, giving the signal to sound the advance. The bugler sounded and Buford's men stood and formed up into their lines. The first two groups filed out of the forest and made two sets of lines, the preferred form of battle in the Civil War era. The group closest to Chase was about forty feet in front of the other group, which was hampered by an uneven tree line.

The plan was working just as planned, and Harden could taste the victory but knew it would be a hard fight. He raised his saber and grunted the command, "At the ready, forward, march," sending his men into battle. They marched forward slowly in the snow; they all wanted to avenge the deaths of their comrades, not just the ones who had died chasing the murderers across the country, but all the men that had died fighting for their state's right to govern itself.

Buford stayed behind the lines while Sergeant Harden led the way, being the leader of men that he had always wanted to be. He didn't resent Buford for staying in the rear; it was what a commanding officer did in a battle. Harden was surprised when his first man fell, the shot sounding like a firecracker in the distance. There would be a lot more men who fell in the snow before they were in range to return fire.

Chase waited as long as he dared to fire, wanting to make sure both sides of the battle committed before he started killing. At the distance that he fired, some of his rounds missed, but two of three found their targets, killing another for God and country. He took aim at the flag barrier. "Why in hell would they carry the Confederate flag into battle?" Chase first took aim at the post of the flag; he wanted to prove a point. He squeezed the trigger three times quickly, cutting the flag and then the man down, both falling in the snow.

The men advanced with skill, disregarding the fact that Chase killed one man after another without taking any fire himself. He had concentrated on the group to his far left, allowing the other group to advance without taking fire. Because of that fact, they were able to make the distance between the two groups up more quickly than Chase had anticipated, and stood shoulder to shoulder with their comrades. All four lines stopped, and Chase heard a mumbled command; he was too far away to make out what it was, but they would fire on his position soon, he knew.

The first group, down fifteen men, wheeled to their right, fanning the line out and creating an opening in the middle. The second group moved to cover the hole, negating Chase's move to the left earlier. The move opened their flank by the river, but Chase couldn't make it to the river safely. Buford had planned the attack well, but Chase had taken his ace in the hole away and felt secure in the fact that if he found cover, he could force them to retreat.

Chase watched as the first line of men knelt and took aim; it was then he knew he couldn't afford to wait anymore to take cover. He pulled one of his last two concussion grenades from his pack and pulled the pin. He counted to three and then tossed it thirty feet diagonally to his left. He had to shorten his left flank. If they got around him, he wouldn't last long.

The grenade exploded, startling Buford's men just long enough that Chase could make it into the small blast crater formed from the explosion. The crater wasn't large, but it created a defilade from the rifle fire. Chase switched to automatic and opened fire. The rifle hummed as he emptied the clip into the line on the left flank. He was extremely worried about that side; they couldn't get around his flank. His preoccupation with the left created an opportunity for the right side of the line to advance and fire unimpeded.

Chase dove into the newly created crater, musket balls and Henry rifle rounds whizzing over his head. He stuck his head above the dirt line foolishly, being greeted by another volley from the left side of Buford's line. *I have to keep up my rate of fire or I will be pinned down and dead without exacting my revenge.*

Dave and Margaret arrived at the site and couldn't believe the size of the battle that was quickly forming. Chase was fending off an entire company of men. Dave tried to get onto his horse and ride to where his friend was fighting, but Margaret grabbed him and wouldn't let him leave her side. She clutched his arm tightly, pulling him behind the bank of the river where the battlefield dipped below the bridge, watching the battle unfold. Quickly, smoke from the muskets made it difficult to see Chase or the men with whom he was engaged in battle.

Dave wanted to move, coming to Chase's aid, but was overwhelmed with the events of the morning. He huddled below the bridge, his M29 ready, but he was too frightened to move, using Margaret as an excuse, who was clutching onto his waist as tightly as she could. They watched as Buford ordered an advance on Chase's position.

Harden heard the advance and came to his feet; his men fatefully following him. The first line fired and then ran forward. The same process happened in little sections along the line. One stationary section would cover the advance of the other sections. Then the group repeated the action for the soldiers in the rear. Chase sprayed his fire along the lines, finding that it was effective in slowing the group down. *He will have to do more than slow them down or he will be overrun,* Harden knew, wanting to negate Chase's left flank. *I have to advance my columns regardless of losses because the advancing columns will eventually encircle Chase's position and make a defense impossible.*

The fire rate from the advancing group increased with their confidence. Some rounds even skipped off the ground, being fired at the perfect trajectory so to ricochet off the frozen ground and into Chase's defilade. Chase was in trouble, having limited ammunition for the M29 and being pinned down under heavy fire. He had to do something to stave off their advance. Chase reached into his bag and pulled out his last grenade and his last two C40 charges that he had saved for a situation similar to this one.

The men were fifty yards from his position, far out of range of his arm. He placed the charges outside the defilade and timed his retreat so that he would have the maximum amount of time between volleys. He stood and ran as quickly as he could, calling every favor he had ever saved up from his body. He made it about thirty feet when the next volley was fired. Chase fell to the ground, unable to breath. He had just been hit by a Mack truck; that was the only thing he could think as he gasped for breath. He had been shot in the vest before and knew the feeling well; the bullet was stopped by his battle vest but did nothing for the pain.

Without stopping to check himself, Chase stumbled to his feet and pulled out his last grenade, throwing it in the direction of his retreat. A piece of shrapnel ripped through his arm, cauterizing the wound as it tore the flesh. In great pain, Chase stumbled into his new position and pulled the burning mettle from his arm. Luckily it wasn't his preferred hand, giving him the much-needed mobility to make his last stand.

He crested the top of the hole and aimed at his charges that were just being overrun by Buford's sprinting men. His first round missed, hitting one man in the foot, but his second was dead on. The explosion stopped the column, the left side all but disappearing in the blast. Chase, who was ready for the explosion, opened fire on the men occupying the other side of the line, who were temporarily disorientated. He was back in charge and able to hold off the attack for the time being.

Buford hit the ground when he heard the explosion. Embarrassed, he motioned his bugler to sound a cavalry charge; he would turn the battle back in his favor. The thirty-two-man cavalry exited the woods on cue, galloping full on to Chase's position. Buford watched as the plan was working perfectly. The cavalry would force Chase to retreat, running into his last group of men, who were waiting for the signal to march.

Harden was doing his part, and now Buford had to come through; he grabbed the signal flag, waving it furiously, telling his waiting men in the forest to the rear of Chase to start their advance. They had a ways to travel before reaching Chase, even with his retreat, so Buford felt it prudent to start them early. Buford's scout watched him waving the flag and sounded the advance on the bugle. They had no idea what was about to happen to them.

Chase spotted the cavalry; he hadn't seen them last night and had no plan for their demise. They could cover the ground much faster than the infantry, prompting Chase to concentrate on them. As soon as he did, the infantry was able to lay covering fire for the charging cavalry. They were going to overrun him in a matter of minutes, having to cover three advancing elements.

The blast didn't badly injured Harden, but he couldn't hear anything except the ringing in his ears. He ordered his men to cover the cavalry charge and advance when they could and he made his way to the rear, disorientated from the blast. He knew that this battle would soon be over; Buford had made the cavalry charge at the perfect time, turning the tide of the battle. When the horses charged, he knew that the flanking infantry would be marching on Chase and the battle would soon be over, giving him an excuse to fall to the back of the lines. He wasn't a coward, but couldn't think clearly from the blast. He had a concussion and couldn't focus on the battle. Both of those symptoms were bad when it came to a battle; he laid down on the ground, unable to advance with his column. Blood dripped from his ears as he passed out from the pain.

Just when Chase was about to try and retreat again, the trip wire was stumbled on, setting off the first charge. The aftershock violently threw Chase back into his foxhole, stopping his forced exit. The charges exploded one after the other, eventually lighting the forest on fire. The cavalry charge stalled as they watched their brothers explode and burn up in the wake of the exploding C40 high explosives. Back and forth the battle swayed, creating an ebb and flow of a full-scale war.

The flanking men had fanned out to the right, away from the charges, saving some of the men from dying in the explosions, but the fires forced them to exit the woods, dazed and completely confused. Dave watched as they erratically stumbled out of the cover of the forest. He seized the opportunity, crossed the bridge, and took a prone position on the other bank of the river. He pointed the laser sight at the first man who had exited and sent him to his maker with the motion of one finger. The other men caught in the fire didn't seem to care about the gunfire that they were taking from Dave; they were more concerned about the forest fire that raged around them. It didn't matter much; they would die either way, both methods violent.

Dave killed each man as they stumbled from the fire, in the process killing his fear and accomplishing the goal he had set back at the Truman house. He looked over at Chase, who had turned to see what the gunfire was all about to his flank. He knew that he had made a difference in the battle, perhaps saving Chase's life.

Chase had told Dave to stay at the Truman place, but was glad to see a friendly face helping him. Knowing that his back was covered, he turned to the advancing infantry; he was far from being out of danger. They had fixed bayonets and were about to charge, trying to overrun his position. If that was not bad enough, the cavalry reformed and began to advance, more carefully than before, but they still closed on Chase's position. Chase open fired with the last of his ammunition, having about seventy rounds available.

Dave was preoccupied and didn't notice the group of twelve men on horseback cross the bridge, charging into the battle. *This is it*, Margaret thought as she watched the men cross the bridge, but to her pleasant surprise, they didn't head for Chase, but headed to cut off the cavalry charge, firing as they galloped to Chase's rescue.

They covered the distance quickly and rode right into Buford's charging horse. Each man had a sword and a revolver. Some had rifles, but being outnumbered, they had to take their counterparts on at close range.

Chase watched as the mystery men charged, literally saving his life. He took the opportunity to retreat from the charging infantry. He was out of ammunition and nearly out of time, but he couldn't leave his new friends out to dry so he decided to use the EP450; he hadn't wanted to use the rifle, but his ammunition hadn't held out as he had hoped, giving him little choice.

He removed the weapon from his pack and turned on the reactor, which took a second to warm up. Bullets from handguns were starting to fly by Chase's head and hit the ground at his feet; he took a knee, preparing to fire, when one round hit his pack, destroying his guidance platform and entering his hip on the deflection. He grabbed the wound and tossed the pack to the ground. *I have no use for the platform anyway*. The bullet had slowed enough so that it only went halfway into his hip. He pushed on the wound, expelling the ball from his side. With the pain of the gunshot wound, he struggled to bring the rifle to bear on Buford's men, but he had no need to take aim; an insane amount of firepower was about to be unleashed on Buford's men.

He hesitated for a moment, feeling unsure about using the rifle, but he had no other option. He depressed the trigger and unleashed the fire of hell on Buford's men. In groups of ten, men fell, the lucky ones scattered, making Chase have to aim the rifle and not just concentrate his fire on the masses.

Margaret, who was still on the other side of the bridge, heard a beeping noise coming from her bag that carried her necessaries. It was a type of purse, but housed items that would save her life, not make her look better, a complete opposite from the start of her journey. She reached in the bag, pulling her guidance platform out. It was beeping, becoming louder with every round that Chase fired.

She took off for Dave, who was unable to hear the beeping over the gunfire of his rifle. Sliding into his position, she landed on top of him, yelling in his ear.

"Dave, the platform, it's on! The fucking thing's beeping."

Dave reached for his, finding that it was also beeping. He placed it on his head, just as Jesse had in the Arab compound. Margaret followed Dave's lead. *Are we about to go home?*

Dave turned to Margaret, touching her on her shoulders. "I have to go after Chase; we can't leave him here." He paused, gathering his confidence and bravery. "Margaret, I love you." He kissed her for the first time and took off running, trying to reach Chase.

Margaret watched as Dave tried to make it to Chase, mumbling her response to the kiss. "I love you, too." She looked on as Dave made it halfway and then they disappeared, on their way back home.

The full spectrum of color caught Chase's peripheral vision and he turned, watching Dave disappear, trying to reach him. He smiled, completing his last mission, going down with a perfect record. Chase turned his attention to Buford's men just as they started to break up.

The seasoned soldiers dropped their weapons and ran at the first sight of the pulse gun. Chase stopped firing and watched as the mystery men killed the last of the cavalry. Chase couldn't imagine who the men were and ran towards their position, pulling his binoculars out and training them on his saviors. It was Jesse and Frank James. He ran at full speed, the binoculars in his hand, to the legendary bank robbers.

"Jesse, what the hell are you guys doing here?"

"Chase, I'm glad to see that you made it. We heard that the posse followed you and your friend. Frank and I wanted to repay the favor you gave us in Liberty. I'm not even going to ask what kind of gun you were firing."

"That probably would be a good idea. Thank you, I'm in your debt now." Chase shook both Frank's and Jesse James' hands.

"Well, we might call on you to help us with our next job."

Chase laughed and thanked both men again, grabbing a horse from one of Buford's cavalrymen and rode to where Buford had his command tent. Both Buford and Harden were still alive; he still had work to do.

Chapter 24

Harden woke up to the smell of death; he had no idea how long he had been unconscious or if any of his men had survived the onslaught. Stumbling to his feet, he surveyed the carnage of the battle, finding his whole company dead, bodies littering the battlefield, body parts missing bodies and bodies missing parts. He staggered to where Buford's command tent had been during the battle, swaying as if he'd had too much to drink with every step. He came to the command area, finding disfigured bodies, but none matched Buford. He turned, looking at the whole battlefield, finding the forest on fire. His fuzzy mind had a tough time grasping the full scope of the battle. He couldn't believe that one person had done all this damage, being unconscious when Jesse and Frank James had attacked his cavalry.

He found a stray horse left over from the battle and started to follow tracks that lead away from the battleground. He had to find Buford, who had run with the rest of his men when he saw the electromagnetic pulse rifle. He went into the woods, still groggy and disorientated. He had a long day ahead of him, hoping that he would survive to see tomorrow.

There were two sets of tracks leading northwest from the river crossing into a dense forested area. Harden struggled to clear his head and focus on finding the only friend he had left in the world. He could only speculate that one set of tracks belonged to Buford and the other to Chase, who relentlessly hunted the hunter.

The weather on the trail was cold and lonely; fortunately, it wasn't snowing outside, allowing Harden to stay on the trail of Buford and his huntsman. The only gloom was in his heart. The sun seemed to run for cover behind the trees, ending a very long and bloody day. Harden couldn't help wondering if his life was coming to an end with the waning day. The setting sun seemed to be a metaphor for his failed mission and life. He had fought on the losing side of a war, lost his land, most all of his friends, and now would most likely lose his life, a fact with which he would have to quickly come to terms.

The easy, self-preserving answer was running for the hills, hiding from Chase, who wouldn't be able to find him while searching for Buford. Harden had pondered taking that very action, running from his troubles and starting his life over. The thought of running was a fleeting one for Harden. *What type of man would I be if I abandoned my best friend so near the end of the journey?* He took pride in being a man of character; he wanted to live, but living the life of a coward wasn't living at all to Harden, who needed to follow the trail to the end regardless of the outcome.

Chase, three times wounded on this excursion into the Old West, had problems tracking Buford, but was determined to find and kill the murderer of his most trusted friend and mentor. The tracks were fresh and newly made, prompting Chase to hasten his pace, knowing that his mind and body were at the extreme limits of their capabilities and would not be able to pursue Buford for much longer.

His thoughts turned to how he would return the favor. Would he be satisfied with just killing Buford, or was something more extravagant called for? Chase wasn't even sure he would be satisfied with the simple death of his prey, wanting to show Buford the hospitality he had showed Jesse in the log cabin. He had completed his last mission for the U.S. Navy, finishing with a perfect record. Revenge, executed with extreme prejudice, was his only responsibility. A responsibility he accepted, not for his country, but for himself, finally ending his battle with the demons that had plagued him on this mission.

The finale to this journey was near as he approached a lake nestled in between two forests.

Shortly before Chase, Buford had arrived at the same small lake fifteen miles into Kansas, needing water for himself and his tired horse. He knelt at the base of the lake in order to fill his canteen. He bowed his head, dipping his cupped hands into the water and moving the water to his mouth. Relieved to have a drink, he dipped his canteen into the water, filling it to the top.

His mount needed a rest desperately, so reluctantly he decided to rest longer than was prudent. After the unprecedented display of power from the new weapon, Buford needed to reexamine the documents from the black box, which were now in his saddlebag. He skipped opening the schematic drawings and went straight to the history book, flipping to the middle of the text and reading the first thing on which he focused.

He scanned the text for a date, wanting verification a theory he had formulated while watching Chase dispense two companies of soldiers. Midway down the page he found what he wanted, a date: September 11, 2001. Buford's head dropped as he realized why he couldn't defeat the men who always seemed to defy his reality. *The most costly mistake I made was dismissing the history book as inconsequential,* he thought, totally defeated.

Buford turned his head towards the tranquility of the lake, contemplating his fate and next move. As he did, Chase's reflection in the calm water startled the war-hardened Confederate soldier. Stumbling to his feet, Buford reached for his revolver, but the laser sight of Chase's 10mm handgun gave him pause.

"I don't think we've met. My name is Buford Jennings Walton."

"I think you already know who I am."

"Yes, I do, but what I don't know is where you came from." Buford slowly raised his hand, tossing the history book onto the ground at Chase's feet, hoping to distract him into picking it up.

"I don't think so. Why don't you just tell me what it says?"

"I'm not really sure; the page I opened had the date September 11, 2001, which would mean one of two things. The first, you and your friends are from the future, and the second option is that the book is fiction."

"I would ask where you got that book, but I think I have the answer. Elizabeth, your spy."

"You would be correct in that assumption, but it still doesn't answer the question at hand."

"I'm done playing with you; it's time for you to pay for killing my friend. It wasn't enough that you defeated him in battle; you had to defile his body. He was a soldier the same as you, and he deserved better."

"Not by my hand; he was in my path and so are you."

The rage in Chase's soul couldn't be contained any longer. "Have you ever heard of the quick draw?"

"Of course I have, why?"

"Because I'm going to give you a chance to live, a chance you never gave my friend." Chase put his gun in its holster and backed away from Buford, allowing him to move away from the lake.

"The quickest draw wins. I think I can handle those odds, but I'm at a disadvantage; my holster has a cover. There would be no way I could draw before you without opening the flap first."

"Fair enough, you may open your holster, but if you make the slightest move for you gun, I will burn you down."

Buford slowly unhooked the flap on his holster and started the motion of tucking it into his belt. Finished, he lowered his hand next to his holster and readied himself for the action. "I believe the odds are a little more even."

"Don't be so sure." Chase circled to his left, his hand resting on the top of holster. He fingered his gun, watching for Buford to move first. He would give his adversary every chance to live.

Buford reached for his gun, drawing and aiming for the kill. Before he could fire, four rounds from Chase's gun greeted him in his center mass kill zone. Mortally wounded, Buford fell onto his back, prompting Chase to run up to him and squat over the dying body.

"That was for my chief, you mother fucker." He stood over Buford and emptied the last eleven bullets in the clip into his already dead body. "That's for making me kill all your men without any regard for their lives." The red of Buford's blood assaulted the pure white of the snow, seeming to engulf its beauty and pureness.

Harden flinched when he heard the first four gunshots ring loudly through the dusk air. He shut his eyes, knowing his friend's fate as he heard a flurry of rapid succession pops that followed. The shots were close and the high number allowed Harden to get a good sense of where they came from. He kicked at his horse, spurring it to a trot, riding to the end of this strange and bloody journey.

He quickly covered the distance to the lake, sacrificing his body to the dense foliage of the forest. There was no turning back; he had come too far to tuck tail and run. Even though he had no desire to die, he had come to the realization that Chase was much too skilled for him and was sublime in the fact he would soon join his family in Heaven.

The thick of the forest lessened with every step of Harden's horse, giving his face some much needed relief from the tree branches. His eyes, free from the onslaught of sharp branches, spotted a clearing seventy-five feet from him. He pulled on the reins of his mount and slowed to a dead stop, wanting to make as little noise as possible.

He carefully made his way towards the clearing, letting his horse go free fifteen feet from the opening, where he could now see the outline of a horse. Harden sighed as he came to the edge of the clearing, finding a duplicitous lake, tranquil and pure to the eye, but deadly to the soul. His eyes fixed on Chase, who, alerted to Harden's presence, stood from rifling through the contents of the black box and turned to face the last of the surviving combatants.

"Joshua Harden, correct?"

"Yes, and you are Chase O'Sullivan?"

Harden nodded at Chase, who was holding his weapon at his side, seeming to contemplate his next move. "I'm sorry about what happened to you friend." Harden was truly sorry Buford had treated Jesse the way he had, but could do nothing to change the series of events that had led to his meeting with Chase.

"Then why didn't you do something about it? You were the second in command."

"I wasn't there. I was following a second set of tracks in the opposite direction."

"I don't know if I believe you, but say you weren't there, do you think because you weren't part of that one battle it will save your life? It didn't seem to matter what happened to my group at the white house; you wanted to kill us just the same."

"Chase, I'm not asking for absolution from my actions. Don't for a second think you are innocent in this mess."

"You started this mess as you call it. I just did what I had to do in order to survive."

"The treatment of Mr. James was unfortunate, but how many men of mine have you killed? You took no mercy on them, hundreds, most with families, gone after surviving a whole war. We're soldiers on opposite sides, not murderers, not mutilators of brave men. Killing is part of our profession, not part of who we are inside."

"Someone once said to me, we are what we are. I'm a soldier, just like you, trained by this country to kill without remorse. I feel no emotion for your men, or your leader, but someone needs to survive to tell the story of our fight. The winning side usually writes history. We only read one point of view in the history books, one reality."

"What do you mean?"

"You and I both know that you're no match for me or my futuristic weapons."

"That would be the safe bet, but you never know."

"We also know that I don't belong here. Who knows what I did to history by killing your men? There is no way to tell whose great great great great grandson will never have a chance to place their mark on history. All of the death we caused because four soldiers had to find out who was the best at their profession. Like I said, I don't belong in this time, but you do." Chase holstered his handgun and turned his back to Harden, who was surprised by the act of hara-kiri by this most talented warrior. "Make it quick."

Harden drew his handgun and pointed it at the back of Chase's head. As he cocked the hammer on his gun, it made the very distinctive double click of a single action pistol. All he had to do was pull the trigger and it would all end. He gripped the pistol, preparing for the heavy kick of this modal handgun. Harden made a last second adjustment to his aim and slowly squeezed the trigger.

The single shot echoed off the hill on the opposite bank of the lake, slowly diminishing until it was no longer detectable to the human ear. It seemed that every living creature and plant was silent after the shot. There were no sounds floating in the air until a small splash rang out in the middle of the lake.

"It seems that I missed. Rather embarrassing at such a close range, wouldn't you say? Unfortunately, these things are unpredictable at best."

"Why? I showed no mercy." Chase turned and once again faced Joshua Harden, who had returned his pistol to its holster.

"It was what you said about history. I don't want any part of writing it. I've placed my mark on history; all I want is to go home, put the war and all of this behind me. Remember, when you write our tale, there were two sides fighting. Right or wrong, we are soldiers until the end." Harden slowly walked to where Buford's body lay, lifeless, on the cold ground, careful not to unbalance the uneasy truce just formed. He loaded the body of his friend onto his horse.

Chase helped Harden secure Buford to his horse and then removed the rest of the black box's contents from the saddlebag. "What are you going to do now, Josh?"

"I'm going to take my friend home and bury him at his family plot. Then,

I guess I'm going to start my life over. Buy some more land and live in peace."

"To tell you the truth, I happen to know from a reliable source that Tom Tidwell is going to stay out West. He said something about the Arizona territory."

"You mean we've been fighting for no reason? How long has he felt that way?"

"Since St. Charles. I think he was thankful to be alive."

"Then why the hell didn't Elizabeth tell us about his change of heart?" Harden was shaking his head in disgust and disbelief at the knowledge he could have avoided all of this death.

"I think she had her own agenda that no one knew about. Between her and Buford, we never had a chance. Good luck, Josh, I hope you find what you're looking for."

Harden mounted his horse and disappeared into the forest. Chase watched him go, gathered the contents of the black box and started back to the bridge on foot. Hopefully, his horse was still wandering in the forest nearby. He had a date to keep with Julia, and it would take him much longer if he had to walk to St. Charles. He would live his life starting today, just like Harden, disregarding everything that he had ever learned and moving forward, trying to love a woman who died almost two hundred years before he was born.

Tom Truman would never see Chase again, but would use the courage, work ethic, and ingenuity that he had learned from him, instilling in his children the correct and decent way to live. He wanted to leave out the rage and death that had followed the two superhuman men, but his son, Harry S. Truman, would certainly know his share of both.

Tom Truman's father decided to travel to Independence, Missouri, sooner than he had anticipated, but wanted to move as far away from the events of the past few days as possible. As promised, he allowed his son to travel along, learning even more about life's vicissitudes.

What the Trumans hadn't planed on was Tom Tidwell and his longing to move out West. He had lost everything over the past few months: his father, money, land, and the woman he loved. Tom Tidwell missed Elizabeth, but knew that Margaret had done what she had to do in order to save the team. He didn't hate any of the time travelers, but hoped that he wouldn't ever have to see them again. He longed to move west, perhaps to the Arizona territory, and start a new life, one of peace and hopefully prosperity. What he didn't know was he would regain his wealth by discovering silver and eventually start a family.

Epilogue

Transporting again rendered Margaret and Dave unconscious, but this time they had a medical crew to look after them, making sure that they were comfortable until they awoke. Margaret was the first of the two to wake from unconsciousness. She was strapped to a bed, unable to move or see Dave, who she had come to love over the time span of their ordeal.

She knew that she was safe, but her emotions got the best of her, calling out, "Dave, Dave." She could care less about the nurses and doctors, who rushed in to see how her health was; all she wanted was to see Dave.

"Madam Ambassador, calm down. It's alright, you're home."

"I can see that, Doctor. Why do you have me tied to this bed and where is my companion, Dr. David Persons? I want to see him immediately."

"He's next door, but I highly advise you to stay where you are until we can run some tests."

"What's your name, Doctor?"

"Robert Willowbee. I'm the ranking surgeon on this base."

Margaret focused on him, finding that he couldn't be over the age of forty, having blonde hair and blue eyes. He was short and slim in build. Margaret focused on his collar, finding that he had gold oak leaves perched on them. *Either a major or a lieutenant commander, depending on the branch of the armed forces in which he serves*, she thought as she was poised to throw a fit. It really wasn't the type of person she was anymore, but it was what everyone expected, and she found that she got better results when she was angry.

"Doctor, this is the second time that I've done this. How many have you experienced?" A lost doctor stared back at Ambassador Knox-Harriman, a powerful person to say the least.

"I haven't."

"That's right, now untie me and go get the ranking officer. I need to speak to him ASAP." The shell-shocked man untied her and hurried to fulfill his orders. Margaret smiled as he tripped over the lip on the doorway; it was nice to know that she still had it.

She walked over to the next room where Dave was just beginning to stir; he would need a few moments to focus his thoughts and his eyes on the fact that he was home in 2100 AD. Margaret took his hand and whispered something in his ear. Dave smiled and tried to move his arms, which were also tied down, just as Margaret's had been a few minuets before.

"It's okay. Dave, I'll have you out in a second, stay calm." Margaret's voice had a calming effect on him and he stopped fighting the straps. As soon as he was untied, he sat up and hugged Margaret, who was very grateful for the affection. When he had run after Chase, he'd had serious doubts about ever seeing her again, or anyone for that matter. There were no words between them, just a connection that had formed over the past few months. They embraced, waiting for Admiral Townsend to debrief them. They wouldn't have to wait long.

Vice Admiral Christopher Townsend entered the room; he had hundreds of questions to ask, the most pressing of which concerned Chase. He needed to find out what had happened to his best solider.

The two survivors turned as he entered the room. Townsend was proud and worried at the same time, harboring hope that Chase and Jesse would make it back to 2100. He would have that hope for only a few more seconds, the time it took him to walk from the door to Dave and Margaret. He stopped right in front of Dave and Margaret, who tried to hide their joy at seeing each other; they would have to convey the bad news.

"My name is Vice Admiral Christopher Townsend. I'm the commanding officer of Navy Special Warfare Operations. I've been running this operation from the beginning." He should've asked a few introductory questions before he asked about Chase, but he couldn't wait any longer. "What happened to my SEALs, Master Chief James and Commander O'Sulliavn?"

Dave still hadn't fully recovered from the transporting effects, so

Margaret reluctantly answered; neither of them wanted to be the bearer of bad news. "Master Chief James is dead; he was killed trying to save our group from Confederate bandits. Chase, I can't account for. When we transported back, he was in the middle of a battle with almost two hundred men. Dave tried to make it to him, but we transported before he could make it out to where he was."

"You have no idea if he was dead or alive when you transported back—" He was interrupted by Cormier, who was running to greet the time travelers. "This is Dr. Cormier; he invented transporting and is the head scientist on the project."

"What happened to you, where did you go?"

Townsend was perturbed at the interruption, but they had to know everything about the mission, so he didn't object to Cormier's line of questioning.

Dave noticed the frustration on the admiral's face and decided to answer his question before Cormier's. "He was alive when we transported, still fighting to save us." He was just about to answer the second question when four junior officers entered the room.

"Sir, there's a man in your office. He said that he has to see you right away; he said he has a letter for you. Apparently, his firm has been holding it for thirty-four years."

The Admiral headed for his office. Cormier and the time travelers ran though the door after him and onto the elevator. All of them traveled the three floors up and then walked down the hall to Townsend's corner office. They filed into the door one after another, finding a young man, just out of law school, holding a briefcase. The man was dressed well, wearing a suit that he couldn't afford on his salary, but looking the part was half the battle.

"Good afternoon, I'm representing Crosby, Coe, and Whitman, attorneys at law. I was instructed to deliver this document to Admiral Christopher Townsend at two o'clock today; apparently, my firm has been holding it for over thirty-four years."

"You're three hours late, son, what took you so long?" Everyone was interested in debriefing the time travelers, not about some letter and had little patience for a cocky kid. Townsend signed for it and opened the letter, paying close attention to the envelope, not to rip the document.

His eyes focused on the letter and filled with tears; he was unable to read the document, intensifying everyone's curiosity about its contents. Dr. Cormier gently took the letter from his hands and started to read it aloud, for the benefit of everyone involved.

"It seems to be from Chase. It's dated November 11, 2067."

"That's the day before Chase was born." Townsend composed himself and added to the conversation.

Dear Admiral Townsend:

I hope that Margaret and Dave are with you, reading along, safe and happy to be alive. If they are, they probably can verify most of what's in this letter, but I can't assume that they made it back. This letter is my account of what happened on November 11, 2099 and the months following our disappearance.

We awoke in Virginia, where Norfolk is today. Petty Officer First Class Fernando Rodriguez was found dead, killed in action. I recommend that the Navy Cross be awarded to him for bravery in the service to his country. At first, the transport disorientated the group, but Chief James and I took charge and I sent him on a recon of a nearby town, finding that we had been transported back to 1865. The date and location was the same, only the year was different.

Because of unavoidable circumstances, we were forced to travel by train to St. Louis, Missouri, with two other people, Thomas Tidwell and Elizabeth Thompson. Both Dr. David Persons and Margaret Knox-Harriman performed well under pressure and earned the greatest respect from Chief James and me.

Ex-Civil War raiders were chasing us across the country, and we were forced to engage them outside of St. Louis. Again, both Dave and Margaret performed well, and we were able to repel the attack and move west. Our mission had changed somewhat with the addition of Thomas Truman, father of the future President Harry S. Truman, to our group. Concerned for his life and the ramification on history, we endeavored to bring him across the state in order for him to meet up with his parents, who had just returned from a wagon train west, in which they were guides.

The mission was a success, but in the process, Master Chief Robert James was killed in action. I recommend Chief James for the Medal of Honor. He knowingly sacrificed his life so that the mission could be completed. He diverted a company of men away from the rest of the group and died fighting with his last breath. He epitomizes what the Navy and the United States Armed Services stand for.

The original mission was completed soon after, with the disappearance of Dave and Margaret. My retrieval platform was destroyed in battle; therefore, I was unable to return home.

The two survivors, who I theorize traveled back to 2100 when the platforms activated, will hopefully augment my report of the events that took place. For some reason I never aged. I lived history from November 12, 1865 until November 12, 2067. For some reason, I knew that I would no longer exist when I was born into this world. I have lived my life righting the changes that we made in history because of our appearance in 1865. In many cases, I was the architect of historical events, using the history text that was sent to us through the transporting device.

Attached with this letter, I have left a journal of my account of the events and actions that surrounded my extraordinarily long life. Undoubtedly it will be classified, but I wanted to leave a record of my actions and how they shaped history.

Humanity is cruel and harsh, wanting nothing more than to leave its mark on history, making life and men follow its lead. If I learned one thing viewing and living word history for two hundred years, it is that we can change and that each man has to look deep inside himself and decide if he wants to ride the roller coaster of life or if he wants to drive it. I've tried to drive the roller coaster and I put the challenge to all of you to do the same; the ride's the best in the front seat anyway.

Sincerely,
Chase O'Sullivan
Commander, U.S. Navy

All four people privy to the letter stared at each other, reluctant to ruin the moment. Admiral Townsend took the journal and placed it in his desk, wanting to hide it from his superiors, but knowing it was impossible. He would make sure that he had the opportunity to read its contents before handing it to the proper authority.

"This will most definitely be classified information. No one outside this room is to know about this letter or the journal; if it gets out that someone from this time has molded our history, a panic will set in and consume the country. We need to get your account of the events leading up to this point, but first I need to be alone. I need to say goodbye."

Cormier, Dave and Margaret exited the office and shut the door. Townsend sat at his desk and opened Chase's journal; he wanted to know how Chase had lived his life. He was happy that Chase had survived the ordeal but had to come to grips with the fact that he was gone, and that would take some time.

Printed in the United States
52349LVS00005B/79-81